Contagious Love

Aishvarya Murali runs The Unbottle Co., India's first 100 per cent recycled plastic-packaged beauty brand. For the last 16 years, she has helped connect India's top brands with consumers through storytelling and marketing at Ola and Unilever. Awarded the 'Most Influential Marketer of the Year' by the World Marketing Congress, she helps start-ups launch their marketing journeys.

Aishvarya loves singing, playing the guitar and running, but all that comes second to important silliness with her kids, Vedant and Antara.

Sriram Emani is an IITian who pursued his MBA from MIT. He is now an actor-storyteller, based in Boston, USA. Sriram founded and runs IndianRaga, the world's largest platform for Indian performing arts. As an actor, he has played principal roles in award-winning indie films and featured in commercials with leading brands in the United States. Most recently, as the first South Asian to play Bob Cratchit in a live production of *A Christmas Carol* at the Hanover Theatre, he is helping reimagine the classic story in a more inclusive way.

In his spare time, Sriram loves treating his friends to elaborate home-cooked Telugu meals over wine and endless banter.

Contagious Love

Love Knows No Distancing

Aishvarya Murali
Sriram Emani

RUPA

Published by
Rupa Publications India Pvt. Ltd 2023
7/16, Ansari Road, Daryaganj
New Delhi 110002

Sales centres:
Allahabad Bengaluru Chennai
Hyderabad Jaipur Kathmandu
Kolkata Mumbai

P-ISBN: 978-93-5702-047-3
E-ISBN: 978-93-5702-072-5

First impression 2023

10 9 8 7 6 5 4 3 2 1

*To everyone who always thinks that
'a little more is possible', every single day*

Contents

Zombie Homecoming

Adele has lost her voice, thought Samyuktha.

There was a gruff voice saying something incoherent in the background of her favourite track, 'Rolling in the Deep.' She tried to ignore it. But then it came again, this time with a hint of anger.

Samyuktha woke up with a start and looked around her. Her eyes felt heavy and she was disoriented. As the world around her slowly came into focus, she realized that the cab had stopped, and a masked man in an army uniform was looking at her through the window.

'Where are you going?' he asked.

Under regular circumstances, she noted, his deep voice would have perfectly matched Benedict Cumberbatch's baritone in a spy thriller. But when someone wearing a thick army uniform, gloves and a mask stares at you with a pistol strapped to his belt, that image gets replaced with Berlin from *Money Heist* instead.

She groped for the button to roll down the window. The warm 6.00 p.m. beach breeze hit her face—a welcome relief from the freezing temperature inside the car and the slight dank smell. 'C-11, Ashok Apartments, Ajay Kumar,' she said, taking out an earphone and trying to open her eyes. 'I'm his daughter, Samyuktha.'

As she waited for the cab to move ahead, she saw Benedict-turned-Berlin make a series of calls. He finally gave a nod and tapped the car to go ahead. As it moved, Samyuktha rubbed her eyes and stared out at the familiar yet eerily quiet TTK Road.

She had never seen the usually busy arterial road so quiet. *Except for the time when we left at 4.00 a.m. to catch that flight to Singapore.* Samyuktha had an eidetic memory, and remembered the tiniest of things that happened years ago, and that too in detail.

After her cab turned at the iconic Sheraton Park Hotel with her favourite The Velveteen Rabbit in the distance, her memory wandered back to the last two days. Samyuktha usually never slept in cabs. But this situation could hardly be called 'usual'. Not only was she excited but also new to such a regime: two nights of no sleep.

Same was the case with the entire country.

The first night of sleeplessness had descended when the country watched the Prime Minister (PM) declare a nationwide emergency, ordering all non-essential businesses and educational institutions to shut down. The army had been requisitioned by multiple Indian states to enforce a peaceful lockdown. It had barely been eight weeks since the outbreak of the novel coronavirus in Wuhan, and it had spread like wildfire after that, from Italy to the United States. At that time, it had felt like a distant catastrophe.

But with the number of infected and dead rising like mercury across the world, it had soon reached India as well. And Samyuktha had had no time to process any of it. The dorm was a blur to her. As the girls had crowded around the television in the common room, there had been a dreadful yet excited uncertainty regarding what was to come next. The verdict had come at midnight through an email. Everyone was to pack and leave within forty-eight hours.

There had been chaos among students the next day. There were tickets to be booked, luggage to be packed. Samyuktha's doting and efficient father had promptly sent her a flight ticket from Mumbai to Chennai. Trains and buses were to be booked for the students who lived close by, like Sharanya, who was from Pune. There were library books to be returned, and frantic parents to be calmed.

Samyuktha had spent the second day washing everything she had with Dettol, as strictly instructed by her mother, who was also a doctor. The night was spent packing every worldly possession she had—from her guitar to her mattress, to her thousand-piece jigsaw puzzle.

She then found herself in a hastily organized end-of-the-world party at Powai Social. What better way to process this news than drown it out in tequila shots while dancing to loud music?

The night had ended, as predicted, with a longish make out session with Rohan by the lakeside in the wee hours of the morning. *Of course.* The distance was about to hit her, for real. She had also had a heart-to-heart talk with Sharanya about how their dreams were about to near an end. They had made the firm resolution of continuing their tradition of watching a movie every Friday, going for beer and night out—even if it meant doing all of that separately over a Zoom call.

Samyuktha smiled as she thought of this…and then sighed at the same time. It was overwhelming to be plucked out of campus life overnight. Her mind wandered back to the time when she had joined IIT in 2018.

It had taken Samyuktha a while to adjust to campus life, and that too in a new city. Away from sheltered Chennai, she had found the newness of campus life to be daunting at first. But once she had adjusted to it, she loved it—her books, her guitar, her lakeside run in the morning, and the time spent in the library lost in a book.

While her friends spent all their money on outfits and parties, most of her allowance went towards paid subscriptions to scholarly magazines, online guitar classes and running gear, much to Sharanya's disgust. FOMO clearly wasn't something she subscribed to. With a dad who was a cybersecurity expert and a mother who was a gynaecologist, she had a lineage that wasn't too worried about missing out.

While her teachers admired her for this, they were also in despair at how frequently she would get into scrapes—yelling at someone because they kicked a kitten or didn't feed the stray dogs on time; going to the PA system and announcing that someone threw a stray tissue or a paper plate in the grassy lawns instead of the segregated trash can; staging a quiet protest by not attending Prof. Himakshi's quantum physics class because she used a diesel vehicle that wasn't tested for emission.

Everyone knew Samyuktha. They either loved her or loved to hate her. She, on the other hand, connected with a few from the bottom of her heart. Sharanya was one of those— her infectious energy, her enthusiasm, her staunch support for whatever Samyuktha did, her ability to toss out a book and force Samyuktha to do something fun instead, her patience to sit and listen to Samyuktha's rant about the planet, the turtles and everything in between...

Sharanya was one of the few people (apart from two glasses of wine) who was able to bring out Samyuktha's crazy, wacky side that very few people knew of. And Samyuktha was her confidante and co-conspirator in organizing karaokes, parties and other such 'extra-cultural' events. Basically, she helped Sharanya put together everything that would help the latter's vote bank for the upcoming elections for the cultural secretary post.

Then there was Rohan, Samyuktha's outgoing and cute boyfriend. Their two-week-old romance was slowly becoming the talk of the campus. Rohan was her exact opposite—a gregarious South Bombay boy, who took her to upscale parties, which her

Chennai upbringing found both baffling and pointless at the same time.

~∞~

He knew something was coming.

It was just another foggy Delhi morning in the cantonment. Lieutenant Abhimanyu Singh woke up, just as the *sahayaks* came in with piping-hot cups of chai. As he sipped his tea, the other lieutenants were woken up, one by one, to get the morning PT started. He made his way to the locker room, which was already abuzz with gruff, off-key singing in the showers (mostly bad attempts at Bollywood songs from early 2000s).

Abhimanyu smiled hearing those who had just returned from their hometowns make others envious by regaling them with tales of *maa ke haath ka khana* (home-cooked food), festivities, toddy-fuelled night-outs with childhood friends and, of course, steamy clandestine affairs. Abhimanyu pulled up Google News as he walked over to the locker room. He frowned as he read the latest on the virus. *Even Tom Hanks?*

`Sab theek kiddo` (All okay, kid)? His sister's message popped above Tom Hanks' face on his phone screen. *How does Didi always know?* he thought as he got distracted by a searing towel slap on his bare back just as he entered. It was Ayaan.

'*Subah subah sexting* (Sexting early in the morning)? Don't get too turned on. Shower time has been cut down to ten minutes,' Ayaan said after his usual guffaw.

'I'm sure it's enough for you,' Abhimanyu said, poker-faced, as he undressed. '*Aur bhai* (and brother), please no singing in the shower today, *dimaag kharaab—(my brain cannot),*' Abhimanyu gave up as Ayaan started singing loudly anyway.

'Why's your mood off?' Ayaan asked as they were putting on their uniforms. Abhimanyu usually had a zest for life, similar to that of a puppy who sees an open front door of their house. It was infectious but infuriating too.

'This virus is spreading everywhere. It's becoming a bigger issue than the Line of Control. PM saab will definitely take action, and our unit is due for our next posting,' Abhimanyu calmly said.

Ayaan stopped short and looked at him as realization dawned on him. 'Holy shit.'

⁖

Abhimanyu was third in a line of brave army men who served India. His father, Retd Brigadier Arjunveer Singh, was a true veteran. As a six-year-old growing up in Ambala Cantonment, surrounded by proud army officers and veterans, Abhimanyu and his older sister Shalini would listen with rapt attention, their eyes sparkling, as they heard the stories for the hundredth time: the march through the Zoji La Pass in -15 degrees, the weekly getaways to Sumur village's restaurants, the prayers offered to O.P. Baba the night before Operation Meghdoot, and the near-death anecdotes that got more dramatic as the alcohol flowed in abundance over weekly get-togethers and dinners.

Back then, Abhimanyu's young mind couldn't help but imagine and play out those scenes long after the others had gone to sleep. Watching *Border*, *Hindustan ki Kasam* and other war movies with his father, he would feel a potent blend of patriotism, bravery, and anxiety, which he was sure his father and grandfather too had felt on the field as men of the Indian National Army.

To become more like his father, Abhimanyu did every physical activity he possibly could. He climbed trees, ran several kilometres each day, even built a mini kayak but gave up after it came apart midstream. He played every sport he could, sometimes with the jawans in the cantonment. He mostly lost, but would always bounce back, stronger and better. Very early on, therefore, Abhimanyu built a unique resilience.

Meanwhile, his sister towered like a shade over him. Shalini didi was his umbrella, his anchor, his balm. Four years older than him, she had partly brought him up, shielding him against many bunked classes and late-for-dinner moments, and had enabled much of his after-school escapades, which his parents would have surely frowned upon.

His peer group at school had truly brought out the geek in him. Most of them were sons of army intelligence officers. From them, Abhimanyu learned a thing or two about cracking codes, using sensors and flying drones. In no time, he was building circuit boards, hacking into email accounts and binging on spy movies.

Yet, the same army life that had built these proud memories had also taken away his and his sister's adolescence, completely.

❧

Samyuktha sat up in her seat, nursing her sore neck. She checked the time. 6.00 p.m. She opened her Whatsapp. There were 174 messages. The college groups were abuzz with lockdown stories, pictures of barren streets, zoom party proposals—it went on and on.

She didn't have the patience to go through all of it. She was averse to using the phone in general and specifically WhatsApp—to be precise—and the groups on it. 'Time spent on WhatsApp groups is the time I will never get back,' she would keep telling Sharanya, who practically lived within her WhatsApp world.

Samyuktha looked around as the cab slowly made its way towards TTK Road. What a different scenario it was! The usually crowded road was starkly empty. The corner autorickshaw stand, usually filled with the drivers haggling, sleeping, or listening to the latest Thalaiva music had fallen silent. There were no twinkly Fabindia lights, and the Health and Glow store, usually abuzz with salespeople, was now deserted. All one could see were shutters. *Like one of those dystopian Hollywood movies,* thought Samyuktha. Was this the Chennai she had grown up in? Her mind wandered back to her childhood...

Mylapore was a haven for cultured, elite folks who woke up to 'Suprabhatham' and filter coffee. Samyuktha's home was no exception. Her mother would light the morning *vilakku* (lamp) and put on the iPod. The routine was standard: 'Ganesha Pancharatnam' on Monday, 'Hanuman Chalisa' on Tuesday, 'Venkatesa Suprabhatham' on Wednesday, 'Oothukadu' on Thursday and 'Aigiri Nandini' on Friday.

Her Thatha would come out from his room, humming 'Ganesha Pancharatnam', and put a small dot of *veeboodhi* on his forehead before entering the kitchen to make coffee and breakfast. Like clockwork, Appa would disappear into his study at 8.30 a.m. As for Amma, she could be called in anytime for work, and there was no knowing when she would return.

Her neighbours, however, maintained saner hours. Usually, people would be back by 6.30 p.m., take a quick shower and visit *Pillayar Kovil* (Ganesha temple) down the road to pay obeisance to the Elephant God. They'd come back without fail to watch the 8.30 p.m. daily soap and the 9.00 p.m. news bulletin.

Samyuktha always said that she didn't mind her parents' hectic schedule. But secretly, she would always get a pang of longing when she would hear her friends in school talk about how their mothers would make them this and that for dinner, or sit with them while they finished their homework. Being an only child, she sorely missed that aspect of her childhood.

Her mother sensed it, and she made a pact with Samyuktha.

On getting late, she would promptly send the car with their driver, Shekhar, to fetch Samyuktha to the hospital, where she worked.

Roly-poly seven-year-old Samyuktha, armed with her teddy bear, her homework and a Harry Potter book, would march into St. Isabel's Hospital and then to her mother's office, as though she owned it. There would be a small chair and table for her. Samyuktha would assiduously finish her homework, and curl up in her mother's large swivel chair, immersed in a book until Dr Anitha Kumar finished attending to her patients.

Anitha's nurses, attendants and junior doctors loved Samyuktha. They'd come in and hug her. They'd gush about how well she focussed on finishing her homework and her ability to read for hours at a stretch. They were Samyuktha's extended family. Once Anitha was done with her work, she would take her out for dinner and to the library, where they would chat for hours on end—about ships, shoes, sealing wax, cabbages and kings…

Samyuktha would talk about her day at school. Anitha would share anecdotes of the delivery room or the gossip around the office. Samyuktha loved listening to the stories. Every so often, Anitha would lapse into her childhood stories (she came from a family of five siblings) and Samyuktha would listen, sometimes wistfully, wishing for a platoon like that around her.

As Mylapore and Samyuktha grew up, they both stayed away from the party culture, choosing to support the network of local *sabhas* promoting Carnatic music and Bharatanatyam. The only difference was that Mylapore did it with panache and Samyuktha did it because her mom forced her to.

Even the doggedly uninitiated could not help wandering into a sabha or a temple *kutcheri* (concert) and marvel at the beauty of India's ancient cultural traditions. And Anitha made sure that Samyuktha was not uninitiated by any means. Samyuktha was faithfully shipped off to learn music from the prolific Suhasini

Rajagopal, who, as luck would have it, lived two floors above Samyuktha's flat in C-31, and unfailingly saw every kutcheri worth its salt in December.

Samyuktha loved music, but hated the training. She could not connect with the never-ending note patterns or enjoy repeating them a hundred times, while slapping the beats on her thigh. While Suhasini aunty was a perfectionist, little Samyuktha was a dreamer. As the lessons moved to songs, she could not keep up with the words and their meanings. 'Lambodara Lakumikara', 'Varaveena Mrudupani', she would get the syllables mixed up by mistake sometimes, but on purpose at other times to break the monotony.

Anitha tried to initiate her into Bharatanatyam as well, but when Samyuktha was found, tenth day in a row, reading a book in the small room next to the main room of the dance class, Anitha gave up.

Fast-forward to high school, when cappuccino unsuccessfully tried to become the new filter coffee: Samyuktha got herself a guitar and started playing her Carnatic note patterns on it. This was her first step in the journey towards embracing multiple cultures.

Pubs started mushrooming and Samyuktha became a more adventurous version of her *chamathu* (simpleton) self. Samyuktha smiled thinking of the times she would bunk school to go to The Velveteen Rabbit.

On the occasions that she could, Samyuktha had always enjoyed spending time with her mother. With time, they had become friends. Anitha was incisive but understanding at the same time. With years of excellent bedside manners combined with a mother's instinct, she knew how to listen, and more often than not, knew what Samyuktha was feeling, spot on.

༺࿎༻

Soon after the officers finished their breakfast at 9.00 a.m., the orders for deployment came in brown, government-sealed envelopes, smelling of fresh wax. Major Verma's company was assigned to Chennai until further orders. Major Verma was Abhimanyu's commanding officer, known for being a stickler for protocol. Enforcing social distancing and maintaining peace was their mission. This was a far cry from the intelligence posting that Abhimanyu had been hoping for since the time he was commissioned.

That was before the virus had reared its ugly head in Wuhan. The next morning, the train chugged into Egmore Railway Station, Chennai.

Abhimanyu had decided he wanted to learn the basics of Tamil when his train had left from Delhi. The other officers made fun of him. *Why are you learning these?* they asked, hooting, as he perused the script with his head buried in his book. He would occasionally look up, trying to string together a bunch of syllables, which no one understood.

'Looking to patao some Tam chick?' Ayaan asked him in amusement.

Abhimanyu looked up. 'Haan, of course, and impress her mom too,' he said looking at his book. 'Sorry, I meant, Amma.'

Abhimanyu thought of everything as an experience. Make today count. No regrets, ever. That was his lifelong motto. Only a few people knew the secret behind why he said that so often, and Ayaan was one amongst them.

He read up about Chennai: its culture, cuisine, music, cinema and history. Abhimanyu was certain that he would not get another opportunity to serve such a long stint in Chennai ever again, and he wanted to make it as memorable as possible. He was surprised to read that the Tamil movie industry was called Kollywood and not Tollywood, contrary to his imagination, since most of the film studios were located in a suburb called Kodambakkam (Tollywood is the name of the Telugu movie industry). Chennai was the home ground of the Mozart of Madras, A.R. Rahman, one amongst the handful of Indians who had won an Oscar. Rahman's impressive list of films caught Abhimanyu's eye. He had seen both *Roja* and *Bombay,* and only later realized that they were made in Tamil first before their Hindi versions captivated the nation's imagination.

As soon as they got out of the train after reaching Chennai, a wave of warm, humid air hit their faces. As the army vehicle slowly made its way through the city towards the Officers Training Academy in Meenambakkam, Abhimanyu looked around. Meanwhile, Ayaan explored Tinder.

'Not a single chick in sight. Or *chiknas* (attractive men), either…wait, let me increase the radius,' said Ayaan, swiping frantically on Tinder, continually increasing the radius as he looked at Abhimanyu wiping the sweat off his brow for the fifth time. 'Abhi, I'm telling you, you should join RAW and sit in AC all day. This outdoor life is not for delicate darlings like you… oh wait, a hot chick finally.' Ayaan's face perked up, before it fell again, '…320 kilometres away! Fuck!'

That was Bengaluru, most likely. Abhimanyu laughed till he had tears in his eyes.

⌒⌒

'*Madam, vandhachu* (Madam, you've reached)!' the driver said in a loud nasal drawl as Samyuktha's cab screeched to a halt. The familiar sign beckoned her.

No. 15, Ashok Apartments, Warren Road, Chennai, 600004.

Even in her grogginess, she smiled. And the smile grew wider when she saw who was looking out for her from the balcony of the first floor.

Thatha.

The earliest memory Samyuktha had of Thatha was when a dog had chased her in the colony. Thatha had come out, shooed the dog away nonchalantly and hugged Samyuktha tight. And then he had looked at her with mock disdain, saying, 'Scared of a dog-a?'

Thatha was a retired paint industry entrepreneur, the president of Ashok Apartments and Masterchef Mylapore. He held the last two posts in high regard. Also, having brought up Samyuktha while her parents pursued their careers, the two had a special *thatha–pethi* (grandfather–granddaughter) bond.

The familiar shriek of her mother as she came bounding down the apartment stairs with 'Samyuktha is here!' made her both smile and frown at the same time. *Where does Amma get her energy from? She's surely going to fall one day.*

Her mother finally reached the bottom of the stairs. After getting engulfed in her hug, Samyuktha smiled.

'Here.' Her mother gave her a squeeze of sanitizer. And then squeezed her arm. She just couldn't resist it. She gave Samyuktha a fresh mask to wear. 'Better to be safe, kanna. How was your flight? And how is college?'

'College is awesome, Amma,' Samyuktha said, picking up the bigger of the two suitcases, heaving them towards upstairs. 'But,' she added hesitantly, 'it feels nice to be back home.'

'What a pack of lies!' her mother said, grabbing hold of the smaller one. They both looked at each other and burst out laughing.

'The times they are a-changin', Samyuktha sang in her head. She was glad she lived on the first floor. It was always easy to climb up during a power cut, or when lifts were banned, like now, to avoid infection. Amma and she lugged the suitcases to the first floor, panting. And there it was. Home.

Bright and airy. There was one large couch in the living room with two smaller couches on either side, in a pale beige fabric. No dark dingy fabric for her mother to hide dust. 'If there's dust, we must clean it,' she'd always say. There was a long, beechwood side table with a family picture on it and another of Samyuktha's grandmother. A set of coffee-table books, carefully curated, sat in the centre, ranging from *F.R.I.E.N.D.S.* to *India's Great Masters.*

But Samyuktha's favourite place in the living room was the large, rosewood *oonjal* (swing) at one end of the living room. The oonjal was from Thatha's ancestral home in Thanjavur. It had been there as far as Samyuktha could remember. She had spent many a day on it, swaying gently to the music, doing her homework, falling asleep on Thatha's lap or just dreaming about her future.

The open French windows in the living room looked on to a large balcony. There was Thatha's vegetable corner on one end and Amma's plants on the other. In the centre was the sacred Tulsi, held in the traditional square pot. Near the entrance was a teak wood rocking chair that Thatha often fell asleep on. And tucked away in one corner, Samyuktha's nemeses: two brown plastic Nilkamal chairs that never gave up. *These will definitely outlast me,* she thought as she grimaced at the eyesores.

Thatha was waiting for her in his standard place on the couch, with that usual half-smile on his face. She was just about to jump on to him with her usual bear hug when she heard a voice.

'*Kulichitu vaa, po* (have a bath now), before you touch any surface, Samyuktha. Hygiene first. Have you not been following the news?' Samyuktha didn't need to trace the source of the voice to know that it was her Appa.

Mr Ajay Kumar fit the archetype of a cyber security expert

perfectly. Most days, he was holed up in his super-secret study, where entry was forbidden to others and which had never been cleaned, as far as Samyuktha could remember. His relationship with Samyuktha largely consisted of signing report cards when Amma wasn't around, teaching her how to solve *The Hindu* crossword and supplying her with an unending trail of books from Giri Stores in Luz Corner, much to Amma's despair.

She ran, pretending to give him a hug. He jumped out of her way. She then quickly scooted to her room, ensuring that she touched nothing before taking a bath.

Twenty minutes later, all fresh, she plonked on the sofa and hugged Thatha. 'Tell me all the *vambu* (gossip), Thatha. Has Sandhya come? Has Mahesh finally managed to lose weight? Has Ahalya become any less annoying than usual?'

Her Thatha grinned and shook his head.

Samyuktha watched her masked parents spray disinfectant on all her bags and suitcases and thoroughly wipe them down. 'Where is Pushpa?' she asked. Pushpa had been their domestic help since the time Samyuktha was a child.

'She doesn't come, kanna. No domestic workers are allowed inside now,' said Amma, as she scrubbed the suitcase vigorously. Samyuktha smiled. Amma was trying to remove an airline sticker mark from two years ago. *Our trip to the US just before I went to IIT,* Samyuktha thought.

'It's just Appa, Thatha and I. We've been taking turns running the house for the last three days. And kanna, I have to go to the hospital every day. Every healthcare worker has a pass. They need doctors more than anyone else during this time.' Amma sat back, satisfied, as the last white remnant of the sticker had come off.

Samyuktha nodded, feeling the all-too-familiar pang of wistfulness hit her again. Her sibling rivalry was with a hospital, fighting over who gets more of her mother's time and attention. *Even a pandemic with forced isolation won't keep her at home*, she thought. The irony…

⌒∾⌒

The jeep slowly rolled into the Officers Training Academy in Meenambakkam. This was to be Abhimanyu's home during their time in Chennai.

'Air conditioned rooms! Not the school classrooms converted into officer quarters,' Ayaan said as he looked out of the window to see miles of arid land peppered with buildings. 'Just curious, does anyone happen to know which Hunger Games district we're in?' Ayaan asked, wiping the perspiration from his forehead for the seventh time.

'LMFMO,' Abhimanyu said, with his laughter subsiding. They stopped and looked at him. 'Laughing My Freaking Mask Off. God. You guys are so NOT updated,' he said nonchalantly, as everyone groaned, taking out his clothes from his suitcase and neatly arranging them.

'God, this posting is going to be the worst,' said Sukhi, bunching up the clothes in a pile to make room to sit down. Abhimanyu didn't flinch. He was used to this by now. 'Have you ever heard,' Sukhi paused for impact, 'of an army posting in Chennai, where there has historically been no invasion?' he asked, watching in disgust as Abhimanyu arranged his perfectly folded clothes in the cabinet and carefully put his toiletries at proper places in the bathroom.

'I'm already tired of being a part of a major historical event,' said Anish, referring to Major Verma's rousing speech about fighting an unseen virus. Anish watched in disbelief as Abhimanyu brought out his carefully packed shoe collection and lined them up neatly in a corner near the entrance. '*Abey*, is this dude planning to move to Chennai? He's setting up a mini home here!' Anish said.

The boys looked around at their home for the next few months. Each room was identical and there was to be no sharing, given social distancing norms. The twelve-by-twelve-feet room had a single bed with a nightstand in one corner, thankfully next to a large window. An air conditioner was at the centre of the room, much to everyone's relief. Near the door, there was a simple, solid wooden desk and chair, much like the ones from school, and a simple cupboard with a single locked drawer to keep one's worldly possessions in.

The boys trooped out, agreeing to meet in an hour to take a walk around the area they were staying in. After they left, Abhimanyu opened a small suitcase his older sister had forced him to carry amidst violent protests by him. As he opened it, he smiled at her thoughtfulness. *Shalini Didi is indeed an interior designer.*

A pair of off-white, green paisley printed curtains and matching bed linen revealed itself. There was also a small off-white Fabindia lamp, followed by a small floor rug and two pale cushions. *How did my Mary Poppins sister fit all this into one suitcase?* he wondered as he obediently put up everything like she had instructed. He did not want to be lectured over a video call later in the evening. Lastly, he placed the bluetooth speaker on the nightstand.

As he surveyed the room, he was amazed at how much those small touches—the bed linen, the curtain, the rug—had transformed the room into a much-needed cozy space that one can come back to at the end of a day of hard work. *Didi's right,* he admitted both grudgingly and admiringly.

Abhimanyu casually picked up his iPhone and remembered what Ayaan had said about Chennai and Tinder. He opened the app and started flicking profiles. They were *different* from Delhi, for sure. As he continued flicking (mostly left), a profile popped up.

A round, smiling face, dressed in the latest couture. Large kohled eyes. *A? Sure, like Madam M, maybe.* On impulse, he swiped right. Instantly, the match sign came on.

Hey! A message popped up the next instant.

Abhimanyu was a bit unsure about his next move. He had come to Chennai on duty. *Should I be doing this or not?* Ayaan's voice flashed in his head. *Bhai, this is Tinder. not shaadi.Com. Have some fun, bro!*

He quickly replied, Hey, nice pic, A!

Yours too, Abhi! By the way, what kind of Abhi are you? Jeet, Ram or Shek?

Abhimanyu smiled and was about to reply, when the others banged at his door, with their masks and gloves in hand. '*Chal* (lets go)!' Sukhi said. 'Let's take a walk around Mylapore. Let's scan the territory,' he said with a grin.

So, the gang drove 11 kilometres from the academy to their assigned area early in the evening, parked their jeep and started walking around. Abhimanyu, who was usually the heart of any conversation, fell unusually silent.

Mylapore. He read the name of the area assigned to them. As they continued walking, he looked around, absorbing in the sights and sounds. A massively tree-lined area, it was a lovely stroll. Every house had a new number and an old number on it. *That must be terribly confusing,* he thought. *How does the mail ever reach correctly?*

He smiled at some of the bungalow names. *Sowbhagya, Magizhvagam.* He had practised the rolling 'zh' syllable during the train ride, but wasn't sure if he had got it right. Some homes had both partners' names on it. *Janaki and Suresh.* He smiled.

A refreshing change from 'Mehtas' and 'Singhs' written in the fanciest fonts.

This place is strikingly different from Delhi, he thought. *It has a certain…stateliness and culture to it, somehow…like stalwarts have come and gone.*

'Can you believe there are more temples than bars in this area?' Anish asked, breaking the silence.

Abhimanyu tried to get a hold on his chain of thought. 'How does that matter?' he said non-committedly, plucking off a leaf. 'Ayaan's room has more alcohol than all of Chennai.'

As they all laughed, a group of swift *mami* (aunty) joggers, wearing salwar kameez and sports shoes, glared at them. It was the last day of freedom for them, and they looked like they intended to walk enough to keep their metabolism working until after the lockdown ended.

One of them was talking about someone called Bombay Jayashree. Abhimanyu heard this and his ears perked. 'Just a minute,' he said and ran to them.

'This Singh will get us killed,' Sukhi said as Abhimanyu sprinted off. 'They'll send us back to Delhi.'

'Aunty,' Abhimanyu asked politely. 'May I ask you a question?'

'Is there an album of Bombay Jayashree that you would recommend to a Punjabi like me? I've read up about her and would love a recommendation,' he said as the strains of 'Enna Thavam' played on the mami's phone.

The women stared at him. One of them suddenly broke into a smile. 'Listen to *Confluence*, pa,' the woman said. 'It's a great album with lots of songs that you may know, or should get to know. '"Vaishnava Janato", "Jagadhodharana"…' She listed out a few more that sounded like tongue twisters.

'Wonderful. Thanks, Aunty!' he said as he gave them a brisk army salute and jogged back.

'What a cultured fellow,' one of the mamis said as all of them walked away.

'Saale, why the brownie points?' Anish asked him, trying to understand what had just happened.

Abhimanyu smiled as he googled *Confluence* by Bombay Jayashree on his phone. 'Just wanted to know, so I asked...' he added in a nonchalant style.

Abhimanyu was an enigma to most who met him—a walking contradiction if there ever was one. He could whistle through a trashy Bollywood masala flick as comfortably as hold an argument on Malcolm Gladwell's *Blink*. During NDA training, he would passionately argue over military strategies in case discussions and at the same time be the most attentive listener to those countering his stance. While intellectual tussles were his thing, ego tussles were not.

Abhimanyu had a resolute optimism, which was admirable for someone his age. His fiery speeches were largely inspiring, sometimes confusing, mostly when he delivered a passionate monologue on the value of filing an administrative report in Meerut that left his jawans trying to connect paper files to patriotism. Regardless of such incidents, every jawan under his command had a renewed sense of purpose and passion after working with Abhimanyu. There was also deep affection.

Abhimanyu's passion had one fallout—he had a terrible temper. He had zero tolerance for pettiness, laziness, shifting the blame and washing one's hands off responsibility. He had been pulled up more than once on losing his cool at his peers and his jawans. His circle knew it was better to not stoke that side of him.

As evening set in, the four officers donned their protective gear and manned their postings. As Abhimanyu walked towards his spot, he started looking out for potential locations. This would be his and the jawans' daytime 'office' over the next few weeks.

More likely months, Abhimanyu thought. He wanted to find a nice spot in the shade. *And a place that doesn't make me hate my job*, he thought.

After a few minutes, he noticed an under-construction building, which had been abandoned by all workers during the pandemic. Just a floor had been completed, and the bricks were visible in the absence of plaster. *In some cultures, this would be home decor fashion,* he thought. *What did they call it? Exposed red brick? Shalini didi would know better.* His sister was an up-and-coming interior designer in Delhi and he trusted her completely on these matters. He went and looked in. The designer had definitely put in some thought while working on the lobby. Even amidst cobwebs of all shapes and sizes, with an occasional dry leaf sashaying glamorously into their midst, Abhimanyu could make out the contours of the zone.

In one corner was a broad concrete slab, which would have probably become the front desk of the building. On the other end was a large waiting room area, where sofas would have been placed for the guests. The entire area was well ventilated, thanks to the French windows.

Abhimanyu picked the concrete concierge space for his office, and the waiting room area for his jawans. Ten minutes later, six uniformed jawans exited a jeep, eyeing the enclave curiously. Abhimanyu emerged from the building entrance, carrying two chairs. He strode towards the boys, rattling out a series of instructions.

As the men got busy setting up the makeshift operational base, Abhimanyu scanned the neighbourhood. Right opposite his post on the other side of the road was a residential apartment. *Ashok Apartments.* He could see the big golden letters etched on a white marble slab. *Fancy*, he thought, *must be some rich folks in there.* He wondered if this was the South Delhi of Chennai.

In about an hour, Abhimanyu came back to his base. The jawans had done a good job of cleaning up the place. He was even able to smell the disinfectant. He did not fail to notice the rustic, rugged mattresses from the barracks on the floors. Dhruv, a particularly bright jawan, had gone so far as to add a few cushions here and there, giving the zone a bright, cheerful look.

The area had been transformed. He saw a few of his belongings placed on the desk—his bluetooth speaker, all the walkie-talkie equipment and a few pictures that he carried everywhere with him. A comfy office chair had been set up for him, which they had ferreted out from the back of the storeroom, still in plastic wrapping. The icing on the cake was that construction workers had been able to complete the electronic work and three giant workers' lamps had been brought in by the jawans, giving the room a warm and rustic, yet an industrial feel to it. Abhimanyu instantly took a picture and sent it to his sister, and air hi-fived his boys. They beamed with delight.

He was ordered to start lockdown enforcement that very day. He checked his watch. It was 6.00 p.m. He picked up one of the books he had brought along and sat on a wooden chair outside the cabin. This spot gave him a good view of both sides of the road, and the one leading to Ashok Apartments. A light breeze had started flowing, which he was grateful for. Wearing a mask was going to take some getting used to. *Especially this*, he thought as he felt warm drafts of air on his eyes each time he exhaled.

He had barely read a few pages when someone approached him.

'Hi,' she said, slightly breathless.

Abhimanyu stopped reading *The Catcher in the Rye* and looked up.

'I'm Ahalya. Can you tell me if the chemist store is open?

Also, can I go there?' A short, slightly plump girl, wearing jeans and an oversized T-shirt, had appeared from nowhere. She had a fair complexion, and donned a short haircut, which was the latest style.

Abhimanyu was surprised. He thought that everyone had been informed that they weren't to go out at all. And here she was, and she didn't even have a mask on. 'No, Ma'am,' he said, standing up. 'You're not allowed to go out. In fact, you're not even allowed up to here. You have a grocery day and that is when you are allowed to go out. Which apartment?'

'C-21, Ashok Apartments,' she said, smiling at him.

Abhimanyu gave a slight smile back from behind his mask and checked his sheet. 'Your day is…Tuesday, Ma'am. From the Ganguly family?'

'Yes. I'm their daughter, Ahalya,' her smile grew wider.

'Oh…okay.' Abhimanyu didn't think he had anymore to say, so he went back to his book. Ahalya stood there, waiting for sometime.

Abhimanyu looked up, surprised. 'Anything else I can help you with, Ma'am?' he asked, genuinely puzzled.

Ahalya shook her head and left. As Abhimanyu watched her leave, he felt she looked familiar. *Where have I seen that face before?*

His thoughts were interrupted by a cab that was slowly approaching. He got up and walked towards it, stopping it midway. He noticed a girl sleeping soundly in the backseat. He knocked smartly on the window of the backseat, but there was no response.

Abhimanyu was observant and noticed the smallest of details within a second. The girl, he noted, had a certain aura about her. Her aquiline nose, like that of Cleopatra, stood out from a mile away. Her slender neck, culminating in her perfectly lined collar bone was even more accentuated as she slept soundly with her head on the seat.

War and Peace, he read the title of the book in her hand. And smiled thinking, *Did the army come here in times of war or for peace?*

He knocked once again, this time slightly louder, and asked, 'Where are you going?'

No response.

He knocked again, this time impatiently.

The girl woke up with a start.

'C-11, Ashok Apartments, Ajay Kumar. I'm his daughter, Samyuktha.'

Lock, Stock and Unbearable

*L*ots of bunnies. Some green, some yellow. Some had headphones on. One was singing 'Vaishnava Janato', another was reading War and Peace. All of them had slender, long necks and a sharp nose. One of the bunnies with a sleepy familiar voice seemed to be shrieking and asking Abhimanyu to let them pass.

Abhimanyu woke up with a start. What was he dreaming of? Ignoring the obvious reference, his mind wandered back to the owner of that aquiline nose. Samyuktha, was it? C-11? Trying to get his mind off her, he shook his head vigorously and splashed some cold water.

As he ran a cursory check on his phone, his thumb flitted to Tinder. He saw a bunch of messages from various blasts from the past and settled to check the three unread messages from A. *Cute girl,* he thought.

`Hey, you there?`

`Are you from Chennai, or visiting?`

`Hey, nice sense of style! Love the Henley Tee.`

Something about the tone of the messages made him click on her profile. He stared in disbelief, for it was Ahalya! That's why she looked familiar the previous day. *Fantastic, so now I'm posted a stone's throw away from that girl. What luck,* he grumbled to himself.

Abhimanyu typed back a message, `Hey A! Thank you so much. You have a great sense of style too! The Chennai heat is unbearable, isn't it?` He tactfully sidestepped answering any questions that involved divulging any information. He quickly flitted back to the usual—Facebook, Instagram and Whatsapp—spending a few cursory minutes on each. As he did, he heard a knock on the door.

His sahayak, a young bright-eyed jawan, Dinesh Yadav, from a village near Lucknow, came in with the morning tea. Abhimanyu smiled and sleepily greeted him. Meanwhile, Dinesh set the tea and proceeded to describe the drill. *What a sincere lad*, thought Abhimanyu, as he happily lapped up all the information he needed to jump straight into his core duties.

He sipped his chai as Dinesh listed the physical training facilities at the academy—where the officers' mess was set up, assembly areas for Abhimanyu's morning briefing with the jawans. Abhimanyu gave him a thumbs up, and to the Indian Army, too, in his mind, for their uber helpful buddy system.

Major Verma's company was assigned to Mylapore across four sections: the neighbourhood around Desika Road, where Ayaan would be stationed with his unit; Luz Corner and the area within the 500-metre radius around it, where Sukhi would be stationed; Mylapore Subway station and the 500-metre radius around it to Anish; Warren Road, Bhaskarapuram, and the 500-metre radius around it to Abhimanyu.

Ayaan was already on the field when Abhimanyu arrived. Neither of them ever missed their early morning PT routines. They usually ended up working out together.

'Are you already done with your routine?' Abhimanyu asked Ayaan, surprised to see him dripping profusely with sweat so early in the day.

'Nope,' Ayaan replied, looking like he had just finished a half marathon. 'I started ten minutes ago. This fucking humidity, dude. I nearly slipped on my own sweaty palms doing push ups.'

Within a few minutes, Abhimanyu, too, was drenched

from head to toe. He wondered how they all would last all day under such circumstances. They ploughed through the routine nonetheless. An hour later, they collapsed on their mats, dead tired.

A cold shower helped. After breakfast, Abhimanyu sped off to his briefing session with Major Verma. Later, as their jeep made the turn from C.V. Raman Road on to Warren Road, Abhimanyu felt a sense of excitement. *Would Cleopatra be there?* He remembered the number C-11, and looked up to the first floor of the building. No one.

The morning passed quickly enough. He explained the daily protocol to his jawans on the route and the frequency of the mobile checkpost, and got some administrative tasks out of the way. He looked at the bunch of masked jawans. They were an eager and friendly lot. Abhimanyu reiterated general instructions about dealing with civilians. It was pretty straightforward. He would be there from 8.00 a.m. to 8.00 p.m. every day. The night-duty jawans would be at limited check posts till the morning hours.

Every once in a while, he looked around for Cleopatra from the previous day. She was nowhere to be seen. Dhruv noticed this. '*Sir, upar kuch hai kya* (Sir, is there something up there)?' he asked, a little cheekily.

'*Aasman* (the sky),' he replied, without blinking an eye.

During his tea break, Abhimanyu saw a string of messages from his sister, the one human being he loved more than anyone else in the world. He immediately called her. As soon as her cheerful voice came through, he updated her on his whereabouts and his first impressions of Chennai. As he did so, he took a sip of the chai Dhruv had so dutifully poured for him. His face contorted as he almost spat it out. *What was this thick concoction? Was it that dust tea that he had read about?* To his refined chai sensibilities, it surely tasted like dust.

'The chai sucks, Didi,' he said spontaneously, 'and the heat sucks the energy out of you,' he replied to her, eyeing the brown liquid with distrust. As his sister laughed at his reply, he strained his ears to catch the sounds around her—a cooker whistle, dishes clanking and running water. She was cooking.

'Done stocking up on groceries, Didi?' he asked as he contemplated whether or not to finish the tea. He heard someone shout in her background. Abhimanyu cursed under his breath and stepped away from the enclave, now speaking in a softer tone.

'Didi, how are the mood swings? Lockdown may...' he corrected himself, '...*will* make it worse. Will you be okay?' he asked as he stared at the layer of cream that had formed on the tea. He gave up and kept it aside.

'I think it's okay for now. He's been having fits of rage on and off, and last week he threw a magazine at me,' she sounded nonchalant as always, having faced the worst. 'But he hasn't gone beyond that. *Tumhara woh Christmas gift wala punching bag kaam aa raha hai* (The punching bag you gave as a Christmas gift has been put to good use). You don't worry about all this kiddo, I'm doing fine. Love you.'

'*Theek hai* (okay). This is an easy posting. I'll keep calling.' Abhimanyu hung up and stared at the phone. *I should pay her a visit after all this. It's been a while.*

∽

It was 10.00 a.m., and the PM was addressing the nation. Ajay Kumar was watching intently as Samyuktha sauntered into the airy living room. She had partially caught up on her sleep, but still felt tired due to the chaos of the last two days.

A lockdown had been imposed. Movement was only allowed between 11.00 a.m. and 5.00 p.m., with children under 10 and senior citizens barred from leaving their homes. No one was allowed to move in groups and it was mandatory to wear a mask at all times in public spaces. Family members were allowed to go on grocery runs only on the designated days allotted to their apartment by army personnel.

Watching the PM address the nation, Samyuktha sat in rapt attention in front of their 55-inch LED television screen and watched his oratorical brilliance cutting through. All the pettiness of borders, religion and money seemed to have vanished in the nobility of the current task at hand—containing the virus at Stage 2—and taking seemingly draconian but highly necessary measures to ensure that.

There was an eerie silence. Thatha interrupted it with his firm yet frail voice.

'Enough of this lockdown *kadhai* (story), the child has just come home!' Thatha said, rebuking the world at large and Samyuktha's parents in particular. He walked slowly towards the kitchen table. 'Come kanna, I've made your favourite tiffin.'

'*Dosai* and *vengaya* (onion) chutney?' Samyuktha smiled, hearing the word 'tiffin'. That was so Chennai and so Thatha.

Since cooks and house helps had been banned from entering homes, on Thatha's insistence, Anitha had reluctantly relegated the reins of the kitchen to him. The 76-year-old warrior had taken it on with some trepidation to begin with, but very soon, had attacked it with gusto. Thatha's sharp attention to detail, unerring sense of taste, smell, and innovations in the kitchen slowly became a delight for everyone in the family, who would wake up every morning to the delicious sounds of mustard and red chillies crackling on the stove.

Over time, one would happily take in the train of gentle aromas wafting in from the kitchen, *jeerakam* (cumin seeds) and then *perungayam* (asafoetida), and then the five friendly members of Thatha's trademark tempering would gently wake one up from deep sleep. Finally, the gentle searing of curry leaves would act as an alarm bell for breakfast being ready, and one's eyes would pop open like breads in a toaster. Messy-haired, hungry warriors would walk into the kitchen to attack the steaming hot preparations that had just come to life.

Growing up, Samyuktha remembered returning home to the heavenly smell of sambar simmering on the stove whenever Thatha cooked. The two minutes it would take her to remove her shoes and wash her hands before Thatha would allow her at the table seemed way longer in comparison to the thirty-minute school bus ride on her way home. Thatha had a penchant for presenting the food beautifully. 'The eyes and nose taste the food before the tongue does,' he would say while placing two fresh coriander leaves in the chutneys before Samyuktha could proceed to eat it.

Breakfast time was an animated affair. Everyone tried to keep their spirits up, but ended up annoying each other. Anitha and Ajay were at loggerheads over their strategy to ensure that there were enough essentials.

'Maybe we should stock up for twenty-one days, Anitha,' said Ajay. 'It's much more convenient and efficient. Why risk it by going out every week?'

'That's not called stocking. That's hoarding,' snapped Anitha. In general, she seemed to snap at Ajay for no apparent reason and Samyuktha noticed instinctively that this had gone up since she had left for IIT. 'We're not doing any of that. We buy for seven days at a time. Let's be sensible about this. We should for sure stock up Appa's medicines,' she said. As expected, Ajay backed down.

Samyuktha, however, was in no mood to intervene. She was more than happy to quietly eat the crisp dosais. She reached out for the vengaya chutney across the table and heaped on a generous helping. Thatha noticed and gave her his toothless grin.

Ajay cleared his throat. *A long lecture,* Samyuktha mentally groaned. *Probably super boring too.* Anitha caught Samyuktha's glance and smiled, to which Samyuktha smiled back. Ajay didn't notice.

And sure enough. There it was—his own Covid advisory. Over mouthfuls of dosa and *thayir* (curd), he spoke of the army personnel standing guard outside. Samyuktha was not to engage in conversation with them at any point. She was not to step out unless it was the designated grocery day. They were to go to the local market with masks and gloves on. They were not supposed to leave the community unless there was an emergency. No gathering was allowed, so they couldn't meet anyone.

'I hope supermarkets don't run out of essentials, Thatha,' Samyuktha said, carefully examining her plate, which she had licked clean. Thatha had once said that Samyuktha's plate never needed to be washed. And since that day, Samyuktha became compulsively obsessed over eating everything on her plate and keeping it super clean. Thatha had his own wisdom and ways of instilling habits into people.

'If they run out, it will be because of the Gangulys,' said Thatha, rounding his 'O's and trying to sound Bengali. Thatha had spent five years in Calcutta, and took pride in his Bengali-meets-Tamilian accent. 'I see one of them at the supermarket whenever I go. Gosh!' he said, now turning British, having worked in British paint companies for thirty years.

'I hope they don't forget to spray Dettol and wipe everything before using them,' Ajay said, smiling at Thatha's way of speaking. 'All it takes is one person forgetting, and all of Mylapore will be at risk.' He looked at Anitha as if trying to reconcile after his earlier gaffe, and continued, 'After all, not everyone is a Dettol queen like Anitha.'

He chuckled at his own joke. Nobody joined him. Plus,

the joke didn't have the intended effect. Anitha glared at him. Samyuktha concentrated on looking at her plate as if her life depended on it. Thatha was suddenly absorbed in checking his WhatsApp forwards.

Anitha had had a long-standing love story going on with Dettol. Ever since Samyuktha could remember, there would be spray bottles with diluted Dettol solution everywhere in the house—in the bathrooms, on the kitchen counter, in the balconies…

Samyuktha always made fun of her mother's Dettol obsession. She would always say, in splits of laughter, 'Amma, if you had it your way, you would have Dettol in the centre of your coffee table, inside the wine cabinet and as your deodorant also!' Amma always laughed when Samyuktha poked fun at her because she knew that deep down, she did not mean any disrespect. With Ajay, however, she always felt that he made fun of her.

'Kanna, do you want to Skype with anyone in the building tomorrow to say hello?' Anitha asked, trying to change the subject. Images of the building floors flashed in Samyuktha's photographic memory. The familiar childhood scenes, like that of the transparent elevator doors, ran across her mind.

On the second floor, there was Indrani Ganguly, constantly dusting her showcase with dainty figurines and collectibles from over fifteen countries. Then there was Ahalya, her daughter, always watching television with the door open. Indrani's son, Arun, was usually seen with his head inside a book, preparing for an entrance exam. *I think it's more to get his mind off the gossip that Ahalya and Indrani are always spinning*, Samyuktha thought, a bit cruelly. Twenty-year-olds can be cruel sometimes. Lastly, there was Abhijeet Uncle, who was always away at work.

On third floor was Suhasini aunty. Samyuktha smiled thinking of her. She was the *joie de vivre* of the building. She was a simple, elegant lady with a powerful gift. Every morning, entire C-31 would resonate with a strong, melodious voice set against a backdrop of reverberating tanpura strains. The voice meandered effortlessly through fast-paced trills, nimble yet purposeful, pausing every so often on a note, holding it with the power and resilience of several decades of training, before gently letting it go. Samyuktha loved listening to Suhasini aunty, but would be equally terrified whenever she would be asked to sing like that.

Suhasini aunty was a stark contrast to Anitha, who could successfully knock down a trail of lamps, books and anything that caught her dupatta's fancy wherever she went. Samyuktha would notice how her mother would come running down the stairs, shrieking in delight at something she was excited about. Suhasini aunty would glide downstairs like an angel, calm and composed.

Every apartment had that one *akka* that everyone would admire. The girl who always wore make-up, the nicest clothes, a slim figure, one who always went to work looking like a daisy, while you would be busy cramming for that biology exam. Well, for Ashok Apartments, that was Sandhya, Suhasini aunty's daughter.

Four years ago, Sandhya and Suhasini were left devastated when Rajagopal uncle passed away due to a sudden heart attack. The way Suhasini bounced back from the grief was nothing short of amazing. She had slowly restarted her singing classes, which also included Zoom and Skype sessions. In the December of 2019, she had sung in Narada Gana Sabha's afternoon slot. Recently, a fast-rising Carnatic fusion channel had invited her to collaborate with them. Sandhya watched with quiet pride as her mother moved from strength to strength in every part of life. Sandhya, nine months pregnant, was now back home and looking forward to starting her journey of motherhood.

Samyuktha shook herself out of her reverie and came back to reality. Her mother was saying something about Skype.

'Thanks, Amma. A yes to Sandhya, but a no to the Gangulys. I really don't enjoy the prospect of having to answer Indrani aunty's questions.' Thatha winked at her. Samyuktha smiled back.

'Poor Indrani, she suffers from anxiety,' Anitha said. 'I saw her almost coming to blows with this woman the other day over the last packet of upma rava.'

Samyuktha burst out laughing. That sounded exactly like Indrani aunty! Ajay frowned. He was very prim and proper like that. Samyuktha saw the frown and quickly changed the subject. 'How do army personnel stand in the heat all day?' she asked.

'Not your concern. Just focus on your classes, Samyu.' Her father's brusque tone once again surprised and stung her. His quick springing up and retiring to his study puzzled her even more.

'Kanna, I think Appa just wants you to be careful,' her mother said as she started putting the dishes away.

⁓

As he stepped into his study, Ajay locked the door and plugged his phone in for charging. The lockdown announcement was bothering him. He stepped over to a grandfather's clock on his left, and set the time to 10.10.

With a soft click, the wooden panel below the face of the clock slid open to reveal a keypad and a scanner. Ajay entered a six-digit code and stepped forward as a horizontal green beam scanned his retina. Seconds later, a panel opened up in the wall and a hidden screen came to life. Ajay stared at it for a few seconds, organizing his thoughts.

Then with a resolute tilt of his head, he started typing. This

is now the second announcement that I was not
made aware of. More importantly, it restricts
movement, including that of our target group.
It is not possible to analyse movement patterns
without movement now, is it? Or am I missing
something about the fundamentals of GPS tracking?
He hit the enter button.

There was no response. He waited patiently. His mind was
whirring as he tried to process alternate options. *Maybe if we
double down on movements during grocery days...but what if it's
the family members who go out and not the target group? Could
we include second-degree contacts in the analy*—his thoughts were
interrupted by a soft ping.

Call me on a secure line, the message read.

Ajay put on his headphones and made the call. A deep voice
in a clear convent-educated accent spoke, 'Ajay, it's we who report
to PM sir, not the other way round. Just wanted to make sure
you are still aware?' Ajay sighed, and was about to respond when
the voice continued, 'I'm aware things are moving fast. There are
political agendas and vote banks to appease, and yes I'm also
aware that it is not *your* problem. I've put in a request to allow
access to more classified information about the target group to
make things easier.'

Ajay's brow relaxed and he grunted in agreement before
the voice continued, 'Most likely, we will get travel information
immediately. I'm also hoping for a messenger app and text
message access, but you know the repercussions of that better
than I do. Give me a few days to massage it in. You have Google
search access already. Are we good?' the voice asked.

'I'm trying my best, Ravi. The new information will certainly
help, but if movement is restricted to a house or a floor, we should
look into expanding the suspect pool beyond the primary. Family

members and immediate neighbours should now be considered too,' he rattled off in an assertive voice, despite knowing the answer.

'We do not have clearance for that yet, Ajay. You know what I am up against. I am trusting you to figure this out. Also, just a heads up, PM sir wants us to cultivate an asset over three years in China-occupied Kashmir, preferably Aksai Chin, to be tapped at the right time. Serious counter-intelligence op would need a new asset, not a previous field agent. Let's circle back soon on that. I'll send a note,' said the voice as the line went cold.

Ajay leaned on his desk and hung his head, deep in thought. *Of course, some sarkari minion dreams up a utopian miracle to impress his boss. His daft bureaucrat boss latches on to it, having no idea what it means or takes. Within minutes, they are rejoicing at their absurd brilliance, and the task of picking up after them is left to us. What a pack of nitwits.* Ajay cringed as he remembered the video of a senior politician earnestly arguing that data should not be stored in cloud because 'if it rains, we will lose it all'.

Despite the setbacks, he knew what they were all up against. He was actually rather amazed by how quickly the Indian government's IT crack team had built an app that traced the movement of Covid-confirmed cases. While that was a major win, the bigger danger was those who were 'potentially-infected', but not showing any symptoms yet, and hence not getting tracked by the app.

With testing kits being as plentiful as common sense in political leaders, Ajay had recommended that they leverage predictive analytics instead of zeroing in on those who were most likely to be carriers. Ajay was determined to crack this problem, for more reasons than the obvious.

If successful, this could help predict at least 63 per cent of cases in the early stages of infection, and, in turn, prevent the spread of the infection by at least 20 per cent, which, in a country like India would be a sizable number and save millions of lives. His boss, of course, was excited that if patented and launched globally, the app would make India a major player in the global Covid-resolution game, boosting diplomacy and international relations.

But for Ajay, it validated the fact that his childhood obsession with technology had not been a waste. It could actually save the country. He leaned back in his chair as bittersweet memories of his childhood flashed through his mind. *Amma and Hari Anna would've been so proud. Maybe Appa too,* he thought wistfully.

꼰

For Abhimanyu, the next few days were eventful. Imposing rules on a population that thrived on breaking rules was both challenging as well as amusing.

There was the nightgown-clad woman who made a sorry face and whined about wanting to deliver her 'medicinal' chutney to the 'sick lady' in the next building.

There was the blue-haired high school punk with stained teeth who wanted to go to the next street to get 'notes' urgently for his pre-board exams. Abhimanyu was impressed with the creativity and conviction. *No wonder we make the most dramatic movies in the world,* he thought.

But the one who took the cake was Ahalya, much to Abhimanyu's discomfort and Ayaan's amusement. She found an excuse every single day to ask him the most inane of questions.

'Should I go buy essential staples with or without a mask?'

'Will the shops be open on Sundays?'

'How long do you feel this will go on for?'

Abhimanyu wasn't sure if Ahalya had figured out who he was. He had a mask on at all times. He was all open to helping people, but this was a bit too much, he thought. Also these strange questions were only posed to him and never to his jawans. At a time when even a few more stray dogs than usual was considered unusual, this became the hot rip-roaring conversation amongst the regiment.

Sukhi and Ayaan put together an open mic for the officers one evening over beer after their shifts. It had a set of A-rated variations of Ahalya's questions and officers needed to come up with what Abhimanyu's reactions should have been. The funnier and racier, the better.

Meanwhile outside, as people slowly resigned to their fate and came to understand the gravity of the situation, the excuses died out. And then it was just empty streets, save the one or two odd instances. Often, people coming out on to their balconies was hilarious in its own way. There was the aunty who puffed and panted as she jogged in one place, the ladies who gossiped from across their balconies, the frustrated uncle attending to a phone call, trying to understand how to log in to a Zoom meeting, and the occasional bickering couple.

Abhimanyu found solace in his open, airy office space, which, with each passing day, became more and more homey with the additions the jawans brought. Some bought their favourite pictures and some their gadgets. A soldier who did *warli* art in his spare time brought his masterpiece and leaned it against the wall. Abhimanyu brought all his books and lined them up at the desk. From *True North* to *Sapiens*, *Factfulness*, *Jugaad Innovation* and *The Catcher in the Rye*, Abhimanyu read a wide variety of genres, and the lockdown served as a time for him to nourish his soul when there was a bit of free time here and there.

Jawans weren't allowed to use phones on duty, so as a sign of solidarity with them, Abhimanyu also left his phone at the Academy; although he carried a burner phone with him, in case his sister needed to reach him in an emergency.

A few days rolled by. Online classes weren't remotely as fun as regular ones. First, there was no one to make fun of. Watching your classmate snigger at your wisecrack in real time is a joy that just cannot be digitized.

Second, bunking and valiantly trying to get a proxy wasn't an option anymore. It was just reams of excel sheets and documents that one had to read, and then reference back to long chapters in Smith and Van Ness.

Samyuktha checked online dating apps to see if there had been any increased activity there. *The usual, just more of it. Guys flaunting their abs, saying, 'I want to be friends first.' (Yes, sure.) Calling themselves sapiosexual. Every one of them! All bios changed to awkwardly include the current situation. 'Let's do a virtual drink sometime. And maybe more. *Wink*' Well. A few hours of swiping every day did no harm to anyone*, Samyuktha concluded, thinking of Rohan. *And I should really stop being so judgemental.*

After a week of enjoying the luxuries of home, confinement started getting to Samyuktha. After the chaos of campus life, the silence and stillness at home felt deafening. She sorely missed her routine back on campus. Rushing to coffee shack in the five minutes between classes for a quick break over Maggi. She missed the endless banter by the lakeside, pointless fights with Sharanya over which of them was always the last one to reach. And there was Rohan, of course, who courted her for three complete weeks before she finally gave in to his surprise proposal by the lakeside. Her rollercoaster campus life was now reduced to a laptop screen and Zoom calls. To top it all, evaluations, submissions and summatives went on unrelentingly and uncompromisingly. Boxes needed to be ticked, after all.

As Samyuktha looked at the online quantum mechanics class screen, she felt a lump in her throat. The dichotomy of the amount of work and the absence of social interaction to make up for it was slowly getting to her. She shut her laptop screen with a bang.

Damn this virus, she thought. *I don't know what the bigger picture behind this is. Is it Thanos? Is it sent by the non-human beings to just wipe us out to the right degree?*

She called Rohan.

He answered on the first ring. 'Hey, baby, how's it going?'

'Terrible. I miss you,' she said as she opened her balcony door and flopped onto her loveseat.

'Me too, babe. From campus life to…this. The army is killing us here.'

'We have hot army men guarding us here,' she told him. She had a bit of serpent's wisdom in her and knew how to make him jealous.

'Baby, soldiers are all brawn,' he replied, chewing something. *Mentos, most likely,* Samyuktha thought. She'd lost count of the number of times that minty Mentos mouth had been on hers.

She laughed, but couldn't stop herself from thinking about the soldier's deep voice—the one who had stopped her at the checkpost. As she talked to Rohan, she walked up and looked out of the balcony. She saw him walking up and down, wearing Ray-Ban over his mask. *Is he the one that stopped me when I came in?* she thought lazily. As she looked intently, he turned and looked at her. *Wait. Is he looking at me?*

Samyuktha quickly averted her eyes. Abhimanyu wasn't to be outdone. He slowly, purposefully removed his Ray-Ban and winked at her. *Did he just wink at me?* As she contemplated, Abhimanyu quelled all her doubts by waving at her. Both hands.

Samyuktha felt a surge of both anger and excitement.

She went back inside, lay down on her bed and continued talking to Rohan.

After 10 minutes, she walked out again, curious to see if Winky was still around. She stood there, looking out from her balcony. It was wide and spacious. A rough, grey stone flooring gave it both a traditional and a rustic-modern look. On one far corner was an open wooden Sheesham bookshelf. It stood like a proud veteran, with its inhabitants from P.G. Wodehouse to Khaled Hosseini to Robert Resnick and David Halliday peeping at her.

Bookshelves were for books, not for mementos and other garbage. Samyuktha was clear about that rule. The only exception she made was for her WiFi speaker, which was placed in one corner of the bookshelf, conveniently near the power outlet.

On the other end was her picture wall. That picture wall was representative of Samyuktha's relationship with herself over the years. In the centre was a family portrait from when Parvati paati was alive, with one-year-old Samyuktha sitting in her lap looking up at her adoringly. Beside it was a black-and-white portrait of Barack Obama, leaning and looking back at Michelle. The perfect couple, Samyuktha always said.

The framed photo of a waddle of penguins in Antarctica was the third proud inhabitant of that wall. Watching any herd of animals walking freely in the wild brought her insane joy. *Poetic justice in these times,* she thought, as she imagined hordes of animals reclaiming their right to live and breathe as equals on Earth.

Samyuktha spent many days of her childhood sitting in her loveseat, deep in thought. The warm evening breeze would lull her to sleep, as the strains of Buddha Bar, the trance music group, or songs of Simon and Garfunkel, the folk-rock duo, played gently in the background.

She loved opening her eyes to see the golden rays of the setting sun streaming through the cracks in the woven wooden blinds. As they gently swayed in the wind, the rays cast dancing shadows all over at dusk. There was the hum of car engines, the occasional horn and the comforting soundscape of unintelligible voices, and, on quite a few ethereal evenings, the soulful choir of Suhasini aunty's music students chanting 'Vanajakshiro' in unison.

Samyuktha gently brought herself back to reality.

Meanwhile, outside on the road, Abhimanyu craned forward to catch a glimpse of The Nose once again. That was his nickname for her. *Shoot. She's gone inside.* He looked over at her balcony. *I can scale that thing*, he thought subconsciously. *Maybe I will.*

There was still no sign of Samyuktha. He got up and stretched. He then picked up the morning's copy of *The Hindu* to solve the crossword. He'd heard about the iconic crossword of the English daily, and got down to trying to solve it every day in earnest. So far, he had never solved any, but came close to finishing it today. Only four more clues were left.

He then swung left and right till he cracked his back, and then nodded left and right and felt a crack in his neck. *I'm going to end up rusting here on this dusty road.*

He started sashaying and imagined he was on a date with The Nose at a restaurant. He then imagined himself as a young desi Bruno Mars, treading with his typical swagger. Just after Bruno met his date in his imagination, his patrol jeep appeared in the distance on Warren Road, and he broke into his regular swagger as his jawans saluted him from the jeep as it passed. *That was close*, he thought. As the jeep sped past, he resumed his Bruno Mars-meets-Prabhu Deva swagger, looking around. His heart leapt. The Nose was back on the balcony!

What the...when did she appear? He turned red with embarrassment and tried switching to a normal pace, like that of a serious military man. *No big deal.* He turned around and The Nose had finished her call and gone back to reading her book. He gazed in her direction. *Mylapore's Cleopatra*, he thought. *That nose could change the course of our history here.* Her hair was tied back loosely with a few strands falling carelessly on her face. He was hoping she would look around shortly, but she remained buried in the book.

Alright then, he thought, *you bookworm. Two can play this game.* He opened *The Catcher in the Rye* and leaned against a tree, trying to rebuild interest in Holden's life. He wasn't sure if it was the last streak of the setting sun, or an intense gaze that made him feel so conscious all of a sudden. He looked at her again.

She was staring right at his book. She was caught unawares and didn't know what to do. He slowly, deliberately took off his mask, looked at her and smiled at her—the same smile that the girls on his Tinder profile loved apparently. It hadn't failed him yet. As their eyes locked, her glare softened, and Abhimanyu knew he didn't need to worry about becoming lonely like Holden, at least not here on Warren Road.

⌒∽⌒

'*Kya soch mein hai, Abhi* (What are you thinking, Abhi)?' Ayaan asked him at lunch, breaking Abhimanyu's chain of thought.

'*First floor wali ladki is quite cute* (The girl living on the first floor is quite cute),' Abhimanyu said, coming straight to the point.

Ayaan whistled. 'Bhai, Singh is in love. Again.'

Anish smiled and said, '*Arre, humaara* (Oh, our) Singh is King. Has he ever been rejected by a girl? That's for losers like us.'

Sukhi jumped in. '*Abe, sun* (Listen now). This is Chennai. People here are strict as hell about these things. You'll get beaten up by the mamis. *Panga mat le* (Don't take risks). Especially if you want that next posting.' Sukhi knew that Abhimanyu's dearest wish was to join the army intelligence corps, where he could put both his patriotism and brains to good use.

'Sukhi is right, Bhai. If any of us can join intelligence, it's you. Don't jeopardize it,' Anish said, chewing mouthfuls of sambar-rice that he tried to unsuccessfully eat with his hand.

'Waise...how cute is she?' Ayaan asked as he helplessly looked at the rasam running all over his plate. 'The amount of risk is directly proportional to the cuteness factor.' He gave up as the rasam spilled all over in the plate. 'Yaar, doesn't this city have the concept of using a bowl?'

'Abe hero, make some space in the middle of the rice mound and pour the rasam there,' Abhimanyu said as he did so. 'Her nose, na...' Abhimanyu said, munching on a papad.

'*Naak pe diwana ho gaya saala* (The man is swooning over her nose)!' said Anish. They all jumped in with an assortment of nose jokes.

Abhimanyu smiled. They were definitely going to pull his leg all night. He decided he needed to know this girl better.

After lunch, he went on a stroll with Ayaan.

'Are you serious about this girl? Bhai, take it slow. Love, shaadi, etc., especially during lockdown...' Ayaan said as he let out a loud rice burp.

'*Shaadi nahin, bro* (Not marriage, brother). Never in life.' Abhimanyu's usually soft face hardened.

Ayaan grew serious. 'How is Shalini didi?'

'She keeps saying she's okay, but I keep on hearing him shout in the background,' Abhi said with a frown. 'Yaar, if anything happens to her, then I can't even reach her on short notice.' Abhimanyu rubbed his nose vigorously. He did this whenever he was perplexed—a childhood habit. He suddenly sat down near a tree.

Ayaan's face softened. He loved Abhimanyu's sister like his own. '*Hamari Shalini Didi na, fighter hai* (Our Shalini Didi is a fighter),' he said as he sat next to him. 'She's smarter than all of us put together, Bhai.'

Abhimanyu looked at him.

'Even you.'

Abhimanyu fell silent. Ayaan knew that he was in deep thought, probably worrying for his sister. Abhimanyu looked at his concerned face and gave him a friendly punch in the ribs. '*Chal. Time ho gaya* (Come. It's time).' He got up and walked away abruptly.

Ayaan watched him as he walked off, and blinked and rubbed his eyes vigorously.

⁕

Anitha knocked on Samyuktha's door.

'Free-a Samyu kanna, or busy with college stuff?' Anitha waited at Samyuktha's door. She knew that twenty-year-olds needed privacy, a privilege she never had for herself in a bygone era in Palakkad.

As she leaned against the door, Anitha thought of the last seven days. The virus and the consequent lockdown had been a double whammy. While Thatha took care of the household as much as he could, with Ajay locked up in his study all the time, Anitha had a lot more work to do. She was unabashedly delighted to have Samyuktha home on two accounts.

First, she was vastly relieved that Samyuktha was not exposed to this maniacal virus in a place like IIT Bombay. Mumbai was leading the count by far on Covid-19 cases, and second, IIT was filled with a representation of all of India's population within close quarters. And who was the boy, Rohan, the one she kept talking to? Anitha wished she could know more, but understood it was better not to interfere in things like that.

But more importantly, she was thrilled because Samyuktha was someone she could talk to about anything. They were each other's...wingmen! She could be crazy, wacky or serious with her and Samyuktha would respond in kind.

'Amma, what are you doing waiting at the door?' Anitha was shaken out of her reverie as she heard Samyuktha's voice, and the noise of shutting the bathroom door. '*Periya* (Big) formality.' Anitha found herself dragged by her not-so-tiny clone to the balcony. It was one of their favourite spots to hang out.

Anitha settled down on the loveseat and looked, with unadulterated happiness, at the lovely space her daughter had created. For Anitha, that balcony epitomized everything she had wanted as a child—the quiet, the openness, a place to dream—which was constantly at a premium, with five siblings competing for everything around, be it space, books or attention. She wanted Samyuktha to have that element of childhood that she had so sorely missed.

'Why so quiet, Amma?' Samyuktha asked as she curled up on the loveseat, and leaned against Anitha like she usually did.

'I've just been running around since you came and we haven't had a chance to talk properly, kanna,' Anitha said as she looked down at her alter ego and tousled her black head of hair.

Anitha was always dressed in crisp cotton salwar suits or Bengal cotton sarees. She was the delight of the dhobi mama because she insisted on having all her wardrobe washed and starched. Since she could be called in at a moment's notice to the hospital anytime, she always wore work clothes at home. Her hair, once long, was now cut short, so that she could tie it in a ponytail easily. It was still black and glossy, though, with no sign of grey. She wore kajal only on her lower eyelid and a big red pottu on her forehead. *Was Amma fat?* Samyuktha often wondered. She was plumpish, but nothing that a well-stitched salwar couldn't take care of.

'Take some time off, Amma. You work too hard,' Samyuktha said as she leaned against her shoulder and sipped her filter coffee. 'Mmmm… Perfect.'

'I wish I could, kanna, but we need all hands on deck in present times. Dr Ram talked of new symptoms noticed by doctors in Manhattan. And I still don't know exactly how it affects pregnant ladies and their babi—'

Samyuktha was listening intently, but Anitha stopped herself short.

'Why am I boring you with all this? You tell me all about your campus life. I keep going on and on about myself. I really should retire,' Anitha said this at least twice every month. Lately, the frequency had increased.

'You'll go mad and drive everyone up the wall. Please don't!' Samyuktha said matter-of-factly.

Anitha burst out laughing. 'That's true,' she said. Her face softened. 'And what about you, kannamma? How does it feel, coming back to your boring old home after all your excitement at college? What a bummer, *illaya* (isn't it)?'

'YES!' exploded Samyuktha as she collapsed from Anitha's shoulder on to her lap. Anitha stroked her hair, just as she did when she was little. 'I'm sorry, Amma, but it really is. I had just figured stuff out, got the hang of things, life was just turning out to be awesome. Don't get me wrong, I love this place. But Amma…! It's unfair, right?'

'Of course.' Anitha had learned long ago not to indulge in the usual 'but you're so lucky' spiel. It was completely unfair from Samyuktha's point of view. 'I understand, kanna. But you know what, we're going to make this as fun for you as possible. No rules, except the ones for hygiene and sanitation. Let's plan some movie nights, bring out the carrom board. Thatha would love that! I'll tell Appa to spend more time with us. How does that sound?'

Samyuktha's eyes brightened. She loved hanging out with her mother. Maybe the lockdown didn't have to be so miserable after all. She sat up straight. 'Awesome, Amma. Let's recreate the ambience of The Velveteen Rabbit at home.' She winked. 'Well stocked on wine, aren't we?'

They both laughed. Just then Anitha got a call on her emergency phone. She picked up instantly. 'Yes, ya...hmm... okay...four centimetres? Okay. Keep her under observation. Call Sunitha. Yes, I'll be there in...' she said looking at her watch, 'ten minutes, thereabouts.'

Samyuktha sighed and collapsed back on the couch. Anitha gave her a tight hug and a kiss. 'Kanna, we'll surely talk tomorrow.'

As Anitha left, she looked back wistfully. *How many times have I done this to my baby, all for other babies.* She had a lump in her throat as she mechanically put on her mask and gloves, and picked up her handbag.

Inside her room, Samyuktha had similar thoughts.

What am I going to do at home during the lockdown? I'm either going to go crazy or drive my parents up the wall. Mostly the former. Amma's going to go off to work and deliver babies. She won't come home before two in the morning. And she could carry the infection to her! What's wrong with her? Does that mean Dad is going to take care of things? Oh man, lots and lots of crosswords, cooking and cleaning. Is this for real?

She stared at the glowy stars stuck on the balcony ceiling from a decade ago, their faded glow reminding her of her fading adolescence...

Desperate Housewives

Abhimanyu became alert. A silver Honda City was coming down the street at top speed. He blew the whistle repeatedly. The car kept coming through. He stood right in front of the speeding vehicle. It was a common technique. Abhimanyu was expert at hurtling away in cases when such speeding cars wouldn't stop. Thankfully, the car screeched to a halt a few feet ahead of him.

Abhimanyu knocked at the window. 'Who is this?' he asked, simmering in anger. 'Don't you know there's a lockdown?'

A few neighbours turned on their lights and came to the balcony. *This is all the entertainment they get in a day*, Abhimanyu thought.

A soft and firm voice answered from the inside. 'Beta, I'm a gynaecologist. I am running late for an emergency delivery at St. Isabel's Hospital. I have a doctor's pass. I'm sorry that Shekhar drove so fast. Could you let me through, please?'

Abhimanyu's anger evaporated. He checked her ID. *Dr Anitha Kumar.*

'I'm sorry, Ma'am. I hope you understand that it's protocol. Please go ahead,' he said in his deep, clear voice.

Something about her look reminded Abhimanyu of something. As the car sped away, he tried to rack his brains for the second time in two days. *Where have I seen that face before?* The woman's face and her voice stayed in his mind.

As the car entered the hospital's driveway, Anitha heaved a

sigh of relief. She had panicked for a moment when the stern-looking masked soldier had stopped her midway. She needed to tell her staff to budget a few more minutes each day for lockdown protocols. *Not that these unborn babies ever give us any time,* she thought in the same breath. She rushed into the maternity ward.

'Vineeta, age twenty-eight. No complications. But she's dilated nine centimetres already, Doc,' the doctor on duty said. 'She came in late. Security issues at their apartment complex. They got delayed getting out.'

That woman is a champion, Anitha thought. *What an ordeal at a time like this.*

There was no more time to think. The baby needed to be brought out and that too fast. The second she entered the ward, a flurry of nurses and doctors swarmed around her as she walked along giving out crisp instructions. One by one, the staff nodded, 'Yes, Ma'am,' and rushed off to do what they were assigned. Anitha reached her office, tossed her bag on the chair and, picking up her scrubs, rushed back out.

'Don't worry, Vineeta. We'll get your baby out, safe and fast. No time for an epidural, you're dilated way beyond that point,' she said calmly, much to Vineeta's consternation.

The delivery went like clockwork. No one was surprised. Anitha Kumar had saved the day on many occasions. The cheerful, high-pitched shrill of her bedside conversation was in stark contrast to her measured, composed voice in the operation theatre, giving precise instructions as she worked like a machine, relaxing only after she heard the war cry of the newborn who had battled all odds and was finally in her hands.

It had dawned on Anitha that she had been doing this for a while when a baby she had helped deliver despite numerous complications sent her a wedding invitation twenty-five years later.

As the car gently rolled to a halt at the checkpoint, Anitha came back to reality. Sukhi, verifying her ID this time, smiled from behind his mask and asked her, '*Aaj itna late, Ma'am*? (Today so late, Ma'am)?'

Anitha checked her watch. It was midnight. 'Emergency delivery,' she said, smiling at the pleasant, masked Sardar.

Anitha was aware that any hospital is a germ factory, with or without coronavirus. Before she entered her apartment, she doubled down on her sanitization ritual. Unfailingly. She had converted her house help's room into a sanitization zone, where she always kept a spare change of clothes.

She would enter the house via the house help's room, and once done with the ritual, she would spray and disinfect the entire room with Dettol spray. There were days when she would be so exhausted that she would just fall asleep there.

Ever since Samyuktha was born, Anitha had been an early riser. She liked being awake as early as 5.00 a.m. When the world outside was quiet, her mind was clear. Her subconscious mind loved the fact that she got a head start by waking up and starting work early. However, by 8.00 p.m., her brain would stop performing logical operations.

Yet, Anitha, despite her brilliance (or maybe because of it), was a complete klutz in general. And she lived and thrived in that klutziness. Samyuktha grew up listening to her mom's chant everyday, almost like an anthem. 'Where's my phone?' 'Where are the keys?' 'Oh shoot, I forgot to water the plants!' While Anitha had saved many babies, she had killed an equal number of plants. One time, she kept her phone at the top of the car and drove off with Samyuktha. They never saw that poor piece of metal again after that.

This was in stark contrast to her perfectionist husband. A man of method, he was always in constant despair at her scrappiness. Little did he realize that her chaos was really her clarity. People called them made for each other because they complemented each other perfectly. While Ajay basked in that compliment, Anitha was not very sure. While he tolerated her scrappiness, he never really understood her brilliance. *Shouldn't a couple understand each other and not just merely tolerate each other?* Anitha thought, every once in a while.

Being the middle sibling in a battalion of five growing up in Palakkad, Anitha was nearly a PhD in sibling psychology from a very young age. Her oldest sister was the 'representative' of the family, the second brother was, well, second in command. Her youngest brother was the spoiled one and her second youngest sister believed she was perfect. And then, there was her. The grand moderator, the peacemaker, like the ghee in the dal tadka to lessen the spice.

So Anitha developed an ideal mix of amazing survival skills. And her high-pitched voice and spontaneous smile ensured that she stood out, in all senses. And stand out she did. She got admission to AIIMS completely on merit, after facing a combination of unbridled anxiety and intense studying for one year. Her dad had sent her off with undisguised pride, putting his foot down when her mother protested that Delhi was too far. And then she ended up falling for a man whose first response on hearing about her degree was a chuckle. *The irony of our lives...*

༺

Two floors above, Indrani felt alone and helpless. It had been a particularly challenging day. Ahalya was in one of her rotten moods, shut in her room all day. Arun's anxiety over the upcoming entrance exam was increasing. It was his third and final attempt.

She thought about her husband, Abhijeet. His solution to

every problem had been money. Tuitions. Shopping. Kitty party. He was up for any and every external factor that could solve the problem. 'Time is money, shona,' he would tell her in jest. But Indrani knew that some problems couldn't be solved with money, and they needed hours of efforts. She had been trying for years to tell him that…

The sound of the gates opening and a car coming in broke her train of thought. *Who could it be?* she thought. As she saw Anitha exit the car, she felt her usual pang of anxiety. *I know what Anitha is doing is noble. Of course, it is. But having a doctor in the complex at this time seems unsafe. I wonder if we should establish some ground rules,* she thought to herself. *Let me check what Ranjini thinks, tomorrow.* She tried sleeping. But sleep evaded her for a long while.

⋄⊙⋄

Samyuktha woke up with a start and checked her clock. 6.00 a.m. *Just in time*, she thought as she went to the balcony to catch a glimpse of the soldier. She looked around in vain, as there was no one to be found. Samyuktha felt disappointed.

That's fine. Let me just admire the world at 6.00 a.m., she thought philosophically. *Is it my imagination, or are the trees greener and the air cleaner?* Birds were chirping merrily along, breaking into song everywhere. *It's almost like they're celebrating the absence of humans around,* Samyuktha thought. Cows were roaming around freely. *What fun,* Samyuktha thought, *to be a cow during these times.*

'Oh, give me a home, where the buffaloes roam,
Where the deer and the antelope play,
Where seldom is heard a discouraging word,
And the skies are not cloudy all day…'
As Samyuktha hummed the song, a part of her mind was

still scanning the streets for Winky, as she had now nicknamed him. He was not in sight. Samyuktha sighed and then perked up as she smelled the aroma of coffee wafting through the house.

As the strains of M.S. Subbulakshmi's 'Om...Om...Om...' started, she knew that either Thatha or Amma was up. 'Oh give me a home, where the smell of filter coffee roams and M.S. music will play,' she sang tunelessly as she sauntered to the kitchen in her giant Winnie the Pooh nightshirt.

Thatha was there, cutting *nellikai* (gooseberries). He was making preparations for her favourite pickle.

Samyuktha smiled at how Thatha thought that her favourite food would dispel all her problems in life. *It's not a bad theory,* Samyuktha thought. *I wonder if I'll do this when I have kids. But for that, I have to have kids. Hmm. Definitely no human kids. Maybe adopt a whale? Or a turtle? Or just adopt a whole forest?*

Samyuktha was prone to getting lost in reveries, which invariably led to a rambling chain of thoughts. Her family called it her 'mind's voice'.

'Samyuktha, can you hear me?'

'No. She's listening to her mind's voice.'

She would be so engrossed in daydreaming that she would usually miss out on many key points in conversations, which she would scramble and ask for later on, much to her father's irritation. 'That girl, she has the attention span of a dog chasing a butterfly.'

'...and so, that's how Amma is going to work, chellam, for the next twenty days.'

Samyuktha coerced herself to come back to the present. *There, it's happened again.* Mentally chiding herself, she started paying attention to what Thatha was saying. He was talking about Amma's work routine. She had switched to doing video calls and phone consultations with her patients, and went to the hospital only for deliveries. Then she would come back and sanitize herself and everything she carried. All other elective surgeries, like hysterectomies, etc., had been postponed till after the lockdown, unless it called for an emergency.

'Okay, Thatha, enough of this coronavirus talk. You want to listen to Selena and Justin?' Thatha's eyes instantly twinkled.

Samyuktha was Thatha's source of anything 'cool' as he said it himself. Be it music, books or gadgets. Samyuktha had taught Thatha how to use Whatsapp, play Scrabble online (she would play the game with him while she was on campus) and had downloaded Candy Crush for him on his phone. She would also play Spotify chartbusters for him.

She was in for a surprise.

Thatha slowly unlocked his phone, held it at an arm's length to see it without his glasses. He successfully identified the Spotify logo all by himself and then tapped it slowly with his index finger. As the interface came to life, he squinted again to find the search tool and slowly started typing 'Shape of y—'

'Ed Sheeran! Thatha, impressive!' While Samyuktha said this, she also played back the lyrics in her mind to see if they were appropriate for his listening. However cool Thatha was, the results could turn out to be negative.

'No, not that Ed chap. This is Vinod and Aditya…Aah this one, correct,' he smiled his toothless smile as the song popped up. 'These IndianRaga fellows are doing a great job, ma. Now tell me which ragam is this.' He beamed as two South Indian boys belted out a Carnatic fusion mix of 'Shape of You' by 'that Ed chap'.

For the thousandth time, Samyuktha looked at Thatha with both admiration and despair. She admired his knack for connecting things in his brain, be it his cooking ingredients or music. But she was in despair, for she did not know what ragam that was. 'Kalyani?' she asked gingerly.

He shook her head and smiled at her. 'No, ma... What a fine way to include Abheri ragam!' They both looked at each other and grinned. In these moments, Samyuktha and Thatha were just two children—excited and happy in each other's company.

⁂

As soon as Abhimanyu returned to his spot in the morning, he automatically started looking for The Nose. His trained eyes saw a mobile phone on the balcony table. *Nice,* he thought with a smile. *She will come back soon to get it.* Little did he know that Samyuktha could go hours without her phone.

As he scanned the building to do the cursory check, he saw Ahalya at the second floor balcony, staring intently at him. He quickly averted his eyes and looked away. *This is getting creepy,* he thought. *She would be a good RAW agent. I wonder who else she's keeping tabs on.*

After a nice long jam session with Thatha, Samyuktha came out to the balcony once again and smiled. Winky was there! He was busy giving out instructions to his jawans, and Samyuktha took the time to observe him critically.

Poor guy must be hot, she thought. *Doing all this work in the heat. Not that he isn't hot, regardless of the weather,* Samyuktha corrected herself slyly. *Five feet eleven inches at least.* He had curly hair and nice almond eyes. His jaw was rugged (she had noticed when he pulled off his mask the previous day). That was a definite plus. Samyuktha just wondered if he was one of those boys who looked nice until they opened their mouths.

Meanwhile, Samyuktha's WhatsApp was abuzz. She checked the messages. There was Ahalya, sending her a cute picture of someone she had chatted with on Tinder. Samyuktha smiled. Ahalya was always chatting with at least six people on Tinder at any given point of time.

But this one is really hot, ya, she had typed. And brainy also. And I think he likes me!

Super, Samyuktha typed back. Looks like there's finally some scenery on Tinder.

The 'Ashok Annettes' group was abuzz with activity. *Annettes.* Samyuktha smiled at this age-old archetypes of apartment kids growing up and parents expecting that they'd all be best friends, like they themselves were. But they were a good gang, who could hang out together and protect each other's secrets.

Arun: Who's up for bored games? :D

Kavya: Aah. Is it summer already, or did you just make that terrible joke yet again out of season?

Ahalya: Wait. We aren't supposed to meet and stuff. That soldier downstairs keeps telling me.

Mahesh: Well if you stopped flirting with him so much maybe he won't have a chance to tell you so many times. :P

Samyuktha quickly typed her own reply.

This is what we do, Samyuktha thought. *If we all don't die from coronavirus, it'll be from an overdose of these WhatsApp groups. Groups for everything. Study, projects, lunch tiffin* (that was important, she conceded), *classes, apartment aunties, apartment uncles, apartment seniors, apartment gossip. Reading through it all is just torture.*

She looked up. Suddenly, she found Abhimanyu staring at her. She looked back, perplexed for a second. Then she gave him a half smile.

Abhimanyu smiled back, she could tell from the way his eyes crinkled at the corners and lit up. He had a sweet childlike innocence in his eyes, which transformed his entire face. Samyuktha couldn't help but smile back, this time with a proper one.

Abhimanyu again tapped his phone. *Give me your number,* he seemed to be suggesting.

Samyuktha felt a little annoyed. *That's direct,* she thought.

She looked around and then above. As she did, she saw Ahalya in the living room balcony on the adjacent floor in the next wing. Ahalya was glancing intently at Abhimanyu, wondering what he was up to. Her eyes then roved around. Samyuktha quickly retreated inside. She wasn't taking any chances when it came to Ahalya. Her phone beeped with messages. They were from Rohan.

`Bored. What you up to?`

`Nothing, sweetie. Just passing time.` Samyuktha felt a pang of guilt, just as when she would check Tinder.

She went back to the balcony. *Drat.* Ahalya was still there. This time, she saw Samyuktha and gave her a wave and a smile. Not to be outdone, Samyuktha smiled and waved back. 'How are you?' she mouthed as she rolled up one of the blinds. 'It's been ages.'

Abhimanyu was looking at this exchange from the corner of his eye. *That looked a little fake,* he thought to himself as he took off his mask to have tea and boiled peanuts—the mid-morning snack. He had read that it was a Chennai delicacy. He respectfully disagreed with the city folks on this count.

The lockdown was boring Ahalya intensely. She loved going out, meeting people, going on dates… After all, if this wasn't the age for it, what was? Once every ten minutes, she would check Tinder, and sigh. *Tinder Abhi hadn't messaged after last night. Cute face. Looked fit too. But this boy hasn't given me any information,* she thought. *Where is he from…what is he doing…* she didn't know that he was downstairs, wearing a mask and military fatigues, and eating boiled peanuts.

Abhimanyu, on the other hand, gave very little thought to

the Tinder conversation. When he had last checked, there were
five more messages from A, most of them attempts at finding
out more about him. Abhimanyu, in general, loathed giving
out details to anyone, especially people on dating apps. He
skilfully dodged these questions each time, hoping she would
get the message. But she didn't, and it quickly became obvious
to Abhimanyu that this was going nowhere. He was wondering
if he should tell her clearly, but didn't want to sound too direct
and impolite.

He looked at Ahalya's balcony and sighed. He wished that
she would go back inside. He wanted to get to know The Nose
better. But Ahalya stood there, stubbornly put. So, Abhimanyu,
not to be outdone, decided to put on his Ray-Ban and observe
Samyuktha better from behind his glares.

She's pretty, Abhimanyu conceded. Not drop-dead gorgeous
like the movies. But this girl had a certain character to her round
face. She had large eyes and lovely delicate lips. And the aquiline
nose, of course. While she had a serious look behind her frames,
how her face changed when she smiled! Her eyes sparkled as
her face lit up, not holding anything back.

Samyuktha checked her phone again. Sharanya had already
started talking about people she knew who had symptoms. A
second cousin of hers in Manhattan, a close family friend in Delhi
who had a hairdresser come to his mansion in Sainik Farms,
an elderly couple in the next building who couldn't do without
house help—the list went on. The WhatsApp groups were abuzz
too, from advisories, to viral videos of a cute Vietnamese boy
showing how to maintain hygiene in the present times. There
were random news articles about youngsters licking toilet seats
and foreigners being made to do squats by Indian police for
venturing out during a lockdown…

Finally! Ahalya went inside. Samyuktha looked at Abhimanyu and her face broke into a smile. *There it was again,* Abhimanyu thought as he took off the Ray-Ban. He looked in Ahalya's direction and wiped his brow in mock relief. Samyuktha's smile widened.

'Where are you from?' Samyuktha asked Abhimanyu, signalling a globe and name tag. *Not bad, she knows mime rules,* Abhimanyu thought. On cue, he signalled 'capital' with a salute and pointed north.

Delhi. Samyuktha smiled and tried to hide her grimace coming from her unwarranted, yet steeped, prejudice regarding North Indians at large.

'You were giving me your number,' he signalled to Samyuktha, tapping his phone again.

Samyuktha wondered what would be the right thing to do. He seemed too forward. And she did have Rohan in her life. But, on the other hand, the soldier seemed fun. *Moreover, if he turns out to be a creep, I can always block him on WhatsApp.* On impulse, she made a decision.

Samyuktha gave her contact number—one digit at a time, with a show of her fingers. He noted it down painstakingly at the back of his crossword puzzle. She was about to ask him something, when a soldier called, '*Oye Abhi, sun bhai* (Abhi, listen brother)!' *Aah so that's your name, or part of it,* she thought as Abhimanyu quickly straightened up, put on his mask and left towards the gate down the road.

Samyuktha sighed. This had been the most fun she had had since morning. She checked the time. It was 11.15 already. How had time flown by? Oh, yes. Ahalya had taken up a chunk of it. She shut her eyes and lazed on the balcony. The March weather was pleasant that morning. Chennai hadn't become unbearably hot, and anyway, her balcony was always cool. Soon after she had started reading *War and Peace*, she dozed off...

⁊☙⁊

Indrani wondered if she should discuss about Anitha with anyone. It did seem petty. But then again, everyone's safety was at stake. She decided to ask Ranjini from B-22 what she thought. Ranjini had both a pre-diabetic husband and an asthmatic seven-year-old son, Aditya.

However, Ranjini was not of the same view. 'Yes, *ma*, I see your point. But, its *namma* Anitha, *ma*. Always careful. Because of her, none of us get Dettol, illaya?' She laughed at her own joke. Indrani didn't find it too funny, but laughed politely anyway.

Ranjini continued on, 'Donntu worry, okay? Also, so good that we have her for any emergency also here, no?' She was absorbed in trying to understand whether to wash her delicates in the washing machine or herself. These were important decisions, especially in times when there were no domestic workers to help.

Indrani hung up and sighed. She looked all around the kitchen. She was trying to fill water and keep an eye on the boiling milk at the same time. She had left the vegetables in the sink, to be washed later. The dal was in a bowl.

'AHALYA!' she called out for her for the third time. She badly needed help now.

Ahalya finally emerged into the kitchen. '*Kya hai, Mumma* (What is it, Mother)?' she asked impatiently. She was not usually helpful around the house, and even more so when there was something interesting to witness from the balcony.

'Mumma, this Samyuktha is back. And she's making eyes at the soldiers from her balcony, right from the morning,' Ahalya said, plunging headlong into her story.

'Arre, her mother just leaves her and goes to the hospital. Poor girl. No one at home to take care of her, na?' Indrani said. She genuinely felt bad for kids who had working mothers, and believed that they were missing out on an essential part of being nurtured.

She ignored Abhijeet's point about working mothers setting a fine example for their kids. She even disliked his American clients, some of whom were single parents, working wives with stay-at-home fathers, or gay couples who had kids. Indrani believed in traditional roles and family structures, and Abhijeet's openness to new-age beliefs on gender roles was a point of conflict between them. He insisted that each style of parenting offers a new perspective, as a result of which the kids learn to have an open mind. Indrani just felt sorry for those kids, and how confused and lonely they must be feeling.

'We should help her, beta, not make fun of her,' she counselled Ahalya.

They both nodded sympathetically. The kitchen continued to be a chaos.

༄༅

Samyuktha woke up with a start. She checked her phone. It was 12.30. *I must be getting old to be taking naps in the middle of the day,* she thought. She went to the kitchen where the smell of *vatha kuzhambu* and potato roast wafted through. Her Thatha was precisely chopping small onions.

It was always a pleasure to watch Thatha cook. He applied all his paint factory assembly-line learning to this task and did so with such zeal. He would start off with the longest lead time activity first, which was the cooker. With that on boil, he could assiduously start chopping vegetables and start prepping. As that would be readied for cooking, he would quickly wipe down the counters, take the milk, make the thayir and set it inside the oven to ferment overnight. He would then start making the sambar or rasam. On hearing the cooker go off, he would mix all the elements of sambar together, clean up, and he would be done. All it took him was forty minutes. Once the food would be ready, he would promptly go and take a bath.

As the day progressed, Samyuktha got busy with her online classes. She was getting used to staring at a laptop and learning. She, however, kept checking her phone every five minutes, which was something extremely unusual for her to do. She saw a message from Sandhya.

My tummy's the size of Krishna's butterball, dude! Eat. Pee. Sleep. Pee. Pee. Pee. That's my life now.

Samyuktha laughed. Sandhya was the coolest akka she knew. She could juggle work, marriage, and was now prepping for a baby—all of that with apparent ease. Under normal circumstances, Samyuktha would have spent a generous portion of her day over at her place.

Dude, I can't even imagine. And to top it all, all of this during Schrödinger's virus time.

Why Schrödinger's virus? Sandhya messaged back.

Samyuktha had no problem typing long messages on interesting, wacky topics like these. Because we can't get tested, so we don't know whether we are already infected or not. We have to act as if we have the virus, so that we don't spread it to others. Meanwhile, we also have to act like we don't have the virus, because if we don't already have it, then we're not immune yet. So we both have it and also not…

As she was typing, a text message from an unknown international number popped up on the screen.

Samyuktha, beware of that guy. Her heart nearly froze.

꩜

The strains of 'Lamberghini' floated out of Abhimanyu's room, amid laughter and banter. This time, the party was in his room. That always meant extra fun because he was one of those souls who genuinely wanted to ensure that people have a good time and enjoy themselves. A peek in the door revealed Abhimanyu, Sukhi and Anish sprawled on the floor, with their buddy, Johnny Walker, placed in the centre. Ayaan stoically supported his old friends, Old Monk and Coca-Cola.

'Cheers to a successful week in Chennai!' said Abhimanyu. They all clinked their glasses together. Abhimanyu ran a cursory check on his phone. No reply from The Nose yet. He sighed. There were two more messages from Ahalya on Tinder. *I'll reply later*, he thought as he noted that there was hardly anything in the texts that tickled his interest.

'I don't know about successful,' Anish said, settling down on the floor, his favourite spot. 'But, it has definitely been interesting.'

'I find these aunties here a little strange, yaar,' said Sukhi, as his eyes gleamed looking at the masala peanuts, a welcome change from the boiled ones. 'I was having chai today, and *yeh first floor waali Aunty* (this Aunty from the first floor) saw me from her balcony. She kept shouting out to me to have more, because it's hot. Now why will I have more chai if it's hot?' He looked confused as Abhi started laughing.

'Paaji, "*mor*" means *chhaas* (buttermilk) in Tamil,' Abhimanyu said, between splits of laughter. As it dawned on the rest, they joined in, laughing louder than usual, courtesy Johnny and Monk.

'Have you seen that driver? The one who thinks he's competing at the Grand Prix?' Sukhi asked, his attention suddenly diverting to the food items placed in front of him. '*Dude, yeh sab kya cheez hai* (Dude, what are these things)?'

The 'cheez' turned out to be a product of Abhimanyu's chefmanship. He wanted to pepper the evening with some 'fusion' culinary delights. His research on Chennai combined with his wacky brain had led to the evening's creative snack menu. While some of the items were appetizing, some were downright bizarre.

Uthappam pizza was the first culinary innovation. Melted cheese sandwiched between two layers of uthappams, with various toppings—roasted chicken, capsicum, onions, green chilly, paneer and was that olives? Ayaan wondered as he eyed the creation with both admiration and suspicion.

Idli chicken chat was the second. Deep fried idli with the traditional *podi* and ghee, combined with fried chicken and topped with crushed papdi, *mudi* (puffed rice), bhujia and coriander at the top.

The star attraction was Vodka Rasam, and it was the easiest to make. Spicy pepper rasam 'peppered' with Absolut. And Absolut Citron, at that, for the lemony effect. With panache, Abhimanyu had brought out all of these and had placed it in the centre of the room for all to enjoy.

'Since the post-apocalyptic era has become current affairs, we may as well make the most of it,' Anish said as he surveyed the food in all admiration as everyone laughed. 'Singh has outdone himself again.'

As they finished their drinks, Abhimanyu refilled everyone's glasses. He was the eternal refiller. No one at Abhimanyu's party ever found their glasses empty.

'Bro, you were talking about a driver, right? I've seen him. He works for the gynaecologist in Ashok Apartments,' one of them said as they all settled down again, considerably tipsier and happier.

'Yes,' Sukhi said, remembering his 12.00 a.m. tryst with her. 'That Aunty is really sweet and has such dedication.'

Abhimanyu smiled wistfully. The alcohol was getting to him. '*Haan yaar* (yes, bro), I've seen her. Super passionate about her work, but as soon as she reaches home, she tries to spend time with her daughter. *Phir emergency call aa gaya* (then there was this emergency call), and then in two minutes she was ready to rush back.'

Ayaan retorted in his tipsy voice, 'Who? The mother, or the daughter?'

Abhimanyu was caught unawares. He slightly blushed. And that was all it took. A collective whoop echoed through the room. Ayaan and his Old Monk were now in form.

'Yaar Abhi, you're way ahead of us, dude. You seem to have become quite the expert. *Tamil zubaan, Tamil khaana* (Tamil language, Tamil food). Is there anything else you need to tell us?' he asked as he finished the last 90 millilitre of his drink in one go.

It was one of the rare instances when Abhimanyu fumbled for words. Similar past experiences told him it was for the best to get to the point.

'I got her number today,' he said, looking intently at his drink like his life depended on it.

The three of them looked at each other incredulously. Here they were, with aunties asking them whether they wanted chaas. And there he was...as much as they loved him, they couldn't help have envious admiration for him.

Abhimanyu was in that dreamy mood, which comes with good alcohol and as a result of being smitten. 'She has a loving family for sure. Mom takes out time to spend with her...her Appa...' he said the word with a smile, 'goes grocery shopping with her. And I see her Nanaji sometimes on the balcony. Down to earth. Quite practical.'

The group fell silent. Singh was not just smitten with Samyuktha but was also reminded of his family. Abhimanyu went on, nursing his glass, '*Ghar wali feeling aa gayi* (It reminded me of home),' he said. Another whoop went around.

'Dude!' Ayaan said rolling over with laughter, '*Gharwali mubarak ho* (Congratulations on finding a wife).'

Abhimanyu broke out of his thoughts and joined the fun. He was good at making fun of himself. They all rolled with laughter helplessly. There was absolutely no dearth of gharwali jokes one could make, and it was simply multiplied into infinity when accompanied with good alcohol. He checked his phone once again. A. had pinged him once again—this time six messages on the trot. He glanced at them, immersed in thoughts, and then put away his phone.

'All you haramis. Don't spill the beans to Verma saab even by mistake, he'll pack me off to Delhi tomorrow itself.' Abhimanyu grinned at his buddies as they wiped their eyes with tears of laughter. They were incorrigible, but he trusted them with his life.

'Bro, as if we would. Just don't do anything stupid. *Else, Verma saab se pehle I'll bash your teeth in* (Otherwise, I will bash your teeth in way before Verma sir will),' Anish said, lying flat on his back, looking at him with a smile.

Abhimanyu nodded. *Nothing stupid, for sure.*

Catch Me If You Can

Samyuktha's mind was in a whirl, on so many accounts. Who was this person? How did he know about Abhi? Should she really stay away from him?

Who could it be, who could it be? The thought kept playing in Samyuktha's mind as she looked around instinctively. The ISD code indicated it was a Dubai number. She didn't know anyone there.

As she looked out of the balcony, she saw Abhimanyu. He didn't look up.

She replied to the message, Who's this?

Just a well wisher, was the reply.

She was about to reply, when she heard a terrible series of clangs outside the room. Samyuktha rushed out. Her mother was furiously opening and closing all kinds of dabbas in the kitchen, and boy, was she creating a racket.

Dabbas are every Indian mother's raison d'être, thought Samyuktha. On the rare occasions when her mother was around when she came back from school, the standard question had been, 'Where is your dabba, Samyu?'

Amma would surely pick a dabba over me, she thought.

'Amma! Why are you punishing those poor boxes?' Samyuktha asked in despair as a giant steel storage tin fell to the ground with a thunderous clang.

Anitha looked around, right through Samyuktha, in agitation. 'I thought I had ordered an extra five-kilogram packet of dal.

Where did it go?' As she said this, Ajay lumbered out of his study, in his usual leisurely way. This infuriated Anitha even more.

For a good part of the past two hours, Ajay had been trying to grapple with which data sets could reliably replace the movement data that had been rendered useless by the lockdown. His mind was racing to find a path through the complex maze, hitting roadblocks each time and having to retrace its steps to find another route. Just when he felt like he was making some headway, the commotion had broken his concentration. He felt the same sense of helplessness that he felt each time, unable to explain the magnitude of what he was working on, or convince Anitha to let go of mundane stuff.

Unable to form coherent thoughts, he simply said, 'Relax, Anitha,' trying to be cajoling but not being able to hide his irritation.

Rookie mistake, Samyuktha thought. Her Appa never learned, despite being married for 20 years. The last thing you tell a person who's furious is to relax, especially when someone was as emotionally fraught as her mother.

'Of course!' Anitha said scathingly. 'That's all you do, all day. Relax. Come for breakfast. Come for lunch. And dinner. This place is a hotel, isn't it? Better still, an AirBnB.' She delivered this last line with what she believed was panache.

Aiyyo. What a cliché, Samyuktha thought. *At least come up with better dialogues.*

Ajay sighed. 'We aren't exactly in the midst of a spring harvest, Anitha. Weren't you the one who said we shouldn't hoard?' he said, putting the steel box back on the kitchen top.

One more rookie mistake, Samyuktha thought. *He's going on and on bombarding her with logical points when she's clearly upset. I think it is not dal that Amma is upset about. It must be something else.*

Samyuktha had hit the nail on the head. That was the truth. Anitha was not upset about the dal. While Ajay was a lot of things—a devoted family man, a good provider, a solid rock to lean on—he hadn't been blessed with high emotional intelligence, or the willingness to learn to develop it. So while his arguments were logically sound, he had little understanding of what Anitha was going through.

'I sometimes just need to talk, Samyu,' she would say to her on many occasions. 'I don't need solutions. I just need people I can pour my heart out to.'

Samyuktha quickly interjected, 'Amma, you need dal, illaya? What else? Give me the list. Today's our designated grocery day. I'll go and get it. Give me the family ID card.'

The tension started dissipating. Anitha gave her the list. Ajay, thankful to his daughter, went back to the study. Thatha lauded Samyuktha with a thumbs up and went back to his siesta. For a second there, Samyuktha felt like Wonder Woman…

⌘

As Ajay sat back at his desk, he tried to shut his eyes as tightly as possible to think about his various options. Instead, he could just see Anitha's face and the sarcastic look on it, accusing him of relaxing. *Relaxing*! He couldn't remember the last time he had done that. *I should have taken Ravi's advice and set up an outside office. It's hard to expect any respect if you're not a man who 'goes to work'*, he thought for the umpteenth time. There was a tinge of bitterness. He shut his eyes again and started thinking hard.

Instead of applying a model across the general population, we should carve out the most likely segments—maybe those who have recently returned from abroad but have no symptoms. Or it could be the frontline workers like policemen, doctors and shopkeepers. It would then also involve Anitha, he thought as his mind furiously segued Anitha from being a source of frustration to an element in his solution.

Ajay had always been a fighter. Being a geek was his 'nature', and he owed his fiery conviction to his 'nurture' growing up in Mylapore of the seventies. His father, Sreenivasa Iyer, was a well-respected school headmaster. He had had a Vedic upbringing, a good command over the English language and a respectable job. That was how guys made heads turn in the streets those days.

'Stop squandering your life away on these western equipment!' roared Sreenivasa Master one morning circa 1981 as he had stepped into the house and seen little Ajay bent over the radio, tinkering at the various knobs and dials, and trying to pull it apart with a steel spoon. The six-year-old had quivered and the sudden roar had startled him so much that he had let go of the device and it had come crashing down on the orange terracotta floor and had broken.

As he cowered in a corner, his mother came to him and held him close, while Sreenivasa Master had continued his rant about how he should be perfecting his grammar and memorizing the Vedas instead. An already shy and reticent Ajay had further retreated into himself, unable to explain his curiosity for technology. Yet, he had remained unwilling to give it up. Even today, if anyone confronted Ajay, he would experience the feeling of being pushed into a corner.

So for ten long years, Ajay wrote and spoke what was needed—an autobiography of a cow, an explanation of the Gayatri Mantra in English and a critical analysis of Subramaniya Bharathiyar's poems. He had recited shlokas by heart, taught them to his annoying younger cousins and sat through overnight kutcheris with his father, all the while dreaming of circuit boards and magical electronics that could fly and take pictures. Even today, he did what was needed or what he had seen his father do for his family.

Outside of that, he had devoured anything and everything related to science and technology. Ajay had also made friends with Hari Anna, who ran a repair shop in Luz Corner. As Brahmin boys were forbidden to visit shops owned by other castes, Hari Anna would let Ajay enter his tiny repair room through a backdoor.

Ajay had spent many afternoons there, tinkering around with discarded devices, dismantling them apart to his heart's content, bearing many a shock that would jolt his tiny body each time a wrong wire would be touched. When he had finally managed to assemble a transistor for the first time using various parts and it had crackled to life, his eyes had welled up with joy as he gazed fondly at the biggest accomplishment of his life so far.

Ajay had learned over the years to absorb the taunts, torments and threats given by his father and channelize it into positive energy, by working in Hari Anna's shop. He did the same now whenever he had an argument with Anitha.

No sooner was he out of his reverie, his eyes shone with childlike excitement. Ajay leapt up and could barely wait for the grandfather clock to go through its motions to open up the panel. He typed out excitedly. Let's add Google search data but go a level deeper and identify key sub-themes. For instance, an alcoholic would google for Covid symptoms differently than a teetotaller. We correlate that with purchase behaviour to validate… for instance whether alcohol was part of the purchase at duty-free. This is preliminary, but it's a start. Requesting confirmation. He glanced at the screen to review the hastily-typed note before hitting the enter button.

He sat back in his chair, his mind at ease. *Why didn't I think of this before?* He wondered. *What are some other sub-themes? What would a doctor, like Anitha, Google about, for instance, if she suspected that she was infected?*

∞

Abhimanyu was impatient and a bit mad at himself. It had been two hours and there was still no reply to his message. *Why did I have to try and act clever unnecessarily? 'Beware of that guy'?* Abhimanyu kicked himself. *'Well wisher'? I could have written, 'Hi. This is Abhimanyu'…THIS has always been my problem. Oversmartness.*

He started typing.

`It's me. Abhimanyu.` He deleted it at once.

`I come in peace. You look like you come in war, though.` Nice. Simple and non-committal. He hit the send button.

Still no reply.

Sheesh. I've scared her off now.

∞

As Anitha sat down with the second cup of coffee (a luxury for her), she reflected on what had happened in the morning. She was glad that Samyuktha was back. *Handling these two men in my home is getting to me*, she thought. *Always trying to be logical and clinical about everything. And here I thought it was my job to be clinical.* Anitha smiled at her own PJ.

'Here you go, Samyu,' she said, furiously scribbling down whatever grocery items she needed. True to the stereotype, her handwriting was no different from other doctors', but she knew Samyuktha would understand it partly from experience. As she was jotting down the list, she saw Samyuktha look at her phone with a smile that continued to widen. *Is it some boy?* It looked like it, from that smile. *I shouldn't pry*, Anitha told herself for the hundredth time. *She's not a child anymore. Let her have her fun and make her own mistakes.*

'Here's the list,' she said, handing it over. Samyuktha wasn't listening.

'Samyu,' Anitha called out loudly.

Samyuktha then immediately took the list from her and noticed that she had been looking at her strangely. *Did she know?* She quickly gave her a hug and scooted off to her room. She typed back a message. She was back in her balcony.

What kind of joke was that?

A relieved Abhimanyu looked up, removing his mask, and grinned at her. *Slightly foolish*, Samyuktha thought.

Abhimanyu typed again, Long story short. I leave my actual phone at the barracks. I have only got this reliable ancient phone while on duty. Hail Nokia 1100. Downside is, only text, no WhatsApp and no emojis. Thank God.

Are you a tech nerd? Or just another mafia don from Dubai?

None of the above. I'm Abhimanyu. He wasn't keen on taking a chance with any more guessing games.

Alright then, Abhimanyu. What else should I know about you? Hope you armymen don't have nano drones flying around peeping into balconies, while us civilians are staying put in our rooms, left with no option but to overthink our life decisions.

Lol. Not as of yet. And yes, you guys should be doing some solid thinking. Has Russia been invaded yet?

Huh?

War and Peace. Isn't that what you're reading?

Oh! No, not yet. Just started reading. *Okay, this soldier is a legit nerd*, Samyuktha thought.

She looked at Abhimanyu. He was still smiling at her. The sun was getting brighter, so he put on his Ray-Ban, but the goofy smile stayed on. *What a nutcase,* she thought as she held up her phone surreptitiously and took a pic. *But a cute one.* She sent the pic to Sharanya.

THAT'S NOT FAIR! He is a HOT mess. I want one too (crying emoji). And girl, two timing with Rohan?

Dude, nothing like that. This is just some lockdown entertainment. Samyuktha felt that pang of guilt again.

As the evening approached, Samyuktha patted herself for getting groceries. That was definitely a case of good karma coming back. She messaged him again.

By the way, I've taken on the grocery run today. We can say hi in person probably.

For sure. Abhimanyu shot back, eating his lunch.

The jawans saw him tapping on his ancient Nokia and wondered who it was. Dhruv shrewdly guessed that it had something to do with the first floor, which Abhimanyu had kept gazing at. But he knew better than to open his mouth about it.

After lunch, Samyuktha planned it all meticulously. Just then, her Appa came out and saw her getting ready to leave.

'I'll come with you, Samyu. You won't be able to carry everything back by yourself,' he said, putting on his floaters.

She hurriedly said, 'No, Appa, I'll manage. I'll do two trips if needed. I could use the fresh air and exercise, illa?' Ajay was relieved and quite ready to let her go by herself. But Anitha was sitting on the oonjal, signing some discharge papers.

'Has this household gone mad, altogether?' Anitha stopped and glared at her. 'If you want to do exercise, go do yoga, or one of those Bollywood dance nonsense online. This is not an exercise routine. It is to get supplies to feed everyone in this house for a full week. I'm done dealing with today's quota of stupidity. Kumar, go with her and that's final. *Seriya* (Okay)?'

Anitha referring to Ajay by his surname meant danger zone. There was no point in even arguing. Samyuktha sighed and nodded. *There goes my moment.* As she and her father stepped out of the main gate, clad in face masks and gloves, like scientists in a lab, Abhimanyu flashed a smile at them (or she thought so, as his eyes crinkled around the corners behind that thick N95 mask). Samyuktha tried to drag her feet and stay a few steps behind her father to try and initiate an exchange with Abhimanyu.

But Ajay, after that rebuke from his wife, was determined to be his efficient best. 'We don't have all day, Samyu. Why are you walking like those tortoises that you're so crazy about?' He chuckled at his own joke. *Turtles*, Samyuktha mentally corrected him, but smiled nonetheless, so he wouldn't feel bad.

Samyuktha sighed again and gave up on the idea of talking to Abhimanyu. It wasn't going to happen. She caught up with her father.

'Appa, you must be busier than usual, right? With so much work from home and data sharing?' she asked, panting.

'Yes, kanna. With everything moving online, the need to protect data has skyrocketed. Did you read about Zoom not being secure enough?' he said as they passed yet another soldier standing guard. Without thinking, Samyuktha asked, 'Why can't the army jawans use their phones, Appa?' Almost immediately, she bit her tongue.

'No idea. Can't they?' Ajay asked as the grocery store appeared around the corner. He scowled on seeing the long queue outside. '*Ammada* (Thank God)…this is going to take forever!' he muttered.

Thank God for the distraction, thought Samyuktha, taking a deep breath of relief. The grocery store was like a zombie apocalypse scene. Everyone had to wait in line, three feet apart at the entrance. Only one family member was allowed inside a store at a time. They were timed, and they had to be out in ten minutes with whatever they needed.

As they waited, they saw some masked marauders heaping up things like their life depended on those. Even with the mask, she recognized Indrani aunty. And there was Ahalya, in another corner of the store, animatedly arguing about a packet of banana chips with her brother. She waved to Arun, who caught her eye and waved back. He blushed. He had had a crush on Samyuktha since puberty had hit him.

Then it was their turn. Ajay was organized as always, marking off items from the list as they found them. They made one quick round of the store and then another to see if they needed something crucial that was not on the list. And then there was a third round to put back guilty purchases that Anitha would consider 'hoarding'.

Father and daughter came out carrying a week's worth of grocery bags in their hands. Samyuktha was impressed by her father walking tall and straight with no sign of fatigue. She, on the other hand, was switching bags from one hand to another, pausing every now and then to put them down, hunching over, doing all kinds of theatrics to numb the pain. *I need to do more upper body exercises*, she thought. As they reached Ashok Apartments, she told her father to go ahead, telling him that she would join him in a minute after catching her breath. She could see Abhimanyu from the corner of her eye. He stood up and waited in anticipation.

As Appa walked ahead, Abhimanyu started walking towards her.

'That's a lot for a young lady to carry,' he said as he eyed the pile of bags she had put down around her. *Lots of vegetables and dal. Eggs. Hmm. One of those fake vegetarian families, who always have debates on how eggs do not qualify as non-vegetarian food,* he made a mental note. *But why so much Dettol? Must be some cleanliness obsession,* he thought, unknowingly hitting the nail on the head.

'Anything for a breath of fresh air, I guess.' Samyuktha tried to stay nonchalant. Up close, she noticed his twinkling eyes. And his physique was not lost on her. 'How has your day been?'

Just as he was about to respond, a shrill voice pierced through the moment. '*Oh ma,* look at all that stuff! Arun, please go help her.'

Samyuktha turned around startled, only to find that Ahalya was walking purposefully towards her.

The Ganguly mother and son duo were behind Ahalya, lugging two hand carts and three more bags. *No wonder the stores are running empty,* she thought, eyeing an assortment of things from chips to veggies to agarbatti packets to…was that an airplane hiding inside, just in case the travel embargo was called off? *I can't tell, there's a mountain on top of it.* Abhimanyu's eyes widened as he saw the assortment. Samyuktha and his eyes met in amusement.

Arun went and helped Samyuktha with all her bags. She had no choice but to follow the platoon in. She gave Abhimanyu a helpless sidelong glance. Amused, he went back to his duty. *I am liking this entertainment,* he thought to himself, making a mental note to get some…*vambu…isn't that what they call gossip here?*

As they walked in, Ahalya came over and whispered, 'What was he telling you?'

'Who?' Samyuktha asked innocently as she took one bag from Arun's gloved hand unconsciously. She didn't notice Arun blushing.

Ahalya disbelievingly said, 'That soldier, of course. Isn't he so cute? I know you've been talking to him, he keeps looking up at your balcony all the time.' She said this last line with a touch of impatience.

Samyuktha hated conversations like these. Her blunt nature took over. 'Don't be silly, Ahalya, I've never spoken to him.' Her impenetrable ice queen avatar kicked in.

Ahalya didn't know what to say after that. Thankfully for Samyuktha, her father came down and took the bags from Arun. Samyuktha raced up the stairs in relief. *What a piece of work she is.*

As Ajay checked off the grocery list, he saw that he had forgotten to get that very thing that Anitha had been upset about in the morning—toor dal. He cursed under his breath. As Samyuktha was about to come in, he accosted her at the door and quietly told her.

Samyuktha instantly smiled. 'I'll get it in a jiffy, Appa,' she said before dashing down the stairs again.

`Forgot the proverbial toor dal`, she messaged Abhimanyu. Heart pounding, she went out. He was nowhere to be seen. As she walked towards the neighbourhood store, she looked all around. In vain. *Why am I disappointed?* she thought. She picked up some pace and went to Select Stores, which was empty, thankfully of people, but alas also of groceries. As luck would have it, a lonely packet of toor tal was sighted in a corner. Samyuktha immediately got it billed and left. She looked around once again. There was no one in sight.

'You looked cute, searching for me like that,' she heard a voice behind her.

Startled, Samyuktha looked back. There he was, leaning

against a tree, grinning at her. Unable to help it, she blushed a little. She was thrilled at seeing him. She didn't quite know how to answer, so she waited for him to saunter towards her.

Abhimanyu looked at her. He tried to hide the admiration in his eyes. She looked just so...fresh. Untouched by make-up. Clear skin. Sparkling eyes. And that regal nose. Was that a hint of red on her cheeks? Was she blushing? He couldn't make out behind her lavender polka-dotted mask. His mind was racing.

'Hi,' she said with a smile.

'Vanakkam, Ma'am,' he said, smiling.

The tension broke and they both laughed. 'What's with the classics?' he asked, referring to the *Pride and Prejudice* in her hand. She carried a book wherever she went. 'Are you afraid that you'll end up an Elizabeth?' *Thank God he had watched the movie,* he thought. Shalini didi had made him.

'Ha ha, I don't have any of her qualities,' she shot back. 'Am more curious to know if you'll end up a Holden.'

Ignoring the question, Abhimanyu went on, 'I think Austen had her male characters way off. Possibly because she was a *she*.'

While Samyuktha rose in defence of her beloved Jane Austen, Abhimanyu just watched and smiled amusedly. *What is she saying? Something about spunk, sensitive... Look at her eyes, how they sparkle when she speaks. Abhimanyu, focus. You have to be strong. And you have to listen, at least enough to have a suitable rebuttal. Okay, just a reply.*

'...and that's why Jane Austen is the epitome of quintessential consumer understanding, in the modern age...' she declared, her eyes sparkling. As she said so, she turned into the street adjacent to Warren Road. Abhimanyu faithfully followed without protest. After all, he still had ten minutes of his tea break left.

'Mills and Boon,' Abhimanyu said, looking around the unfamiliar road.

'What?' Samyuktha shot back.

'Now that's a great example of consumer understanding,' Abhimanyu offered. 'Those guys, they know their readers. They know their motivations. They know how to get them hooked. They create the right tension points in the story. They create a need. And deliver on it. And leave the reader wanting more. That's why it's the longest running series since…sliced bread.'

'Trash and substance,' Samyuktha said with a twinkle.

Absolutely. 'Let's be honest. Sex has and always will sell. The trashier, the better. *Kama Sutra* and *50 Shades of Grey* have proved that beyond doubt.' Abhimanyu looked at her a bit daringly, waiting to hear what she had to say. Samyuktha smiled, but refused to acknowledge beyond that.

As they were talking, they circled back to the entrance of Warren Road. They both nodded in implicit agreement and went their ways, Samyuktha clutching the toor dal and Abhimanyu clutching on to the memory of her striking face, up close and personal.

Anitha came home and was happy to see the fresh supply and started animatedly examining them as Ajay told her all about which groceries were over and how he had figured out smart replacements instead. Samyuktha stared at them, for a moment, in half-amusement, half-disbelief as the two giggled like teenagers in love, but over groceries.

She gave up and took out her phone and started typing a message to Abhimanyu. Mental Note: If you ever find your moment of joy in a bag of toor dal and brinjal, hang yourself.

Abhimanyu read this and guffawed as his jawans were returning from dinner.

Dhruv looked at him and asked, '*Hua kya, Sir* (What happened, Sir)?' Abhimanyu shook his head and continued smiling.

He texted, LMFMO.

What's that?

When he told her, Samyuktha groaned and smiled. *Nutcase*, she thought.

⌘

'Yeh Abhimanyu has fallen in love with his phone,' Ayaan commented, watching him stare at the phone.

Abhimanyu, who was deep in thought, was startled at the mention of his name. He looked at the boys seriously. 'Bhai,' he said. 'I met her today.'

Sukhi's rice mound suddenly collapsed and the sambar flooded the neighbouring beans *poriyal* (vegetable). Sukhi and Ayaan looked blankly at each other, and then back at him. '*Kaun? Gharwali* (Who? The wife)?' Ayaan asked loudly. A few jawans at the other tables looked at them.

'Shhh,' Abhimanyu signalled them to lower their voice.

Ayaan waited until the others went back to what they were doing. 'Dude, how? Here we are, dying in this heat, with Chennai aunties barking orders at us. I can't believe you met her *already*,' Ayaan said, with emphasis on the last word. When Abhimanyu wanted something, it usually happened. It was just a matter of when.

Anish looked at him incredulously. 'How did you, bro?' he asked, his voice rising with every syllable. Now more than a few people looked up.

The four of them kept quiet, gobbled their food the best way they could and hurried outside for their customary walk. Abhimanyu took a deep breath and rubbed his nose. The others waited silently for him to say something.

'She came outside for groceries. I met her during my chai break. We roamed around a bit and talked,' he said, glancing at the four of them with a nonchalant look in his eyes.

'He has his I'm-so-cool face on, dawg,' Sukhi said, decoding nonchalance in the terms he knew. He smiled at his buddy and slapped on his back. '*Ja Simran, jee le apni zindagi* (Go, Simran, live your life).'

There it was. Their implicit understanding. Abhimanyu knew if anything ever happened to him, they'd have his back. Amidst laughs, the four of them walked off.

⋙⋘

GoT, Samyuktha messaged. Another example showing that sex sells, she messaged Abhimanyu later in the night. I hate to say it, but I think I agree.

Attagirl, came the reply after a few minutes. Fiction is just an exaggeration of inner desires. And all of this just flies in the face of this whole monogamy thing, don't you think?

Samyuktha was surprised at his directness. Did he think she was promiscuous? She thought for a moment and replied. Not entirely true, she replied. Everything has a place under the sun.

True, Abhimanyu replied. Having said that, I doubt our generation will ever vouch for getting married. Marriage is that perfect thing which ruins a good relationship. Just a random musing.

Does one need to get married if they wish to adopt a whale? Samyuktha asked quickly, changing the subject.

Abhimanyu looked at his phone. It was getting really tiring for him to type from his battered Nokia. He looked at his sleek iPhone, and on an impulse, dialled her number and put on his AirPods. After a few rings, she answered.

'Are you sure you want to be talking to that soldier?'

Abhimanyu asked. 'He's bad news.'

Samyuktha smiled, recognizing his voice. 'I agree. I think I should hang up,' she said, her smile growing wider as she sat up in her bed.

'Okay, before that. Tell me what's the deal with the whale?'

So, Samyuktha told him about how her love for the environment had been ironically sparked by a dog chasing her when she was tiny, and how she had cowered in fear at the sight of animals ever since. However, the more she had watched them warily while passing them by, the more she had noticed hungry animals eating out of waste bins, stray dogs being shooed away and baby elephants clad in chains within temples. Her fear had turned into pity as she saw the look of helplessness and despair in the eyes of those poor animals. Growing up, she started asking questions and reading up as much as she could.

'I still can't believe that we pay such obeisance to Ganesha as the Elephant God in our music, dance, paintings, weddings, pujas...basically in every way except the one way we should,' she told Abhimanyu, surprised at how she was talking so freely to him about one of her deepest passions. 'I want my education to mean something, and use it to make a penguin do a happy dance,' she said with a smile, adding, 'and maybe dance with it. I am hoping to join the EDF.'

Abhimanyu didn't know what EDF was. So she explained how the Environmental Defense Fund worked on advocating for and solving issues related to global warming and ecosystem restoration. He listened intently, admiring her passion and commitment.

He looked around at his airy room and the windows outside, where he saw miles and miles of nothingness except a stray cow meandering around. 'You know what, when I'm at my post every day and see these cows and dogs ambling along, I always think they have this look in their eyes that seem to be asking, "Wait, why are humans wearing muzzles now?"' he said, with a laugh.

Samyuktha smiled as Abhimanyu went on, 'I never thought about jobs like the one at EDF, it sounds so cool!' He paused as he sat down on his bed with his Glen on the rocks. 'Our generation thinks that video, animation, design are the cool things to do. But how will we do all these things,' his eyes flashed, 'when our world will have nothing natural, nothing green or blue left?' he asked, looking outside his window. 'Sometimes, I feel our parents' generation had it better,' Abhimanyu continued as he leaned back and stretched. 'Good work–life balance, no information overload on WhatsApp, *mast zindagi* (carefree life).'

'True,' Samyuktha said as she got up and started pacing around, smiling at his ability to put things so cleanly. 'We aren't really letting any moment sink in and appreciate it. Everything has become a selfie moment. Although I'm glad that we also don't fall in love with the first guy or girl we meet and get married.' Samyuktha was surprised at herself for saying the last line. It was very unlike her to speak so freely to someone that she had just met that evening for the first time. Abhimanyu smiled and nodded as he sipped his drink and set the glass down.

'You have a lovely smile,' Abhimanyu said after a few seconds of silence, half-shyly, half-earnestly. 'I could catch a glimpse of it today behind that translucent mask.'

Samyuktha blushed. 'Thanks,' she said, smiling, but a little awkwardly. 'It's my Amma's smile. My Thatha calls us a carbon copy.' She sent him one of her favourite pictures, a selfie that her Thatha had taken of all of them when she had gotten into IIT. Abhimanyu sat up as he clicked on the image. It was a dorkier-looking Samyuktha with a smile that lit up her eyes. Abhimanyu smiled wider. He loved that she had a beautiful family, something that he missed and always craved for. The birthday celebrations, decorations at home, family trip pictures…and through them, tracing the slow metamorphosis of a child's face becoming more like that of their parent.

'Okay,' said Abhimanyu, finally. 'Lady, my chai break is between 4 and 4.30 p.m. If you want to come for your grocery run tomorrow, or any kind of run, you could perhaps tell me a bit about what else your Thatha tells you. And I could catch a glimpse of that smile firsthand, perhaps.' He paused and waited.

'I'll think about it,' Samyuktha answered untruthfully as she leaned against the loveseat. A big thumbs up emoji had already popped up in her brain.

'I may change my name if you don't show up,' Abhimanyu said in mock despair, 'and I like my name.' He laughed. Abhimanyu had a spontaneous, hearty laugh. Just listening to it made her want to laugh.

What am I doing? Samyuktha asked herself. She didn't want to answer that question. Not right away. As she hung up, she heard a low rumble of a car from below. She turned around and saw a car slowly pass by her bedroom window before turning to the main gate of Ashok Apartments.

Who is it this late? Samyuktha wondered as she glanced at her phone. It was 12.23 a.m. She stepped out from her bedroom. Quietly, she crossed the kitchen and the living room to go into the balcony of the living room which was right above the entrance to C wing. A suited man got out, and waited for the driver to open the trunk and lift what looked like a heavy suitcase with a white tag. Samyuktha couldn't recognize the silhouette. The man tipped the driver, quietly unlocked the gate and stepped in. She could see him lift the suitcase as if to avoid the noise it made while rolling. He was then out of her sight.

Step Up

Samyuktha woke up to a loud and incessant knocking on her door. 'Kanna, is everything alright?' Anitha asked, concerned. 'It's eleven in the morning and your phone is switched off. Sharanya has called me thrice. She's worried you're dead, apparently,' Anitha laughed.

Samyuktha rummaged around sleepily for her phone, squinting at the sunlight streaming from the balcony. She found the phone finally under her pillow as she sat up lazily. Dead. *Of course.* She had forgotten to charge it before falling off to sleep. *Again.*

'I'm fine, Amma,' she said. 'I was up working on an assignment last night. That's all. Just coming,' she lied. She felt a bit guilty, but excitement took over the guilt.

Samyuktha's mind went back to last night and she unconsciously smiled. They had talked for three hours on the phone after she had noticed the midnight visitor. It was like some cheesy Bollywood movie. Except that it wasn't. *It was totally* vera *(different) level,* Samyuktha thought. That was high praise in her lexicon.

She had talked about penguins waddling curiously around South African towns. Then she had explained why Sharanya was so keen on becoming a cultural councillor. Then there was her Thatha. He had talked of his enduring friendship with Ayaan. They had woven imaginary theories around a post-pandemic world, and wondered how soon movie actors would agree to do intimate scenes again. Neither had had any idea of what time it was. Samyuktha had stopped short of mentioning her angst about Amma being away at the hospital all the time. She had noticed that Abhimanyu did not volunteer to divulge any more information about his sister either. *Too soon,* she had thought.

At 2.00 a.m., Abhimanyu had hesitantly said that he needed to hang up. Samyuktha had agreed. As a parting note, she had happened to ask him what he thought of Chennai, and before she knew it, another hour had flown by. She had found his outsider interpretation of Chennai fascinating. The houses, the music, the culture... She secretly admired how much he knew about most of it. Parts of what he said were new even to her. She was not aware why temples had red and white stripes on them. She, in turn, had told him about Marina Beach and how she loved running there and why. As they had neared 3.00 a.m., they had both hung up, almost half asleep as the dark sky was about to start getting aglow with the first rays of the sun.

Samyuktha dragged herself back to the present, out of bed and straight to the washroom. Samyuktha *had* to brush first thing after waking up, no talking without brushing. It's weird how the things one most resists growing up are the ones that become staunch habits. The girls in the hostel would make fun of Samyuktha, calling her Arthur Dent's lover.

As she sauntered for breakfast, the intercom rang. It was Suhasini aunty. Her otherwise calm and melodious voice sounded worried.

'Hi Aunty!' She said in a warm voice. 'Yes... yes...sure, Aunty... Amma, she wants to speak with you.'

Anitha picked up the phone. 'Yes, Suhas, tell me...yes... Oh, is it?' Anitha checked her watch. 'Yes, I'll be there... Ten minutes...tell her to relax, ma, okay?'

Anitha briskly went to her cupboard, picked a set of operation gowns and another crisp, starched kurta. She was used to the drill by now.

⌐∽◯∾

Abhimanyu had been up since 6.00 a.m. to start his morning workout, thirty minutes late, but brighter than usual. Lack of sleep never bothered him, lack of inspiration did, and last night, he had got more than his fill of the latter. Bright eyed and bushy tailed, he finished his rigorous workout. He decided to go for a run. As he jogged, masked, showing his badge to all the police folks who stopped him, he turned a corner at the Marina Lighthouse and stopped short in his tracks at the sight ahead.

Abhimanyu had reached Samyuktha's favourite Marina Beach. The vast water body that lay ahead of him gurgled softly in the morning low tide as flocks of birds flew over it, revealing how endless both the sky and water were. Samyuktha had sounded regretful that the beach was usually too littered, but Abhimanyu found it pristine, with not a speck of dirt or stray paper. *Absence of humans has a definite advantage,* Abhimanyu thought and wished Samyuktha could see what he was seeing right now.

Nothing can calm your mind and impulses like a beach can, he realized as he felt like a dot amidst the soundscape of waves and seagulls as the salty breeze enveloped him. He filled his lungs with it as he started his jog again, finally knowing what it meant to be able to let go of all thoughts. He splashed around like a child.

He smiled as Samyuktha's vivid description of the beach came to life in front of him. Miles of sand and water on one end, and the iconic landmarks of the city on the other. And there was the perfect running track at the centre. As Abhimanyu jogged, he saw Queen Mary's College, the majestic Madras University, the Kannagi statue and the grand Presidency College. As he turned the other side, he saw miles of unending water. *She's so right,* he thought. *I wish she were here jogging with me.* He took out his phone and sent her a panorama picture, accompanied by a GIF of a child with its eyes wide open in wonder.

Clamping down Samyuktha thoughts, he plugged back his earphones, listening to 'Club Can't Handle Me', and raced across the Marina, until he came to the majestic Napier Bridge. He stopped at that point, panting and gazing at the majestic bridge. What a brilliant work of architecture. Far in the distance proudly stood the War Memorial, which, as Samyuktha had correctly said, had a 'lovely, misty feel' to it of heroes who had fought and were long gone. Abhimayu felt his eyes turn misty as he thought about his father. As he jogged towards the memorial, he found tears freely rolling down his eyes. He made no effort to stop them.

He crossed the road and went quietly to the Memorial— dignified, tasteful, with a patch of grass at the very centre of it and surrounded by marble epitaphs. Abhimanyu took a deep breath, stood up as straight as he could and gave a full army salute. The pride on his face was palpable, but the wistfulness behind it could have been visible only to the discerning eye.

Ayaan was already on the field with Sukhi and Anish. The minute he sighted Abhimanyu, he broke into an all-knowing smile. Abhimanyu groaned. He knew what was coming next as he stifled a yawn and braced himself. Ayaan jumped up like a pogo stick, leaving behind his push-ups set.

'Abhimanyu Singh late for his workout? Anish, has this ever happened?' Ayaan asked in an extra dramatic tone as he looked at Anish, who was busy doing jumping jacks.

'Never in known history,' Anish solemnly replied. 'Maybe he finished his workout already?' Anish looked at Abhi with a wicked smile and went back to his push-up routine.

'Why does Abhi need this *cardio-vardio* when his heart is pounding anyway?' Sukhi chimed in. 'It's called,' he paused for impact, 'the gharwali feeling.' The rest of them burst out laughing and collapsed on the floor.

Abhimanyu knew they weren't going to let him go without details of some sort. So, as quickly as he could, he told them about the phone call and about his chances of meeting her again.

Abhimanyu was basking in the glow of last night. Reliving those with his buddies left him beaming like a child. He mindlessly ended up doing two extra rounds of push-ups much to Ayaan's amusement. Samyuktha was yet to read his message. He noticed the time. 7.30 a.m. *Probably not awake yet.*

༄

As Anitha walked upstairs to the third floor, she passed by Ahalya sitting on the stairs, busy on her phone. Anitha idly wondered how she was allowed to sit outside the home during these times. But the scatterbrain that she was, it didn't bother her for long.

'Hi, Anitha aunty,' she said morosely. She stared at her stethoscope and was about to ask her something. Anitha didn't have the time to ask her what was wrong. *Probably something about not being allowed to step out. Ahalya was a social butterfly. Poor girl.*

'Good morning, Ahalya! Sorry kanna, in a bit of a rush, will talk to you later, okay?' she said as she passed her. Ahalya looked at her, open-mouthed. *Where was Anitha aunty going?* Ahalya at this point was absorbed in figuring out what she would say next to Abhi on Tinder. She checked to see if he had replied. No message yet. She felt a pang. *Should I send him more pictures?* She wondered.

Suhasini had already left the door open in anticipation. Anitha went through her usual sanitisation protocol. She scrubbed and washed her hands thoroughly, wore the face mask, gloves and the disposable surgical gown.

She checked Sandhya, who was writhing in pain. After checking her pulse and BP, she felt her stomach, and then shot off a few questions to her in a clear and professional voice. After five minutes, Anitha turned back to Suhasini and addressed both of them.

'It's a classic case of Braxton Hicks, Sandhya. It means you get false labour, which mimics contractions, but you're not really in labour. But...' smiling with a knowing look '...the time isn't far away, kanna.' She patted Sandhya's head with her gloved hand. She had much fondness for this girl. She had seen her grow up in front of her eyes.

'Thanks, Aunty,' Sandhya said, smiling amidst her pain. 'It's a blessing to have a doctor and...*you*...' she smiled, 'rolled in one. I wish I could give you a hug now.'

'Don't,' Anitha said with a laugh.

'Anitha,' Suhasini said, her melodious voice tinged with gratitude. 'You have no idea what a help...'

'Suhas, leave all this formality,' Anitha cut her off. 'I'm just glad I hadn't left for the hospital yet.'

Suhasini smiled as Anitha bounded down the stairs in her usual graceless manner. *What a darling,* she thought.

Anitha didn't notice Ahalya peering down from the balcony intensely. As soon as she saw her leave in her silver Honda, she went up to her mom. 'Papa, Anitha aunty just went to visit Suhasini aunty,' she said, panting. 'Is that allowed?'

As Indrani placed the *luchi* and *chholar dal* in front of Abhijeet, she started to feel her usual anxiety coming up. Abhijeet Ganguly sat as usual, with his head buried in the newspaper, sneezing, as the aroma of spice-laden chholar dal wafted around the room. Arun looked equally disinterested.

Abhijeet looked up as he sniffled. 'Yes,' he said clumsily, waving the newspaper, 'I don't know.' He looked at his daughter, who was looking at him for an answer. 'But shona, she's a doctor, na? If Sandhya has pains, who else would she call?' Arun nodded in agreement between mouthfuls of luchi. 'And Anitha is intelligent,' he said, with a slight smile.

Indrani caught onto that quickly. 'She will definitely be careful.'

Indrani sat down, quietly. This wasn't the first time she had seen that smile or that look of admiration. Indrani knew how highly Abhijeet thought of Anitha. As did Indrani, of course. But somehow, she always felt...*lesser*...than Anitha in Abhijeet's eyes. There was always that pang of jealousy that came about, which she had been trying to suppress for years.

'Yes,' Indrani agreed. 'Knowing Anitha, she definitely is. But it's still a little uncomfortable, na?' she asked her husband, who was by now again immersed in his newspaper.

'I don't know all these things, Indrani,' he said a tad impatiently. And continued to eat, reading the newspaper. Many years of wisdom had taught him not to respond or fall for something that meant incessant back and forth, where there was no right answer. But was it wisdom, or avoidance of conversation?

꧁꧂

After breakfast, Samyuktha finally switched on her phone. As the messages started popping up, she groaned. There were around two hundred messages on the college WhatsApp group; Zoom party invites from her campus tennis club; Netflix watch-together plans and more forwards—videos of hoarding of groceries after the PM's lockdown speech; police resorting to lathi charge in several cities; and more dance videos with each dancer throwing an object to the next person. Samyuktha rolled her eyes. It was cool when the first one came out, but then a few hundred more came out over the next week.

The one forward that did make Samyuktha smile and prompted her to watch the video was that of a group of penguins in Chicago that had been taken to a museum.

She then saw as many as fifteen 'are-you-dead' frantic messages from Sharanya. And then there was that one message that made her smile some more. It was from an unknown number. It was the only one she bothered opening. *Probably his phone,* she thought. *The one that he called me from last night.* She smiled when she saw the landscape picture of Marina Beach, and laughed when she saw the GIF, which as she had been told many times are the new way of communicating.

Samyuktha opened her Instagram. Amidst stories of Zoom parties, various pictures of the sun and sky, pets, lockdown cooking pictures…she quickly searched for Abhimanyu. She saw at least thirty, and she couldn't make out which was Winky. *Oh well…*

She went to the balcony. There he was, bright and cheerful, looking as handsome as ever in his crisp uniform. Just as Samyuktha was about to send him a message, a group of stray puppies wandered up to him. Her heart did a double flip as he knelt down to pat them, talk to them and give them some biscuits. Samyuktha didn't want that moment to end. She watched him, her face softening.

And at that moment, he glanced up, saw her and broke into that crinkly smile. She smiled back and blushed. She had rarely felt such a warm rush of emotion like that before in the twenty years of her life.

Sharanya called again at that moment. Samyuktha had to answer. She dragged her eyes away from him, went inside and hit the answer button.

'Finally!' the voice on the other end screeched. 'I've been trying to reach you since morning! Tell me everything!'

Samyuktha smiled. Sharanya must be pacing around frantically tugging her hair like she always did when she was excited. *We all need that friend*, she thought. *When you say, 'I've murdered someone,' and they reply with 'Okay, let's go find a shovel and bury the evidence!'* She told her everything, sparing no detail, and they spent two hours discussing the conversation she had with Abhimanyu.

From what she could decipher, Sharanya was impressed by his intellect.

'You're so lucky. I am so jealous!' she said, without a hint of jealousy in her voice.

'Sharan! I've just had one phone call with him, dude.' But she smiled. *Men who communicate well are rare,* she mused, and then the thought of her father crossed her mind. Just as she was about to end the conversation, her phone started beeping with another incoming call. It was Abhimanyu. She hurriedly hung up, tapped the answer button and went quickly to the balcony.

'Are you still trying to figure out the best response to my GIF?' he asked as he looked up at her, smiling.

'Wha—oh!' Samyuktha realized she had not responded to him. 'I'm so sorry. I was going to but...'

'It's okay. I have that effect on people. Don't be too hard on yourself,' he said, smiling wider now.

'Really? You get ghosted all the time?' came the retort.

'I walked into that one, didn't I?' Abhimanyu said, clutching his heart dramatically. *She's witty,* he thought.

Overgrown child, she thought, exactly at the same time. *Overgrown child, but one who can communicate well.*

'Seriously, though,' she said hesitantly, 'It was fun. Didn't realize how the time flew by. But I overslept and got no work done all morning. How are you holding up?' she asked, surprised at seeing him not show any signs of sleep or fatigue.

'I'm sure I have filter coffee instead of blood in my veins by now,' he laughed. Samyuktha loved that carefree laugh and wished she could be so spontaneous.

'In that case, we're on for the 4.00 p.m. jog, I assume?' she asked, on impulse. She noticed Abhimanyu smile as he put his coffee glass on the desk and looked up at her. He looked at her intently for a few seconds.

'Of course,' he said with a smile. 'Looking forward to beating you hollow.'

ॐ

Once breakfast was done, Indrani started pacing up and down. She couldn't let go of the niggle. Of course, Abhijeet was right. Sandhya needed a gynaecologist, and Anitha was the best person right now, given that poor Sandhya couldn't step out.

But the human mind works in strange ways, right? *What if...Anitha has Covid? What if...she is healthy because she is asymptomatic? She is, after all, what people call a super-spreader. All healthcare workers are. What if...when she travelled upstairs, she sneezed, or talked loudly and passed it on to Ahalya? Even a loud voice can release the virus into the air, and it can spread around the air upto twelve feet, if the latest guideline released by WHO is to be believed.*

She wished she could discuss all these things in detail with Abhijeet. Indrani, beneath her anxious facade, was a keen researcher. She knew all the latest guidelines on Covid. She read up frequently on it and was usually the most updated on it. However, with her anxiety and overthinking combined with research, she would often make up stories and tales around facts. Doing so, it would only become unrealistic. It didn't help that

Indrani did not have too many friends who could bring out the best in her.

What she needed was someone who could sit her down and help her get rid of her anxiety, while still appreciating the depth of her research. And Abhijeet unfortunately was not that person. A smart savvy salesman who knew how to make slides and sweet-talk to people, he had risen in his career. When it came to their marriage, he always overshadowed her, with people believing that he was the catch and she, the reacher. Her insecurity had built up over the years, combined with the feeling of being misunderstood, leading to anxiety attacks and some pettiness, even when she tried hard to suppress all of it.

So, here she was, pacing around and trying to understand what to do. She decided to call Ranjini again.

'Anitha went into Suhas's house-a?' Ranjini's friendly drawl took on a shade of worry as Indrani told her. The rhythmic slash of her knife had stopped as she put away the vegetables.

'Yes, Ranjini. Ahalya was sitting on the steps. She just crossed her in a mad rush. And…' she said in a worried voice, 'she spends all day at the hospital meeting hundreds of infected patients.'

'Maybe it is for Sandhya…' she said, logically hitting the right conclusion.

'If Aditya has a slight fever tomorrow, will you ask Anitha to check him, Ranjini?' Ranjini looked out of the window and saw Anitha leave in her silver Honda City.

She thought for a moment and replied. 'Maybe not. I would just do a phone consultation to be safe.'

Ranjini was already a bit shaken by a WhatsApp forward that Ganesh, her husband, had sent her that morning—it had disturbing visuals of a young boy on a ventilator in the US. Her husband was pre-diabetic and the only earning member of the family. She was anxious enough.

⌒∽∽⌒

Abhimanyu was eating lunch in the mess, but his mind was in Dreamland, where he was jogging next to Samyuktha on Marina Beach. His brain couldn't think of anything else at that point. It was abruptly forced to, however, as it broadcast images of raging fire when he mindlessly bit into a ferocious green chilly lurking in the *avial* (thick stew) on his plate. He coughed and downed a full glass of buttermilk as he came back to the present. Sukhi was talking animatedly as Ayaan was trying to interrupt him.

'...*haan, par* (yes, but) once the media branded an entire community over an event, and splashed sensational headlines, no one is talking about other religious gatherings anymore,' Sukhi finished saying what he had to.

Ayaan jumped in, 'Yaar, Tablighi needed to be blamed. They had religious leaders from abroad at a crucial point in the initial stages of the pandemic. I'm not saying other religions were not congregating, but their participants were not from abroad. It's different.' They were talking about the Tablighi Jamaat conference's role in super-spreading the contagion in India.

'Whatever it is, I think Sukhi's point is that this has become a convenient mouthpiece for the ruling party's agenda. Muslim residents in Chennai are already being targeted, and I think we need to pay closer attention. Would we know if residents in Mylapore, for example, are ganging up on them?' added Anish as he curiously eyed the South Indian style dahi vadas on his plate.

'One mami on Desika Road already asked me,' Ayaan sheepishly added. 'The moment she realized I'm Muslim and had come from Delhi, she took two steps back and rather politely asked if I had been at the congregation.'

'That's exactly what I'm saying,' fumed Sukhi as he put his spoon back without eating from it. He was clearly annoyed by the flames of religious bias that were gently being stoked in the background and that no one was really talking about.

᙭

'Amma, I feel really lethargic since I have been back,' Samyuktha said, stretching, her head on Anitha's lap. It was one of the few afternoons that Anitha was free—her shift started in the second half of the day. So after lunch, mother and daughter lazily spent their time in the main living room balcony, looking at the diffused afternoon sun on the vast avenues of Mylapore.

Samyuktha could hear the birds chirping excitedly and it reminded her of the IIT Bombay campus. *That's why I took to campus life so quickly,* she thought. *The sounds are the same!* Although the air in Chennai felt a tad heavier than Mumbai, Samyuktha felt at peace in her Amma's lap. The ceiling fan was cooling enough.

Anitha shook out of her reverie. 'I can understand, kanna,' she said as she checked her ears for dirt, something she did when Samyuktha was a kid. Samyuktha hated it and would always flinch, but this time, she didn't say anything. She had an agenda.

'What can we do about it? You must be missing the Powai runs, illaya?'

Samyuktha liked that her mother came straight to the point. Here was her perfect opportunity.

'Yes, Amma,' she said. 'I really miss the runs. We can anyway head out between ten and five, if we're alone and wearing a mask. So why can't I just go for a run here?'

Anitha gasped. In this heat? Are you mad? You'll come back like a fried potato,' she said, though Samyuktha hardly had any potato-esque features about her.

Samyuktha laughed. 'Amma, I won't. I'll wear sunscreen,' she said, hoping her Amma couldn't sense her increasing heartbeat.

Anitha then looked at her daughter long and hard. *Poor girl. Cooped up in the house all day long. And going out between ten and five is allowed, after all.*

'Wear medical sunscreen, seriya? Tell Thatha or Appa I said okay. Come back quickly.' Anitha systematically gave instructions as if she was talking to her junior doctors. 'And...' she smiled at her younger clone, 'Have fun, kanna.'

Samyuktha grinned with relief and a wee bit of wickedness, and raced inside to get ready. Anitha smiled. As she got up to leave for the hospital, she saw Ranjini, who had come out to hang clothes on the balcony. She looked at Anitha and waved to her. Anitha waved back warmly. She was fond of Ranjini. Though a considerable number of years younger than her, Ranjini was a brave mother, who had been quietly battling her son's asthma for the last four years and not to mention her husband's diabetes.

'How are you, ma?' she asked. 'And how's Adi?'

'All good, Anitha,' Ranjini called Anitha by her name, not 'Aunty'. Anitha had strictly forbidden it. 'Adi is actually much better. Maybe the lower pollution levels. Illaya?'

'For sure, Ranjini,' Anitha answered. 'Seri, ma, I have to rush, okay? Need to go to the hospital. I'll talk to you soon. Take care, ma.' She waved and disappeared, knocking down a small innocent rose pot in the process.

Ranjini smiled at the clumsiness. Then her brow furrowed as she thought of what Indrani had said. *What if Anitha, in her clumsiness, forgot to sanitize on some days? Was that even possible? No,* she thought as she hung up Adi's dinosaur T-shirt. *She's careful. I trust her.* She hung up the rest of the clothes, deep in thought.

෴

'You're really a turtle, I hope you know that,' Abhimanyu said as Samyuktha tried to keep up with a resolute look. *This girl is good and gives me stiff competition*, he thought as he noticed her practised, systematic breathing and her stamina.

Samyuktha opened her mouth to start talking about her speed and stats, when Abhimanyu stopped and cut her off.

'You're a metaphorical turtle, Turtle,' he said, panting and taking a break to walk instead. 'You have access to everything you will ever need and yet you are the eternal procrastinator,' he paused and blinked, 'I don't exactly know what I mean by that, but I mean it as Holden would have said. So, henceforth, this becomes your name,' he said as he sanitized his hands.

Samyuktha opened her mouth to defend herself, but chose not to. She started running again.

'Wait up!' he said, panting, as he caught up with her. 'May I ask how old you are, so that I know that I'm not toying with the boundaries of the law?' he asked this directly, looking straight into her eyes.

'Twenty,' Samyuktha replied equally directly. 'I'm not underage, if that's what you're implying. At least not in my state. I don't know when and how Delhi girls...well...come of age.'

'They age like wine,' Abhimanyu replied tongue-in-cheek.

Samyuktha smiled. 'I would not like to know much about anything said in that sentence,' she said, panting and trying to catch her breath. 'But tell me more about the metaphorical turtle thing.'

Abhimanyu paused before he answered, trying to frame it right. 'I may be totally wrong,' he said, 'but I can see it in your eyes, how much you love the environment. You live for those penguins. And the whales. You crave clean air. And the olive ridley sea turtles...'

'So, now I am a turtle?' Samyuktha shot back.

'Yes,' Abhimanyu said. 'Last evening you talked about the Environmental Defense Fund. And I checked online,' Samyuktha went red because she knew what was coming. 'IIT Bombay has a collaboration and internship partnership with them.'

'I know,' Samyuktha said, 'and I am going to apply. I have all the forms...'

Abhimanyu's eyes grew serious. 'What are you waiting for, Samyuktha? I'm sure you were planning on it anyway. But,' he smiled, 'like Nike has said for years, just do it. I don't know you very well yet, but I know that you would be one of the better candidates.'

Samyuktha replied, 'I will, for sure. I might not be the best candidate, but I will do it.'

'Tell me about your Amma,' Abhimanyu said, changing the subject. He didn't want to sound preachy. They had lapsed into a walk now, briskly across the quiet bylanes of TTK Road. *Sriram Nagar,* Abhimanyu read.

'Amma is a rockstar, Dad is a rock,' she said. Abhimanyu laughed his usual wholehearted laugh. 'One of those providers without an emotional backbone, I take it,' he said, incisively hitting the nail on the head. Samyuktha was amazed at how he instantly got it.

'Yes. Exactly. How did you know?' she asked in amazement.

'Story of Indian marriages throughout the world,' he said.

Amidst laughs, they continued the chatter. They both found it easy to talk to each other. Samyuktha found Abhimanyu cute and funny. Second, he was well read and could add back a different dimension to almost every conversation. Third, he had a sweet way of just listening—head tilted to one side, with half a smile, and a nod every once in a while. She loved the way he caught her little jokes. Samyuktha's heart skipped a bit as she looked sidelong at his sculpted silhouette.

A text message that popped up just then made him frown. 'While on the subject of marriage and family...I need to take this. I hope you don't mind.' He returned the call.

'Everything alright?' Abhimanyu sat up as he turned away from Samyuktha. 'Yes…you can tell me, Didi,' Abhimanyu calmly said. But Samyuktha knew from the tone of his voice that something was up.

'Of course, Didi,' he paused again. 'Don't bottle it up. Waise, aren't the medicines working?' A small frown started appearing on his forehead. Samyuktha had this sudden urge to kiss it away. She shushed herself.

After a few minutes, Abhimanyu hung up and then stared at his phone for a bit.

'Is…everything alright?' Samyuktha asked, noticing Abhimanyu breathing slightly heavier than usual, and that was not from the running.

Abhimanyu snapped out of his thoughts and looked at her. 'Sorry about that,' he said as he smiled at her. 'It was my sister, Shalini didi,' Samyuktha noticed him glancing back at the phone quickly. 'She…just needed to talk,' he said, looking at her with a hesitant smile.

One can tell the difference between a goofy smile and the one where one's eyes become a window to their soul. Samyuktha didn't want to pry, but she tried to do what her mother did. She looked at him with an earnest smile. She waited. *Three… Two…One…*

'Staying at home is getting to her…husband,' Abhimanyu paused as he said the last word, and his smile rapidly waned. 'I don't know why…he's not bad, but…' he paused again. 'I'm sorry,' he said as all pretence vanished from his face and he slouched like a five-year old sulking in a corner.

Samyuktha held back a sudden urge to hug Abhimanyu in the 'it'll-be-alright' kind of way. It took her some resilience to stay away. She found it sweet that this bold, audacious, macho soldier boy was vulnerable when it came to his sister.

'It's okay, Abhi. We don't have to talk about it if you don't want to,' she said, finally, a poor substitute to what was actually playing in her mind.

He warmed up to her calling him 'Abhi'. He looked away again, and then closed his eyes as he took a deep breath and smiled, and said again, 'So ironic...just when we were discussing marriage,' he tried to coax himself back into his goofy mood.

Abhimanyu and Samyuktha walked on in silence for some time. They were just content being next to each other, looking around, taking in the sights of the quiet, peaceful CP Ramaswamy Road. Samyuktha looked at her favourite stores as they lay eerily quiet—Fabindia, Brass Tacks and even the Nilgiris, which was the closest 'large' supermarket near her home, that she used to go to as a child. She told Abhimanyu about how her mother would let her put little things into the basket, pretend not to notice, bill them in the end and pretend she didn't know where it came from. Abhimanyu laughed when he heard this.

'Your mom is really cool, you know?' Was there a hint of wistfulness as he said it? Samyuktha wasn't able to make out. He told her about the under-construction building that he converted into his office. As he described it, it reminded Samyuktha of the home in the iconic Mani Ratnam movie *Alaipayuthey*. She told him about it excitedly, and he smiled at her enthusiasm. He made a mental note to look it up.

Finally, they approached Warren Road just as the sky was turning a shade darker. As a light midsummer drizzle began, Abhimanyu looked at her and gently said, 'I guess we have to go.' Was that disappointment in her eyes? He hoped so.

Samyuktha said nothing. After a moment, she smiled and said, 'See you soon.' She looked up at the sky again as the sweet smell of the first rain hitting the parched Earth filled their noses. Samyuktha let it into her lungs eagerly, and at the same time reluctantly dragged her feet towards Ashok Apartments, looking back at Abhimanyu just before turning the corner. He was standing there, smiling at her, getting wet in the rain. As soon as Samyuktha got home, she ran straight into the balcony, pretending to do some post-run stretches. But her eyes were glued to the lone soldier walking in the rain, turning his head upward to take in the welcome rain. A long thirst finally quenched, if only by a drizzle. Their eyes met again, and Samyuktha's heart did a flip as he ran his fingers through his wet hair. *Play it cool*, she instructed herself sharply before giving him a quick wave and dashing back inside the house.

The Wolf of Warren Street

Ajay was in his study, poring over the new information that had just come in. His team had been hard at work, identifying sub-themes in Google search results and correlating it with credit card purchase data. The results showed promise, but weren't strong enough to make a correlation yet. This was going to be trickier than he had thought. He wondered if his own apartment's activity could be taken as a case study.

Ajay imagined Ashok Apartments as a series of boxes that could be taken apart and their contents examined, just like he used to do in Hari Anna's shop as a child. He imagined a miniature world with finger-sized Ramesh, Ranjini, and the Gangulys walking around with their cell phones emanating tiny shootlets of messages and searches into the world. *If one of them had symptoms, what would they be doing?*

His mind wandered back to his childhood, as it often did when he was stuck with a problem that revolved around people's motivations and behaviour. Ajay was able to relate better to characters from his childhood when interactions were plain and direct instead of today's convoluted world of social media messaging, where words were twisted to appear politically correct. Whether it was his father's displeasure with western values, Hari Anna's extreme care not to be caught harbouring a Brahmin boy in his shop, or Amma's visionary outlook despite her secondary status in a patriarchal house, everyone's motivation was clear and their behaviour consistent with it. Especially Amma's.

In 1991, when Ajay was completing high school, the PM had liberalized India's economy, and the markers of social status had started shifting overnight. Much to his father's chagrin and with the IT sector's rise to prominence, private sector jobs had upturned the social hierarchy—they only cared for knowledge and skill, and had no regard for caste. Amidst all this, Ajay had secretly written the entrance test for IIT Kanpur and got selected with a full ride. When he had told his mother, she had taken one look at him and had known what she had to do. She had taken the offer letter and given it to her husband, and had *told* him that Ajay will be leaving for Kanpur soon and would like his blessings. That was her trump card and she played it well. Sreenivasa Master had heard her tone, seen her body language and had known better than to challenge it—he had placed his hand on the boy's head and wished him success. From there, there had been no looking back for Ajay.

Ajay had lapped up every bit of it. Having access to laboratories with cutting-edge equipment, a peer group of India's best from every corner, who were all intellectually stimulated and ambitious, and world-class faculty, had been an explosive combination that had chiseled and sculpted him into a tech wizard.

And *that* is what being an undergrad had meant to Ajay. It had liberated him from his predestined fate and had given him the tools to change the course of his life. So when he had passed by his 15-year-old daughter a few years ago, standing outside a loud, overpriced eatery, amidst youngsters smoking, drinking and wearing outlandish attire, he had wondered, *would they ever truly know what their passion is, and would they understand what it feels like to pursue it against all odds?*

'Why can't the armymen use their phones, Appa?'

Ajay shot back to the present, going over Samyuktha's

question from a few weeks ago in his mind. *How did she know they could not? She must have spoken to one of the soldiers. The mind always wants to break rules, especially those that are stated explicitly. What other rules have been imposed explicitly? Lockdown, groceries...what else?* He opened his eyes as a wave of realization hit him.

Ajay typed into the messenger window, `Can we narrow down search results to focus on location coordinates, especially originating in or around Meenambakkam? I want to look at sub-themes of Google searches, purchasing behaviour, movement if available, reports from police visits to enforce quarantine and anything out of the ordinary. If we can focus on this sub-group and identify a pattern, that would be a big win.`

◦≫◦

The doorbell rang in flat number No. 35.

Suhasini was puzzled. Who could it be? In the age of lockdown, a doorbell ring was a mystery. She slowly made her way from Sandhya's room and gingerly opened the door. There was no one, but there was a bright red parcel, wrapped up and tied in a big bow, lying on the floor. Just then, her phone rang. It was Indrani.

'Hi Suhasini, how are you, shona? How is our Sandhya doing?'

'All good, Indrani,' Suhasini said in her usual cheerful voice. 'How are the kids? How are you keeping busy during the lockdown?' Suhasini was fond of the children and they had both spent some time learning music from her. In fact, most kids in Ashok Apartments had.

'Don't ask, Suhasini. *Yeh lockdown, na* (this lockdown), it's been hell for me. Arun has an entrance exam once again. And

Ahalya, you know her na, she loves going out. Both of them are in the house all the time. And no maid. Can you imagine?'

Suhasini could, given that she didn't have any help either and a pregnant daughter at home. But she chose to say nothing, and clicked her tongue in sympathy. Indrani ploughed on.

'Anyway, did you see the red parcel on your floor, Suhasini? It's from us for you and Sandhya. I asked Abhijeet to order a few things for you,' Suhasini heard the sound of the tadka sizzling and could smell the mustard oil.

'He also brought a USB mic that you can connect to your laptop, to record your songs. Also, there are some nice children's books for the baby.' Indrani was genuinely fond of Sandhya, and had carefully researched all of this before asking Abhijeet to pick gifts for her.

Suhasini looked at the lovely red package and smiled. She was touched. 'Thank you, Indrani. That's so thoughtful of you. I'm sure Sandhya will love it,' she said, placing the package on the kitchen counter.

Just then the loud cooker sound interrupted them. As the noise abated, Indrani continued.

'So Suhasini, Ahalya was on the steps yesterday,' Indrani paused, 'and told me that she saw Anitha visit you. Is everything okay with Sandhya?'

Suhasini smiled. If an extra crow flew through Ashok Apartments, Indrani would know it. Between mother and daughter, they were the RAW of the apartment complex.

'Sandhya had some pains yesterday, Indrani, and we were concerned,' said Suhasini. 'That's why we called for Anitha's help. It's so great, illaya? To have a doctor in the complex? And that too an excellent one like Anitha,' Suhasini added the last line on purpose.

'Of course. I know Sandhya's due date is approaching. You

both must be so anxious,' she paused briefly and continued, 'And I know we are all so lucky to have Anitha right here, but sometimes I wonder how safe it is with her being at the hospital everyday.'

Suhasini paused. She knew this was coming. She was, incidentally, one of the few people who knew how well-read and well-researched Indrani was. She had known her for almost fifteen years. But she also knew that when Indrani's anxiety caught on, it tended to surpass reason. Usually, Suhasini would have sat down and explained this in detail to Indrani. But with zero sleep last night, her patience was also wearing thin this morning.

With an air of finality she said, 'Indrani, if there is anyone in the building I would trust to be extra careful right now, it is Anitha. Yes...' Suhasini paused. 'Anyway, ma, Sandhya is calling me. Thank you so much for the lovely gifts. Take care, ma.'

Suhasini hung up and continued sipping her coffee. Sandhya was fast asleep in her room.

꧁꧂

Samyuktha woke up, bright and early at 7.00 a.m. As she opened her eyes, Abhimanyu's sulky schoolboy face came into her subconscious mind and she shut her eyes again with a smile.

Turtle? Was that what he had called her? Samyuktha sat back and thought. Was she really a turtle, procrastinating what needed to be done? Samyuktha took these things very seriously and would slip into introspection mode when someone would give her a feedback.

Going to EDF was her dream. And she *had* been putting it off for many weeks. It was not that she didn't intend to apply. But she always got the feeling that she wasn't good enough. Abhimanyu's words came back...'and I still know that there's no one better for it than you, of everyone I've met...'

She sprang out of bed, and on an impulse, opened her laptop and went out with it to her balcony. She curled up on the loveseat and opened the website. There it was. She could see the deadline flashing. *5th May.* She copied the form questions and pasted them in an open document. And just like that, she started typing. She poured her heart out. This was always her process of writing. She never worried about language, punctuation, etc. She just needed to get the emotion out, as raw as she possibly could.

After forty-five minutes, she looked at the draft and smiled. Every possible emotion in her heart about why she wanted to save the environment had been expressed, albeit crudely written. She checked her phone and tapped on Abhimanyu's profile picture. As he loomed up with his smile, she blew him a kiss, mouthed a thank you and went to brush her teeth. This was the first time she had ever done anything before brushing her teeth. As she looked in the mirror, she realized that there was something important that needed to be done.

∽

'You sent the parcel to Suhasini's home? *Tumi ki pagol* (Are you mad)?' Abhijeet asked. 'She has a pregnant girl in the house...' The conversation was starting to get heated.

'But shona, I just wanted to give her the mic, the books...' Indrani honestly didn't think it was a big deal. She had not even realized that she had subconsciously decided to hand over the gifts that very day, so she could get a chance to speak with Suhasini to find out about Anitha's visit. But hearing Abhijeet's strong disdain for this stung her. *When Anitha actually visits Suhasini, it's alright. But when I send her a parcel, he has a problem with it.*

She raised her voice. 'If anyone, it should be Anitha Kumar. It's one thing for her to come from the hospital to her house, and another to mingle with other residents. She passed by Ahalya while she was studying. What if she catches the virus from her?' she said, trying to fight back tears.

Abhijeet instantly replied, 'Ahalya should be inside the house and not out on the stairs. If our PM can get a billion people to stay indoors, surely we can control two teenagers?' he said, scathingly.

'You weren't around, Abhijeet, and managing her temper tantrums and mood swings is terrible!' Indrani started working herself up. 'I had to pick my battles, else I was afraid I'd lose it.' Tearing up, she had to sit down momentarily, and started breathing heavily. Abhijeet realized it was another of her anxiety episodes. He calmed down and went over to comfort her. 'We don't have to talk about this right now. Why don't you take a nap? I'll talk to the kids and set a few rules.'

Indrani wanted to tell him how she was feeling, but she realized that he just wouldn't get it. She went into the room and tried to sleep, but couldn't. No one really understood her concerns.

Finally, she couldn't take it anymore. She picked up her phone, opened the Ashok Apartments' WhatsApp group and started typing.

Dear Friends,

Hope everyone is keeping safe and staying indoors. I'm sure you're following the news. Things are getting really bad out there. We have been instructed to stay quarantined, but I understand that certain professions still require people to step out into crowded infected places with a permit. Would you feel that it's unfair and dangerous for them to be mingling with other residents? Please let's get together and collectively establish some

```
ground  rules  in  this  regard.  In  everyone's  best
interest,  Indrani.
```

Mr Ramesh, Mahesh's father, wrote after a few minutes.

```
Indrani,  thanks  for  your  message.  As  the
secretary,  it  is  my  responsibility  to  ensure  that
we  all  adhere  to  the  lockdown  measures  strictly.
I'm surprised to know that the rules are not being
followed.  If  you  know  of  anyone  in  particular,
please  feel  free  to  bring  it  up  with  me  in  a
personal  message,  and  Mr  Ramanathan  and  I  will
do  the  needful  to  address  it.
```

Suhasini saw the message and muttered softly under her breath, *this Indrani is becoming a bit of a troublemaker.* She was about to pick up the phone to call her when Sandhya woke up and asked for a cup of hot milk.

Ganesh, Ranjini's husband, also picked up on it. He sent a WhatsApp forward he got a few days ago about a doctor who infected five people in the community of condos he lived in, after he visited them.

`Sometimes  noble  intentions  come  to  naught,` he typed, clicking his tongue. Ranjini was in the other room with Adi and read the message. *He has no concept of what to send and what not to.*

She promptly replied with, `All  of  this  is  utter nonsense.  I  would  urge  all  of  you  not  to  create false  panic.`

`Plus  one,` came Sunil's message with a thumbs up emoji. Sunil Taldar lived in A-32. He was a young finance professional, posted from Mumbai for a stint as the finance head at Unilever's Chennai office.

Ajay and Anitha were both busy at work, and did not see these messages. The other residents of Ashok Apartments were surprised. They were not sure as to who was being referred to. It set off a string of internal conversations among them. Some of them reached out separately to Indrani asking her about it. She, remembering what Abhijeet had said, did not give out any names.

The Ashok Annettes group was buzzing with a different topic altogether.

These soldiers are so cute no? Who do you think is the cutest? @Samyuktha? typed Ahalya.

Samyuktha was messaging Abhimanyu when this popped up. She frowned. *Why me? Why does she keep doing this?*

Why are you asking me @Ahalya? I think you have a much keener eye for this. (Wink).

Evidence suggests otherwise. The balcony sightings are making top page news. (Wink Wink.)

Samyuktha was boiling. She sent the message to Abhimanyu.

He replied, Tell her… Gossip is always welcome in these boring times.

She smiled and did just that. No reply.

Samyuktha browsed on her phone and came across the eight unanswered messages from Rohan. She gave him a call on WhatsApp. Samyuktha, being a very open and fair person, realized that there was no point leading him on. It was better to cut it, clean and simple. *Will this thing with Abhimanyu ever go anywhere? Maybe not. But will it be fair to lead Rohan on in the meantime? No.*

It wasn't pleasant. He was hurt, upset and more than anything else, bewildered. Samyuktha tried to explain the long distance, the situation, not knowing how long the lockdown would last, and hung up feeling like a jerk. She called Sharanya and told her. She also cried a bit.

'Sweetheart, don't worry,' she said. 'If you don't feel it, you don't feel it. It's worse to lead him on than do what you just did.'

'But Sharan,' said Samyuktha, 'I don't know what this thing with Abhimanyu is even!' She gave up on the online class entirely. Both of them had switched off their videos and were lying on the beds in their respective rooms.

'I know,' Sharanya said, but you want it to go somewhere, right?

Samyuktha was silent.

Sharanya smiled from the other end. 'That's your answer.'

Samyuktha smiled between sobs.

∽

Abhimanyu finally opened Tinder once again. Ahalya's messages were lying unanswered. And she had sent two more messages a short while ago.

How's your day going? If you prefer talking instead of typing, we can chat on a Zoom call too! Don't be shy;)

Usually, Abhimanyu would've been up for some harmless fun as that was most of his Tinder life in Delhi. But Ahalya had been trying too hard. *Or is it me just wanting more of a chase*, he wondered in self-doubt. Regardless, he also found her questions and style of talking rather weird. Not to mention, he was also creeped out a bit by her staring at him incessantly from the balcony.

He quickly typed, Hey A, don't really want to reveal any more about me. My name or my whereabouts for now. Hope that's alright? He checked WhatsApp once again. No new message from Samyuktha. It was Sunday, a half-day at work. So the plan was a sundowner party in Ayaan's room. He placed his phone face down next to him as the boys sauntered in.

Ayaan's sharp eye noticed the phone at once. 'Oye,

Abhimanyu's made friends with his phone again! How come?'

Sukhi joined in. 'Again? He's been in love with it for the last three days,' he said as he sipped his Glen.

Abhimanyu smiled. 'Yeah,' he said as he filled his glass with ice, looking wickedly at them. 'I wanted to give it a "ghar waali" feeling.' Amidst everyone's laughter, Abhimanyu stole a quick glance at the phone again. No message from Samyuktha yet.

As he took a large sip of his drink, the phone rang. It was Shalini didi. He left the room and answered instantly. Only Ayaan saw who the caller was. His sister was sobbing as she explained how her husband's mood swings were getting worse. He had had a history of getting violent and had also beaten up Shalini a few times. Abhimanyu had offered to help her get away, but she was hopeful that he would change with therapy and counselling.

Abhimanyu looked at the phone helplessly, and kicked the door as she narrated the day's events. *What can I do?* He looked at his phone again and the tears stung his eyelid. He couldn't bear to hear her so afraid and heartbroken.

'Didi,' he said softly. She continued crying. 'Didi,' he said once again. 'You're brave. Do you want me to send someone there? I can ask Maasi to go there.' But she declined vociferously.

As he hung up and turned around, Ayaan was standing outside the door. Abhimanyu rubbed his nose and quickly updated him.

'We can get our army connections in Delhi to go and get Didi out of there, Abhimanyu,' Ayaan said in anger. 'Just say the word.'

Abhimanyu smiled. 'I will, buddy.' He locked arms with him and went inside.

The theme of the party seemed to be 'North Indians Dancing the South Indian way'. Sukhi was dancing to 'O Podu' and Anish was unsuccessfully trying to gyrate, ending up looking like

Chandler from *F.R.I.E.N.D.S.* Abhimanyu saw him and started laughing. He downed his glass and joined in the fun. *If Samyuktha saw me now, she'd leave me,* he thought as he pictured her slender face. The vision of that combined with two glasses of whiskey made him feel warm all over.

It was a lovely evening, surrounded by friends and banter. And then there was Samyuktha firmly ensconced in Abhimanyu's mind. He wasn't able to stop thinking of her.

A few hours later, he finally received a message from her.

`Want to do a Zoom call tonight?`

He didn't bat an eyelid before replying, `Yes, Ma'am!`

~◌◌~

Back at the Ganguly home, Abhijeet was turning mad. He had now seen the series of WhatsApp messages. *Why did Indrani start this?* he thought. *A mountain out of a molehill?* Little did he know that the solution to Indrani's problem was just listening to her, allowing her to vent out and understanding the depth of knowledge that she brought to the table. She needed to be treated more than just a woman who brought up his kids. Instead of doing what should be done, he tried frivolous solutions. He would ask her to go for kitty parties, take pottery classes, join the Bengali Women's Club. Throwing money at the problem was something that had never failed him at work. However, this was not a one-size-fits-all solution, especially not when it came to human emotions.

'Shona, I asked you to go and take a nap. And what did you do? You put such a petty message on the group? We've known Ajay and Anitha for so long now. Are you really going to let this frustration kill our friendship?'

Indrani was tired of her husband blaming her all the time.

'Abhijeet, Ahalya has been exposed to Anitha in close quarters.

Anitha, however careful, is by her profession, a superspreader. They're saying this virus has no cure, and it could take more than a year before a vaccine is available. Also, do you know that while it's aerosol borne...'

Abhijeet always zoned out when Indrani started talking like that. He cut her off quickly. 'I understand, shona...' he patted her and told her to take a nap. Indrani took a pill and sat down on the bed, doing a deep breathing routine that had been prescribed to her for her anxiety. Abhijeet put on some meditation music, closed the curtains and within a few minutes, Indrani was asleep.

༺༻

Only five minutes were left for the Zoom call. Samyuktha quickly brushed her hair one final time. She had already brushed it a hundred times before that. She wore a Fabindia kurta, with blue ikhat and red piping, paired with a pair of jeans. She put on some lip gloss, a special addition, and just a slight trace of kajal.

As they connected on the call, she noticed Abhimanyu in his non-work clothes for the very first time. The thick fatigues had been replaced by a brick red Henley T-shirt. His hair was slicked back. As his handsome face appeared on the screen, Samyuktha got a sense of deja vu.

It was the same smile and shirt from the Tinder profile. However, she played it cool.

'Nice outfit,' Samyuktha said, breaking the silence. Abhimanyu smiled. He had tossed six T-shirts before picking this one, but he wasn't going to tell her that for sure. 'Do you go shopping with Shalini didi or Ayaan?' she asked, teasingly.

Samyuktha's guy friends were usually awkward when discussing the subject of shopping. However, Abhimanyu's response was a surprise to her. 'Honestly, I love being sharply dressed,' he said. *No airs, no pretence.* 'I read,' he looked at her

to gauge her reaction, 'my weekly GQ digest and stay updated.'
He then sheepishly smiled.

Samyuktha, too, smiled. *I love the fact that he's so bindaas
about it.*

She looked at him. With a gentle breeze rustling the leaves in
the background and the balcony lit up by the moon, the setting
was perfect. Abhimanyu was sitting at his desk by the window
and she could see the moonlight shining on his face and the
curtain behind him gently flapping. *Must be the AC*, she thought.
She asked him to show his room, and he turned around his Mac
for a better view of the immaculately organized space. She was
impressed by the well-made bed, neatly arranged shoes, and the
sense of calm the place reflected. Little did she know that just
an hour ago, it looked like the place had been hit by a cyclone,
with glasses and snacks strewn around, and the bed and pillows
in complete disarray after the raucous party.

'Get a drink, will you?' Abhimanyu asked. He showed her
his glass of Glenlivet on the rocks.

Samyuktha smiled. 'All my alcohol is in the living room,' she
said. 'Give me some time. Need the older babies to go to sleep.'
Abhimanyu smiled at her use of 'babies'. Abhimanyu could hear
the television playing faintly in a neighbouring home all the way
via the Zoom call. *Must be the Gangulys,* Samyuktha thought as
she heard the familiar strains of 'Maula Mere'.

'I love that song,' Abhimanyu said. 'It's one of my go-to
comfort songs.' He then started whistling the tune. Samyuktha
listened on. He was insanely good!

'Which are the other ones?' she asked. Her ears always perked
up when it came to music.

'Well...' Abhimanyu mused. 'There are a few. "Time of
Your Life" by Green Day. "A Million Dreams". "Tubthumping"
by Chumbawamba. "Monta Re"... What are you squealing for?'

'I love "Time of Your Life". Insane life perspective, no?' she asked, slipping into the Tamil habit of adding no to the end of every sentence.

'Absolutely,' he smiled, looking at her enthusiasm. 'What are yours?' he asked her, taking a large sip of his drink.

'"Audition" from *La La Land*, "Chinna Chinna Aasai" from *Roja*, "Top of the World" by Carpenters, "Heartbeat" by José González ..."Aaoge Jab" from *Jab We Met*.'

'*Jab We Met*,' Abhimanyu said, 'was a cute flick. My favourite movie of all time has got to be *Memento*, though.' He took a large sip again. The alcohol, the breeze and Samyuktha on his screen was starting to get to him.

'Get your drink now,' Abhimanyu ordered her, as he nursed his precious Glen and ice.

Samyuktha quietly crept out to the living room, poured out some wine and came back, both glass and bottle in hand.

'Mine is *Definitely, Maybe* and *Pulp Fiction*,' Samyuktha said, remembering where the conversation had been left off... She smiled as she heard 'Tu Cheez Badi Hai Mast' from Ahalya's house.

'By the way, you must know all about our interesting habits by now, considering you get to see everyone who steps out. What's the word on our street?' Samyuktha asked him, taking a sip of wine.

Abhimanyu smiled. 'That kind of stuff costs money, Turtle,' he said with a twinkle in his eye.

'I'll pledge all my future earnings as an underpaid environmental scientist to you,' she said. 'Now spill the beans.'

Abhimanyu smiled. He got a refill of his drink and sat down again. He then leaned back on his bed and stretched his hands. Samyuktha couldn't help but notice his taut muscles. He looked at Samyuktha. She was looking intently at him in anticipation. *The girl loves gossip*, he thought. *Why not?*

'The Gangulys use more oil than anyone else in the building.

Actually, they use more groceries per person than I have ever seen. I wouldn't be surprised if they were smuggling a human inside one of those heavy bags. Someone called Suhasini Rajagopal is obsessed with sambrani stick. One of my jawans thought it was weed and wouldn't let her go till I intervened. There's a creepy guy on the fourth floor who whispered whether "blue films" were part of essentials, and the building secretary, Mr Ramesh, wanted to know if he could pay me for an Old Monk,' Abhimanyu said all this with a flourish, taking in a large sip of his drink like a treat to himself.

Samyuktha burst out laughing. What a fun way to get gossip about people she had known for years! She could never look at them normally now. Imagine Suhasini aunty smoking up…she couldn't unsee it.

'Wait, I'm not done yet,' Abhimanyu said solemnly. 'The Vishwanathans only want to step out on odd-numbered dates for numerological reasons, and Mrs Swaminathan does this exercise routine on her balcony everyday wearing a nightgown. Very bizarre. And those Kumars on the first floor…'

'Yes…those hooligans,' Samyuktha said smiling. 'What about them?'

'They consume sanitizers by the gallon! I'm sure they drink them,' he winked. 'And soap. And detergent. And Harpic.'

'That's my paranoid Amma and her cleaning routine,' she explained the routine to Abhimanyu. He was impressed.

'That's something. Stay at work all day long, come back home tired, go through the sanitization routine, make food, take care of spoilt brats like you… Dr Anitha Kumar is a champion, for sure,' he said, looking at her mother's picture in the family portrait he could see behind her.

'Amma is a rockstar, for sure,' she said. 'She's always been. She's such an amazing doctor, you know.' Samyuktha felt pride surge in her chest. She was again speaking freely, thanks to the wine. 'Her entire unit worships her. All her patients love her. And her staff would die for her.'

'And you never get to spend time with her, isn't it?' Abhimanyu asked, looking at her intently.

Samyuktha looked up in surprise. 'How do you know that?' she asked.

'I can see it in your eyes a little bit,' he said. 'You're proud of her, but you wish she'd be around a little more, for you.'

'Is that wrong?' Samyuktha asked, looking a little wistful.

'No, of course not,' Abhimanyu said. 'Your feelings are justified. But look at it from her perspective too. She is highly educated and ambitious. Should she forego her career for you or anyone else?' he looked up at her.

No one had said this with so much directness before. 'True,' she looked back and said, 'but I wish she would be around a little more, you know?'

'I know that. So, do what she does, no?' Abhimanyu replied, mimicking her slightly. 'Wake up early. Spend time with her in the mornings. Help her around the house...'

'For sure,' Samyuktha replied. 'For your information, I washed all the plates today.' She looked at him challengingly.

'*All?*' Abhimanyu widened his eyes in mock admiration. 'You don't say! Your hands must be worn out.' She held them up for him to inspect.

As Samyuktha imagined Abhimanyu taking her hands in his to examine them, she felt an electric sensation in her body. She looked at him. *Could he see the look in her eyes?* She hoped not, but also hoped he did. The heart works in funny ways.

Abhimanyu was going through much of the same feeling. Here was this beautiful, witty girl in front of him, and he couldn't even reach forward to hold her soft, delicate hands in his. *Abhimanyu, beta, yeh toh achcha mazaak hai* (Abhimanyu, boy, this is a good joke).

'You know...' he stopped himself short. She looked at him expectantly.

Abhimanyu resisted what he was about to say next. 'I—I'm going for another peg,' he said instead. 'Try to catch up, Turtle!' he said as he looked away and got busy refilling his glass. Samyuktha, not to be outdone, downed all her wine till the last drop, and even stuck out her tongue to get the last drop. She grinned at Abhimanyu with that million watt smile.

As the wine got to Samyuktha's head, she felt she had been transported back to her dorm room night-outs with Sharanya. She had been sorely missing the carefree banter where they could just vent and blabber mindlessly without any judgement.

Then she thought of Abhimanyu. He was well read, had an incisive perspective on most things. He was very much in touch with his emotional side, thanks to being so close to his sister. And he was funny, too, thankfully not in the stereotypical Delhi boy way, but in a very subtle, Farhan Akhtar in *Zindagi Na Milegi Dobara* kind of way, and 100 per cent genuine.

Abhimanyu was enjoying himself to the hilt in a way he never had with another girl, or even with his male friends for that matter. The best part of Samyuktha was her lack of pretence and her ability to see genuineness from a mile away, and then respond in kind. He found he could say anything to her and she would respond, scathingly sometimes, but without judgement.

Abhimanyu's childhood had been hijacked way early, his innocence forced to give way to adulthood too soon. While his sister was his shade, she was also his responsibility. Books had become his best friend, his way to build perspective. High school was a blur, quite a far cry from the heady sex-and-romance action of teen romcoms.

One can sympathize with a kid who is both nerdy and looks nerdy. But one barely talks of the guys who are nerdy and never fit the nerd label. And that was Abhimanyu's happy yet unhappy problem. Girls fell for Abhimanyu, but he had no idea why. While he would be looking for deep conversations, they would be looking for something frivolous. While high school life might establish clear boundaries between braininess and hormones, it does not teach one how to deal with an accidental mix of the two.

And then before he knew it, he was off to the army at seventeen. On most dates, whenever they were possible, he would let the girl talk more. He wasn't sure what he would say about his family, his geeky passions, his personal life (or the lack of it).

But such was not the case with Samyuktha. He could tell her things very easily. And she just…got it all. And the best part was that she helped him think and talk more and more.

'You know…' Abhimanyu said, slightly sleepily, as he stared at her.

'Hmm?' Samyuktha answered as she brushed the hair from her face. *Again. Why am I so conscious?* she thought to herself.

'I would sleep so peacefully if I could see your face like this every night,' he said flashing his smile. Abhimanyu's eyes were twinkling, both seeing her and the alcohol.

Samyuktha couldn't help blushing. 'Why do *I* care if you sleep or not?' she asked, in stark contrast to how she felt.

'How will I guard your building if I don't sleep well? This is for your benefit,' he teased her back, sitting up on his bed and sipping his drink.

'Well, in that case, let's not do any afternoon jogs, I say. You should use your break time to catch up on sleep instead,' she said as Abhimanyu looked on helplessly. That was not where he wanted this to go. She continued, 'Also, no looking into balconies and winking away. Grab one of those bright red pillows in your

Bohemian den and take naps,' she laughed.

'What! You can see all of that?' He went bright-eyed before sheepishly admitting, 'By the way, I checked the *Alaipayuthey* home and it does have a striking resemblance, I must say! The only difference is, my boys did it up.'

'Yeah, they did a better job than a wife would have,' Samyuktha shot back. 'I think you should also add some balloons, party caps, blue satin sashes…cream-coloured ponies,' she added, quoting lyrics from her favourite song 'My Favourite Things' from *The Sound of Music* as her eyes teared up from laughing.

Abhimanyu glared at her, stupefied, 'You're horrible!'

'I know,' she said mock-seriously, 'I am horrible.' She smiled and winked at him. Abhimanyu felt his stomach churn and it was not the alcohol.

It was 3.00 a.m. when they both downed the last of their glasses and in Samyuktha's case, the bottle as well. Abhimanyu watched in horror as she took the slender Jacob's Creek bottle and started pouring water into it.

'Oye! What are you doing?' he groaned as he saw the heinous act unfold.

'Relax. Amma doesn't keep count of bottles, but Appa is definitely going to notice. Need to fill it back to the level it was. Thank God, it was white,' she added nonchalantly.

'You know you're completely mad, don't you?' he gaped at her. Samyuktha smiled, winked and then hit the 'end meeting for all' button.

⟨∞⟩

Samyuktha woke up with a start in her balcony. It was 10.17 a.m. She had slept the whole night in the balcony. As her eyelids flickered and she took in the scene outside, the glasses and the water-filled wine bottle, she smiled as she recalled last night. It was easily the most fun, heartwarming, sparkling night-out she had had in a long while.

Nursing a slight headache, she went into the living room. She saw her mother drinking coffee. Samyuktha, basking in her happiness, jumped on her and gave her a tight hug, and then a giant kiss on the cheek.

'SAM-yuk-THA!' Anitha yelled as she pulled herself from her embrace. 'I love you kanna, but this is absolutely not done, kanna. I am a doctor. I am staying three feet away from everyone. Taking all sorts of precautions here.'

The professional in Anitha was genuinely disturbed. Samyuktha wondered what had come over her mother, whose lap she had been ensconced in just the day before. Remembering Abhimanyu's advice from last night, Samyuktha said, 'Really sorry, Amma. Don't worry. Going by the amount of precautions you take, I think even Covid hates you by now. Your sanitization ritual is apparently the talk of the town in Corona Land, too. Even those microbes know it,' she joked away.

Anitha lightened up. 'I'm sorry kanna. There's a silly WhatsApp war going on in the apartment complex, and I'm just bothered by all of it. I'm really looking forward to that time when I can put my feet up and go back to being overly affectionate to everyone like I usually am.'

'Thank God for Covid,' Samyuktha shot back, recounting the times when her mother would smother her with hugs and kisses, and just not leave! 'I think I like this version better. What's the apartment nonsense?'

'Nothing.' Ajay walked in at this point and as usual, he had the 'she's-too-young-for-this' protective vibe on.

'I think she's old enough,' Anitha snapped, and then proceeded to tell her the entire story. Samyuktha was shocked to hear that the apartment could make such a big deal out of something like this!

'Doctors around the world are being praised for their hard work, but also suspected of spreading infection by their own neighbours. Such hypocrisy, *pah*!' she spat out.

Anitha smiled at her daughter's spirit. Deep down, she felt good that someone was standing up so vociferously for her. Somehow, hearing this from Samyuktha made her feel appreciated and validated.

'Amma, maybe you should send them all a video of your cleaning ritual every evening when you get home. No one who sees that can ever accuse you of spreading infection,' Samyuktha said as she struggled to bite through the idlis. 'Where's Thatha?' she asked, looking at his empty place.

Ajay and Anitha looked at each other.

'Just a small cough, kanna, he's just resting up,' Ajay said quickly.

Samyuktha's heart skipped a beat. 'Is everything okay?' she asked.

'Nothing to worry about, Samyu. It just seems like his usual dry cough. But I just told him to take it easy.' Just as Anitha said this, a message popped on her phone. It was Suhasini. *It's a bad attack this time, Anitha,* it said. Anitha sighed. Remembering Samyuktha's hug, she went in, took a shower again and left for Suhasini's house.

'Ajay, leaving for Suhas's house. Sandhya has contractions again,' she said before leaving.

'Shouldn't you be more careful, Anitha? After all this furore on the groups?' Ajay asked, placidly.

Anitha had mulled over that as well, and had no straightforward answer. All she knew was that there was a pregnant girl who was suffering and sending her to a hospital at this time was far riskier. And here she was just two floors below. It seemed obvious to her from a humanitarian point of view to go visit her.

'Trying, Ajay,' Anitha replied, a bit impatiently. 'I just took my third shower of the day. Will take another when I return. She needs me, and it's better than her going all the way to the hospital, isn't it?' she said and then left.

Ajay knew better than to try and reason with her at that moment. *She is so headstrong,* he thought. *What do I do? She just doesn't listen. Going to visit when she has a sick father in her house.*

Ajay's team had just told him that someone from or around Ashok Apartments had shown up as a potential suspect in their searches. This person had suddenly started googling obsessively about Covid symptoms. Ajay was wondering who it could be. It could be a resident or even a soldier standing guard outside, but everything was still nebulous. That's why he didn't want Anitha taking a chance when there could be a potential superspreader in the building.

Samyuktha, blissfully unaware of all this, agreed with her mother's logic. A pregnant woman needed help and Amma was helping! It seemed fairly simple. As she left, Samyuktha sat down and started work on her internship application. She opened the document in which she had poured her heart out. As she read it and quickly edited the grammatical mistakes, she felt the passion firing up again. Just then, a Pinterest quote popped up. *Do more things that make your heart beat faster.* On cue, she got to work immediately and started dividing her cover letter for the internship into clear sections. She worked on perfecting it and looked at it with satisfaction an hour later. It was nearly ready. She decided to check it again a day later with a clear head, before making any final changes and sending it in. She stretched and went out to the balcony.

There he was, looking fresh and chirpy again. Abhimanyu was engrossed in giving a set of instructions to his team. When he was done, he gave a cursory look at the balcony. Samyuktha smiled, her heart beating. *How cute he looked in his uniform!* It was a different level of closeness knowing that the smart officer, who was taking care of the entire apartment, had spent the whole night drinking virtually with her.

⁜

Back at Ranjini and Ganesh's house, a very different breakfast conversation was taking place. Adi had suffered an asthma attack that morning, and Ranjini was helping him with his nebulizer in his bedroom.

Ganesh was relaxing on the couch, with his newspaper and a cup of filter coffee, and the television on. His phone buzzed. He looked at it lazily, and suddenly became alert. He called out to his wife from the living room loudly.

'See! I told you this virus is not to be taken lightly. Now, it is being said that Covid is affecting kids under ten in the US and causing a cyclo…cyto…some terrible storm in their body. The doctor's threat isn't to be taken lightly, Ranjini kanna,' he clicked his tongue. Ranjini tried to ignore it, but then realized that this was not getting any better. Since Adi had started feeling better, she tucked him in and went into the living room

'Ganesh, I get it. This is all true. But what does Anitha have to do with any of this? Why are we creating such a big ruckus over her going to see a poor pregnant girl, who genuinely can't get out of her house? Seriously, don't we have better things to do?' she asked, looking at him, knowing the answer already.

He glared at her and switched off the television. 'Do you realize you have an asthmatic son and a diabetic husband, Ranjini?' he asked pompously. 'Family should be first, you know,' he said.

Ranjini sighed again. Ganesh lived in his WhatsApp world

and considered himself the resident expert on most things, based on a few forwards and videos that the world, at large, generously threw at him. He also took intense pride in selecting the best few and forwarding it to the rest of his groups. 'Ganesh's Gems' he called it. He got a lot of praise on the groups for doing so.

Ranjini wasn't as educated or well-read as him, but was well versed with the basics—fresh air, exercise, good food and, most importantly, hard work. She looked at her overweight husband moulded into the shape of the sofa and mustered to bring forth every bit of her patience. 'I have been taking care of Adi all morning after his asthma attack. As for your diabetes, if you could *konjum* (little) move and do some walking, it will be better than those insulin injections,' she said, more than a little irritated.

'You don't understand how the world works, Ranjini. You will regret it,' he said, looking at her wisely and shaking his head.

Never Have I Ever

A few evenings later, there was another breaking news on television. The lockdown was being intensified. There had been a sharp rise in the number of cases, amounting to almost six thousand a day. Witnessing an increase in the spread at an alarming rate, the news anchor announced, Italy had already announced a curfew.

India, too, was taking strict measures. Amongst the many, was that all essential groceries would be rationed and brought to civilians by the army.

The PM also announced the seven steps that every citizen needed to take to tackle coronavirus. *Did he get inspired by Abhijeet uncle and Indrani aunty?* Samyuktha wondered as the directives were listed out. Care for elders, use home-made masks, follow the health ministry's directive, install Aarogya Setu app, help the poor and deprived, don't sack employees and respect corona warriors.

Samyuktha found it impressive how science was always clad in the sheepskin of morals and tradition to get the 1.3 billion people to follow orders. Then there was an announcement to join the candlelight vigil the next night on Sunday. At 9.00 p.m., the entire country was to come together in solidarity and light a lamp on their balcony to pray together for the corona warriors—the community workers who toiled for us. Samyuktha almost burst out laughing watching the look on her mother's face.

Ajay turned off the television. The entire family looked blankly at each other.

'Nonsense!' declared Ajay. 'This is all a result of those idiots spreading the virus in the US.'

Anitha continued staring at the blank television. At that moment, Thatha came out hearing the commotion, asking what had happened.

'We can't go out for groceries anymore, Appa,' Anitha said, her brow furrowing as she tried to process what this meant to her family. While Samyuktha was concerned about the overall situation as well, her mind, in her characteristic style, tuned out the conversation gently, like a frequency change.

She was wholly absorbed in figuring out how she would meet Abhimanyu. For her, the 4.00 p.m. jogs and nightly Zoom calls had become the highlights of her day. She could feel a strong chemistry with him that surprised her. But there was more she had to figure out. It was annoying that they couldn't just go on an actual date. *It's so easy to get to know someone in person! Maybe I'll just walk over to his den and we can sit amidst some red pillows and imagine it's a date*, she thought as she tried to visualize the setting and the jawans cluelessly staring at them.

Did you see the news? she texted. The lockdown will be intensified.

You mean essential groceries will be rationed and brought by the army?

Samyuktha was surprised. Then she typed. I forgot. You are an important army man and all that.

Nothing like that. Army personnel were briefed in the morning. So we aren't caught unawares by panic-stricken civilians. ;)

I'm not panicking.

Not you. I'm talking about the woman who just came to her balcony and yelled at my poor jawan to get milk urgently.

Samyuktha burst into laughter. Amma looked suspiciously at her. It was the first time that Samyuktha's phone had been a reason for so much entertainment.

I am panicking, though. How am I going to meet you?

Just as she hit the send button, her phone buzzed again. It was Ahalya. There was a screenshot of a chat on Tinder. The bottom most message on the screen was an Abhi telling A. that he found her cute and liked her sense of style. Ahalya's message popped up below.

Hey, don't you think this handsome soldier outside looks like the guy in this profile? it read.

Huh? How would I know Ahalya? Samyuktha typed back after thinking for a moment. I've not seen him without a mask, and like I already said, I haven't interacted with him, she lied as she scrolled up again to re-read the chat.

She zoomed in on the display picture in the chat. That was Abhimanyu's face, staring at her. She got up, went to her room and sat down on her bed as she stared at that familiar rugged face with smiling eyes and chiseled features.

Ahalya meanwhile typed, This is his profile pic, and he appeared only recently when the lockdown began. That soldier wears a mask most of the time, but I can swear it's him. What do you think?

Samyuktha didn't know what to say. Ahalya continued, He said he finds me cute and stylish, but hasn't responded since. Maybe he wants to take it slow or isn't much of a talker if you know what I mean. (Wink).

Samyuktha stared at the phone in shock. *Is this what Abhimanyu does with every girl he comes across? Am I just one of those girls he is courting at the same time?* she thought, imagining him on jogs with other girls. She had to stand up and pace around to calm herself as all kinds of thoughts flooded her mind.

Hey, are you there? came Ahalya's message.

There was a message from Abhimanyu's too, We'll find a way to meet, don't worry.

Samyuktha was fuming by now and the walls of the room felt like they were closing in on her. She typed a hasty reply to Ahalya, Not sure Ahalya, but all the best! and then put away her phone.

She ignored Abhimanyu's message. Her mind was racing. *Is he just looking to get some, any action? Was the jog, the Zoom call, everything a set-up?* She had heard that armymen were always looking to hook up, but had somehow felt Abhimanyu was different. *I am an idiot to have been so naïve,* she admonished herself as she buried her head in her pillow.

Back in his room, Abhimanyu was blissfully lost in thinking about Samyuktha. He kept checking his phone. *Why has she stopped responding?* he thought. *Maybe something came up.* The responsible soldier Abhimanyu was in conflict with the 23-year-old boy whose hormones were on fire. Not to mention, she felt so close and yet so far.

Ayaan knocked at his door and then Abhimanyu joined the gang for dinner. However, he kept checking his phone every so often. *This was unlike her,* he thought. Finally, at around 10.00 p.m., he decided to call her. He stepped out into the field to walk in the moonlight as he spoke with her, but she didn't answer. He texted her a few more times. Then, a few more calls. But there was no response.

Samyuktha was still seething. She heard her phone buzzing, but couldn't get herself to look at it. *Why did I trust him in the first place? I've known him for what, a couple weeks at most?*

She thought of her break-up with Rohan. *It serves me right, its poetic justice at its best.*

Samyuktha's phone kept buzzing till she finally answered. Abhimanyu knew instantly that something was wrong. *Really* wrong. There was silence on the other end. He began, 'I've been trying to call all evening. What happened suddenly?'

There was silence. *Was that a sniff? Is she crying?* Then her voice came through, 'Abhimanyu, I'm not sure what impression I gave you, but I'm not one of those girls. I'm sorry if I led you on, we should end this right here.'

Abhimanyu was completely flabbergasted. He asked, 'Wha—wait…what are you talking about? What do you mean one of those girls, what girls? I don't get it.'

'Ahalya showed me your Tinder chat with her. I really don't mind you loving her style and cuteness. I'm just not sure I'm looking for a quickie with a casanova here,' she said as she cut the call.

Abhimanyu stared at the phone in disbelief. Clearly, a lot had happened. He called her back relentlessly till she answered again. 'What is this? Is this a Bollywood film where the guy has to keep getting ignored? Don't you want to hear what I have to say?'

'Okay, what do you have to say?' she asked plainly.

'Nothing. Because there is nothing! This is ridiculous. It was a random thing that popped up the day I reached Chennai, and once I saw her in person, I realized I'm absolutely not interested. Surely you're not upset about me being on Tinder, are you? Haven't you ever met a guy on a dating app before?' he asked, trying to sound earnest and hide his irritation at the same time.

The clarity and conviction in his response calmed her down. 'I'm not upset about anything. You do you, Abhi,' she said this scathingly, pun fully intended. 'If you aren't interested in her, why are you leading her on? You are calling her cute and stylish, and then making her wait for your reply? Who does that?' she spat out.

Abhimanyu was taken aback. He had really not put in any thought into this. It was a Tinder chat! Who takes that seriously? He tried to form a cogent response and continued, 'Listen, I was being polite. I haven't replied to her in days. I thought she would get the hint and stop. Plus my iPhone is at barracks all day, so it's not like I spend time on the app. At least not since I met you. Please don't tell me you actually think I'm some two-timing asshole,' his voice conveyed a strong sense of disappointment.

Samyuktha took a deep breath and stayed silent for a moment. Her mind was in a whirl. *He does sound earnest, am I overreacting? Ahalya did say he hadn't been replying.*

'Abhimanyu, I know we've barely known each other and this is all happening too fast. I don't even know what this is. You shouldn't be leading someone on if you are not interested. I know that much,' she spoke clearly and firmly.

Abhimanyu's heart sank a wee bit, but he knew when to stop. 'Alright, Samyuktha. Good night.' He stayed on the line, though.

'Good night.' Then the line went cold.

෴

The next morning, the army unit was abuzz. Now they had to make deliveries too?

'Quiet!' Major Verma said in his deep voice. He proceeded to give them a pep talk on how they were at war, at war with a pathogen that was infecting thousands as they spoke, and there was a need to enforce army-level discipline on civilian life before it was too late.

'Boys, this is exactly what Italy and then the United States did not pay heed to. And look at what that has led to. It's too late for them now, even if they want to do anything. Every gathering you can stop right now can save up to five lives.'

Roused by the pep talk, the men proceeded to deliver the rations. *This is not a peacekeeping operation,* Abhimanyu thought, *we are at war, though with a pathogen, but still a war. But is the pathogen at war with humans because humans are at war with the world?* This question often surfaced in Abhimanyu's mind. *Us humans have always plundered Earth and deprived it of everything. The virus doesn't attack animals. Why is that? Has this virus been sent to set the balance right? Is Covid our very own Thanos?*

Abhimanyu transferred his attention to Major Verma. He was describing the delivery process. There was one supermarket and one pharmacy assigned to every 500-square-metre zone. Every apartment would give their lists to the supermarket or chemist directly via call. The supermarket would bundle everything neatly, with the apartment name on it and place it in a designated, sanitized place in the store. The army jawans would then come, pick up these supplies and deliver it to the respective homes.

Abhimanyu and his jawans got to work quickly. They hauled parcels and started the work of segregating them as per the buildings they were meant to be delivered to. As they were doing this, he noticed a parcel for C-11, Ashok Apartments. Wasn't that Samyuktha's house? His heart jumped.

Abhimanyu had promptly written to Ahalya the night itself, saying 'I'm out' in as gentlemanly a way as he could. He had sent the screenshot to Samyuktha in the morning, but she had not responded. He shrugged thinking about that. *There's only so much a guy can do,* he thought. Then an idea struck him.

It seemed they had been delivering supplies since forever. Sowbhagya Apartments. Chaitanya Apartments. Ram Apartments. Abhimanyu had supervised his jawans to ensure they maintained social distancing norms while delivering the supplies. Finally, as they reached Ashok Apartments and entered

Samyuktha's block, he volunteered to deliver the goods to help his jawans out, *of course*. He felt excitement run all over. Would he get to see her?

As he set down the standard supplies—milk, curd, bread, potatoes, spinach, rice and eggs—on the first floor landing, he rang the bell, and Samyuktha opened the door. She looked at him briefly and then looked away. She looked very different than when they had met—a mix of anger and hurt was visible on her face.

'Balcony,' he said quickly.

'What?' Samyuktha said, puzzled.

'I'm coming to your balcony tonight. After ten. We need to talk this through. *Theek hai na* (Is that okay)?' he asked, nonchalantly, leaning against the wall. It would have been a perfect *DDLJ* scene, minus the three packets of *thayir* (yogurt) five packets of dal and a cabbage that he was holding.

'Wait. What?! No!' Samyuktha was alarmed. The humour of the cabbage was not lost on her, so she had to try very hard not to burst out laughing.

'Don't worry for my safety. I can climb well.' Abhi tried to maintain his swag.

'Climb?' Samyuktha was flummoxed as to whether he was serious or joking. In her sheltered life, she had only heard of such things in the movies, and that too in the cheesy ones, of course in the ones like *Romeo and Juliet* and *Rapunzel*.

'Yes. After my shift gets over. That's okay, right? I thought it's important to ask you for permission on these things. *Theek kiya na* (Was I right)?' Abhimanyu had an innocent-meets-daring face at that moment.

Samyuktha's mouth opened and shut like a goldfish. As she gaped, Abhimanyu looked at her in amusement. Anitha called out for her in that opportune moment.

'*Jaa Simran jaa. Raat ko milenge. Tata* (Go Simran, go. See you tonight. Bye)'. So saying, he elegantly disappeared.

୧୭ୡ୬

Back in his room, Abhimanyu turned up the AC full blast and headed for a shower. It was one thing to stand in the heat all day and another to lug around packages and climb stairs. As the hot water hit him, he realized he was whistling the tune of 'Oonchi hai building'. He grinned to himself.

But as the hot water calmed him down, he started thinking more clearly. *Climb into a balcony?*

As he was soaking his clothes in hot water to sanitize them, he wondered if he had been careful enough that day. It was hard to resist touching your face in such humid weather and the masks made it worse. He wasn't even sure if he had inadvertently wiped his forehead or adjusted his mask during the delivery. These things had to be kept in check if he was to actually meet a civilian.

Meanwhile, Samyuktha was in her balcony—thinking hard. She was considered the bold, daring girl on campus, but this was a bit much even for her. Not to mention, she was still rather upset.

As she looked around at her balcony, she suddenly felt a lot more exposed and accessible. She walked along the railing, looking out to see how many units could directly look into it. *Not if I roll down the blinds*, she thought as she untied the knots.

On the right, a series of pipes ran vertically and she leaned over to see how far it was from the ground. She wondered if he would use some kind of rope and harness, or were his bare hands just enough.

Let's assume he does land up. What do I do? The thought of him coming over sent a shiver of anticipation up her spine. Her Tamil upbringing firmly tried to shush that shiver and think practically. The two Samyukthas were sitting in her head, fighting it out.

Abhimanyu was having very similar thoughts, added with a heightened sense of duty. *Just remember what the boys said, and adhere to the rules.* At 9.30 p.m., exactly, he set off in his jeep towards Warren Road. He messaged her on the way, `Coming in 20 minutes. Keep the balcony open.` There was no reply. Abhimanyu wasn't too worried. If it was shut, he would come back. Simple.

As he drove up to the checkpost, the night duty jawans of his unit recognized him and came up.

'Jai Hind, Sir,' one of them said, assuming Abhimanyu was the duty officer that night.

Abhimanyu smiled and nodded. He drove into the night towards Warren Road purposefully.

He reached Ashok Apartments with a minute to spare. He went in slowly and purposefully, scaled the floor like a monkey, and was standing on the pipes below the first floor in no time. The sliding doors were shut. He knocked on it. First softly. Then a little louder.

There was a shuffle. And the doors slid open. *Not bad,* he thought. *She's got spunk.*

As he jumped in softly, he noticed Samyuktha was not her usual happy self. She looked super angry and held a broom in one hand. And what was that? A kitchen knife in the other? It took all of Abhimanyu's restraint to stop himself from smiling. *What a cutie.* Instead, he maintained a poker, even a slightly scared face.

'Leave or I'll call my parents,' she said in a low, warning tone.

Abhimanyu took two steps back and his back touched the wall. 'Arrey, aunty, don't kill me. And also, please call your parents, but next time. I'll make chai. Proper Punjabi chai,' he added, thinking of the dust tea with disdain.

'Would your parents approve of you doing these...' Samyuktha struggled for the right word, '...blasphemous things?'

'Blasphemous?' Abhimanyu couldn't stop himself from smiling. He looked up at the sky. 'Parents, do you approve?' he asked.

Samyuktha was puzzled. 'What—' Abhimanyu gestured her to stop. 'Wait. I'm trying to listen.'

Samyuktha inched closer with the ever dangerous mop and knife. 'I'm calling my parents. Jogging and Zoom is fine. But isn't this trespassing?'

Abhimanyu, his back to the wall, said, 'On second thoughts, *bula lo* (call them). Since I don't have any, it'll be a pleasure to meet them.'

Samyuktha, despite her anger, asked, 'What do you mean?'

Abhimanyu put his hands up in surrender. 'Okay! I'll tell you. But only because I think you'll kill me...' He paused. Samyuktha inched menacingly closer. *Cute,* he thought. *Her angry look is even more adorable.* But he maintained his scared look.

'Papa was martyred in Kargil. Mumma heard the news and... had a heart attack. Since then, it's just been me and Shalini didi...' Abhimanyu shook his head, unable to go on for a second. Then he shrugged his shoulders. 'But after that, na, I realized something. We can plan everything, but everything can still be taken away in a second.' He slowly put his hands down.

Samyuktha asked him, 'So you stopped planning, is that so?' a little caustically. But she had already lowered the dreadful, dangerous weapon, the mop, a little.

Abhimanyu smiled slightly and moved a step forward. 'I knew you would say this. Terrible logic. Life isn't a pendulum to keep swinging from one extreme to another.'

'Then?' she asked.

Abhimanyu smiled at her. 'You're smart, right? IIT, EDF and all. Use that brain that you're blessed with.'

Samyuktha lifted the knife. 'Will you come to the point?'

Abhimanyu took a step forward and spoke with conviction, 'The point, Samyuktha, is that you can't swing from enjoying a full night of a Zoom conversation with me to suddenly accusing me of being some wayward loafer. You know how much I love and respect Shalini didi, and I have never consciously done anything to hurt a girl in my life. I was honestly trying to be polite with Ahalya and had no idea she was mistaking my silence for a yes. But I heard you and it gave me a new perspective, and I've politely told her I'm not interested. What else do you want me to do now to get things back to where they were?' he stared at her.

She didn't know what to say to such an eloquent testimony, so he continued, 'I, too, have self-respect and I'm not going to stand here and let you paint this terrible picture of me. Ask what you have to and I'll give you the answers you want,' he said as he concluded his dramatic monologue.

Samyuktha lowered her knife ever so slightly as she stared at him, impressed with his eloquence, yet a bit reluctant. 'Alright, so how many girls are you seriously chatting with or meeting right now except Ahalya?' she asked him with a straight face.

'None, Samyuktha,' he looked at her earnestly. 'And I already told you there is no Ahalya. There never was. You're an intuitive person, did you ever feel like I was just leading you on just to have a hook up? Just think about our conversations. You know I was honest with you at every step, don't you?'

He is right about that, Samyuktha thought. *Maybe I'm just being too impulsive. Or maybe it's the fact that it was Ahalya, of all people.* She couldn't bear the thought of Abhimanyu even remotely liking Ahalya. *How mature, Samyuktha, well done,* she thought of that last bit as her inner self rolled its eyes at her.

But she was also not going to apologize. After all, he did lead Ahalya on and that was not cool.

She continued, 'Abhimanyu, maybe I did overreact. Given the information I had, it definitely seemed like you were leading her on. I was going with the flow, so this suddenly hit me and made me wonder what was going on. I'm still not sure what this is. What *we* are. We are in the middle of a global pandemic, the worst ever in decades. Is this really the time to be exploring something like this?' she asked him in a less threatening yet serious tone.

'If I agreed and said "No, it's not", would that really make you happy?' he shot back, staring at her, his face expressionless.

Samyuktha had not seen that coming. She froze, unable to answer.

'That's what I thought,' he concluded.

Abhimanyu's eyes roved around the balcony, taking in all the small details around. The bookshelf. He caught sight of a set of neatly arranged frames. The waddle of penguins. The Barack and Michelle poster. He slowly cleared his throat, and started speaking, clearly and concisely.

'Life is nothing but a string of moments, and every moment's a decision, isn't it? And we should make that decision, after weighing the pros and cons. We should not wait to do that later in life, when we're old and wrinkly, if we ever get there, that is.' He laughed a bit sardonically. 'That has to be done in the now.'

Samyuktha fell silent. Abhimanyu knew he had her. He ploughed on, 'Like when I saw you sleeping in that car, and you told me that you're in C-11,' he said, wickedly.

Samyuktha knew something good was coming. She didn't even pause before asking, 'What about that?'

Abhimanyu laughed. 'Pro: Beautiful girl. No...' he shook his head, seriously, correcting himself, 'not just beautiful, but bursting with personality...lives on the first floor, nice balcony....'

Samyuktha blushed, ever so slightly.

Abhimanyu noticed and continued with a smile. 'Con: I'll get caught and beaten up by Mylapore mamas… So…I took the decision.' He winked.

Samyuktha interrupted, 'You'll get Covid…'

Abhimanyu cut her short and rattled off, 'The WHO guideline on Covid asks us to stay at least one metre away. Check. Sanitize hands every three hours. Check. Gawk at the beautiful girl from a distance. Check. Sorry, the last was inaccurate. Or was it?' He winked.

'By the way, I have a gift for you,' he said.

He pulled out a small parcel and gave it to her. She noticed his hands were gloved. It was a pocket hand sanitizer with a ribbon around it.

Samyuktha smiled and used some of it and so did he.

Abhimanyu smiled his usual, infectious smile. '*Yeh hui na baat* (That's the spirit),' he said cupping his face and placing his elbows on the table, looking at her, wishing he could cup hers instead.

Samyuktha felt his eyes on her. She smiled, despite herself. 'Why the intense gaze?' she asked, half shyly, half intensely. She had surrendered, with both mop and knife now hanging down from each hand.

I want to kiss you, Abhimanyu thought.

'You look beautiful,' he said as he looked at her delicate face shining in the moonlight. She blushed beetroot. 'Drat this social distancing,' he said with a mock sigh. They looked at each other and laughed. That moment cleared the air of all residual animosity.

After a moment, he looked up, with a twinkle in his eye. 'Did you ever think that something like this could take over our lives the way it has?' he asked, taking another generous dose of sanitizer absentmindedly.

Samyuktha shook her head.

Abhimanyu continued with a poker face, 'Had you ever thought *ki tumhare cute boyfriend ki jagah I'll come and steal your heart* (Had you ever thought I would have replaced your cute boyfriend and stolen your heart)?' As he said so, he looked at her intently.

Samyuktha looked up at him in surprise, 'What?'

Abhimanyu smiled. 'That was a guess, but good to know.'

Samyuktha blushed a little.

Abhimanyu looked at the sky lined with stars, which were so clear and visible in the absence of the usual air pollution. 'Here you are, on your balcony talking to me. And over there,' gesturing towards the world outside, 'far in the distance, the olive ridley turtles are happier—'

Samyuktha interrupted him, 'The animals are roaming freely again, the birds aren't breathing polluted air...' They both laughed and with that, the last bit of tension flew out of the balcony.

Abhimanyu's eyes caught sight of the family portrait where a one-year-old could be seen staring up at Parvati Paati. Next to it was the framed photo of a waddle of penguins in the Antarctica.

'This is cute!' he said as he touched the picture. Samyuktha felt a rush once again as she saw his boyish face smiling at one of the things she held dear. Watching any herd of animals walking freely in the wild brought immense joy to her, and she loved that she could share her happiness with him.

'How's that internship application coming along?' he asked, still looking at the picture.

'It's going alright,' Samyuktha replied. 'You want to see the application?' she asked half eagerly, half shyly. In a flash, she realized that that's what she had been waiting for—for him to see it. She opened the document on her phone, sanitized the gadget and handed it over to him. He read it without betraying any expression. Samyuktha felt the jitters, and she realized that his opinion mattered to her.

He finally looked up. 'I think I can stop calling you Turtle now,' he simply said. That sentence and the look of deep admiration in his eyes said it all. Samyuktha suddenly felt a catch in her throat. If there was no social distancing, she would have thrown herself at him and given him a giant hug. His heart proceeded to beat at a million beats per minute. Of course, he then proceeded to tell her about the portions that could be reworked to make it better, and they argued about some of it.

Samyuktha and Abhimanyu were both oases for each other. Amidst all the pettiness and the chaos, and the mundane and the drudgery, here was a person she could talk her heart out to without the fear of judgement. And he always had something to add to every conversation, something Samyuktha rarely found with others. It could be an interesting perspective, perhaps, or a twist to the theory.

He listened intently and actively. He always looked at her in a way that made her feel like she was worth it all. At the same time, he wasn't patronizing. He would praise her to the skies when he did. But he would equally call out her bullshit when she was being overly dramatic or going off on a tangent.

For Samyuktha, his sense of duty and responsibility, along with his efforts to not compromise on anyone's safety, even in their meetings, only heightened her intense attraction for him.

And as for Abhimanyu? What started off as an innocent escape from the monotony of guarding an empty, lifeless street from an unseen virus was turning into something very special. Samyuktha wasn't like the other girls he had met in Delhi. There was a spark about her that he was both attracted to and also curious about. He loved the intensity in her eyes as she took in every word that he spoke, her eyes narrowing to focus when she heard something she didn't know about or her eyelids drooping when he said something silly. She was attractive, hell yeah, but without having to doll up—her confidence and intelligence were what he was drawn to.

Abhimanyu remembered the first time he had seen Samyuktha and the game of stares that they had played. There had been a playfulness to it that he loved. *Boy, come to think of it, she does have an intense gaze.* He had loved Samyuktha's aura. He felt noticed, heard and understood. Conversations with Samyuktha went beyond the mundane, and he didn't have to pretend to be someone else or pander to the usual stereotypes about soldiers. Samyuktha was beyond all that. He could just be himself in every moment with her, and that was precious to him.

He had dated several girls, and there was a pattern to each relationship, with each turning monotonous very soon. It was a formula and he played his part well. With Samyuktha, all rules were being reinvented, even being broken more than being followed. But he was enjoying discovering a new dimension to their attraction for each other every day.

Abhimanyu, of course, craved for this relationship to go beyond conversations, and his fantasies were only getting wilder each day they spent apart. All Samyuktha had to do was offer to break the rules and he would be down for it. But she had not done so and he loved her for that. He wouldn't be able to respect himself, and hence her, if he did something irresponsible that would endanger the very thing he was tasked with protecting. He couldn't wait for this lockdown to end, when there would be no rules.

They spent the entire night like that. There were long moments of silence, interrupted by a few words here and there. They were so close and yet so far. As two souls, they couldn't have been any closer than in that moment. And they did not need to say anything to fill any void.

Finally, at four, Abhimanyu gazed at Samyuktha. She had dozed off into a gentle sleep, with a lock of her hair windswept near her eyes. It took all his resilience to not move that lock aside. He looked at her for a long while.

He quickly took out the sanitization wipes he always carried with him, cleaned the entire balcony with those and climbed down deftly, his heart both light and heavy at the same time.

⌒∽⌒

The day of the candlelight vigil finally arrived. The PM's words had definitely mesmerized certain residents of Ashok Apartments. All WhatsApp groups were buzzing with activity. Ramesh applauded the PM and said it would be lovely to have all the apartment residents turn off the lights and light diyas in their balconies.

It will lighten up the mood, he said, chuckling at his own joke.

Indrani typed, Why not do an arati at 6.00 p.m. to ward off all this evil? She felt pleased with herself.

Ranjini helpfully chipped in with, Sure. Great ideas, everyone! She also added two thumbs up emojis for extra effect.

Sunil, however, was not a fan of the idea. Let's please not go overboard with the diyas people, else we'll send more folks to the hospital and increase the work of our healthcare providers.

Anitha chuckled as she saw this. *At least someone is sensible in this group,* she thought.

Ahmed chipped in, We will do a pre-Ramadan iftar on our balcony, Allah be merciful. Anitha gave a thumbs up to this, and so did Sunil and Ranjini.

Abhijeet was the most cheerful. He was posting on the group

about how the ruling party once again was leading the world in solidarity and unity by getting a billion people to pray together and create positive energy.

He wanted his family to come together and do something special. He sensed that the events of the last two days had left everyone jittery, especially his wife and daughter. So, Ahalya was tasked with making a rangoli, and organize the lamps and leftover fireworks from last Diwali. Indrani was busy preparing delicacies and planning their outfit for the evening. Arun was the designated videographer.

Indrani got to work. She got so busy preparing gulab jamun and chhole, it took her mind off the Kumars for a day. As she sat down to catch her breath and relax for a bit, the news about the UK PM flashed on their TV screen. He had tested positive and so had Prince Charles a couple weeks ago. The UK health minister, too, had tested positive. The world started shifting around her. An anxiety attack was coming on. *The heir to the British throne, the PM of one of the most developed countries and the minister tasked with protecting their health, none of them were spared.*

Abhijeet quietly left the house, stepped down to the gate after 8.00 p.m. and beckoned the night shift jawan over. It was Dhruv.

'Can you keep an eye on the balconies tonight please? C-11, 21 and 31?' he asked in a plain voice, although Dhruv was quick to notice the frown over his eyebrows.

'Is everything alright, Sir?' Dhruv asked as he quickly eyed the three floors.

'Yes yes, all good. Just with all the lights out tonight and everyone busy lighting lamps, I'm a bit concerned. I've lately heard some rumours of people climbing balconies after dark. I'd be very grateful if you keep an eye on the balconies,' Abhijeet cleared his throat as he kicked a cigarette stub out of the way.

'Sure, Sir, no worries. I'll make sure to keep an eye out tonight and let you know if something comes up,' Dhruv assured him.

'Really appreciate it.' Abhijeet saluted him with a Jai Hind and the soldier did so likewise. *Strange request,* Dhruv thought.

꧁꧂

What a complete waste of time and energy, Samyuktha thought. She was completely against such ways of warding off the virus. *It must be laughing at us,* she thought.

She messaged Abhimanyu, `Looks like we won't be able to meet tonight, thanks to your supreme commander-in-chief`. She was already groaning at the mere thought of receiving more pictures on the WhatsApp groups after the lamp lighting.

`That's the President. I think you mean our Prime Minister,` the soldier shot back.

`Stickler, :P!` she wrote, sinking back into her chair.

`How do I blow kisses on this stupid Nokia?` he typed, trying to remember what the code was.

`Well, you just did,` Samyuktha replied, smiling as she imagined him kissing her.

Abhimanyu smiled.

꧁꧂

Sandhya had been asleep for most part of the day. She woke up in the afternoon to see that her mother was flipping through pages of a magazine, wearing a mask and gloves.

'Are you afraid that the magazine will give you Covid, Amma?' she asked, amused by the solid blue mask and gloves contrasting awkwardly with her mother's elegant baby pink Bengal cotton saree.

Suhasini laughed. 'This Indrani has a way of transferring her panic to everyone. Just feeling a bit paranoid today after all the WhatsApp conversations. With your due date approaching, one can never be too careful, right?' She looked at Sandhya, her glasses misting up every time she exhaled.

'Amma, you're crazy. As usual, being paranoid.' Sandhya felt both scared and angry at her. 'You really need to stop listening to what everyone says. Just like Ammamma.'

'I remember when I went to stay with Ammamma,' Suhasini swiftly and tactfully changed the subject, seeing a mood swing coming along. 'Pampered is an understatement. Those days, we never had these maternity leave issues. I went to my amma's place after the second trimester itself. Almost everyday, some relative or the other would come with baskets of sweets and fruits, give me tonnes of advice, and pray for my and your good health. All I would do is sit and sing all day, hoping you could hear and recognize my voice.'

Sandhya's face softened, and she broke into a smile looking at her mother innocently wave her hand in the air expecting the mist to clear.

'You're going to be a doting grandmother, Amma. I can already tell. And I am so lucky that my baby, too, gets to hear you.' Sandhya smiled.

Suhasini was relieved. *Moodswing averted.* Suhasini loved her daughter, but since the ninth month had started, Sandhya had become a walking minefield, prone to go off at any time.

'Just promise me that you will get that voice back in shape and sing me a perfect *alapana* in Kalyani. We want nothing but the best for the baby now, don't we?'

Sandhya laughed, 'Maybe at the delivery table, Amma. What do you say?'

☙

Anitha came back early from work for a change. Sitting down comfortably, she sighed. 'Phew! A night at home, for a change.' Ajay was also in the living room, watching the news.

Samyuktha sat next to her and put her head on Anitha's lap. 'Amma, please don't feel badly about all the backbiting. You do know that you're doing something that not everyone can. You risk your life every day to help others.'

'I know, kanna. It's just the overall unpleasantness.' Anitha patted her daughter's head. By habit, she started examining her ears. Samyuktha squealed just like she used to when she was a kid. Anitha smiled.

Before she could say anything, Samyuktha laughed and added, 'By the way, we consume the most detergent in all of Ashok Apartments put together, thanks to you.'

Anitha laughed as she sat back feeling happy that her daughter's ears were clean. 'Where did you get this important data point from?'

'Just,' Samyuktha said guiltily, 'I would assume so, don't you think? Come on, let's face it. Our house smells like a combination of Dettol, Lizol and Surf. It always has and even more so now.'

'Would you rather it smelled of deep fried puris?' Anitha asked caustically, flipping through a magazine.

'You know, sometimes, I wouldn't mind that, Amma. Better than the rock-like idlis, illaya?' Samyuktha smiled wickedly.

Anitha swatted her. Cooking was not Anitha's best skill. *Eat to live, not the opposite*, was her motto as the family dreaded the dystopian delights she doled out on the rare occasions when she cooked.

'So, no diyas tonight, Amma?' Samyuktha asked.

'You can light diyas and lamps or whatever you want. You know what, let's call it New Years' tomorrow and open that bottle of champagne!' Anitha was in The Velveteen Rabbit mode. She would always end up doing this. First, she would just want to put up her feet and rest, but her natural enthusiasm would take over everything by the end.

Ultimately, she ended up lighting diyas, drinking champagne and staying up late.

∽

As 9.00 p.m. approached, lights across the city were turned off. All balconies of Ashok Apartment came alive with lamps and sparklers. Chants could be heard. Instagram was full of celebrities wearing their best kurtas and taking soulful pictures in portrait mode. The city looked serene, dotted with millions of lamps looking like fireflies in the dark. Ajay was reminded of his childhood, when there would be power cuts in his village after dark, and everyone in the street would light diyas and sit on the porch. There were no cell phones to bother them, just cups of hot filter coffee, the warmth of a porch that hadn't yet cooled down after the long day, and lots of conversation. Some of his best memories were from those times, when his mother used to tell him about her childhood and his father would tell him stories from the Mahabharata. He missed them both.

Samyuktha looked at her watch. It was 9.45. Her mother was busy with her glass of champagne. *Amma is hilarious when she's drunk, and I so love spending time with her...but...it's nearly ten...*

Ajay came by and sat down next to them. He poured a glass out for himself.

Samyuktha groaned inside.

'Let's go to Samyuktha's balcony,' Anitha said, springing up and almost knocking over the champagne bottle off the table in the process. Samyuktha just about held it before it toppled over. 'It's lovely there. And the skyline will look so beautiful with all that revelry.'

Anitha knocked on her father's door. 'Appa, you also come. *Romba naal aachu* (It's been a long while). Let's sit in the balcony like old times.'

After a few seconds, Thatha came out with a grin. He was always up for some fun. He looked a little weaker than usual, but nothing alarmingly worrisome. Ajay also faithfully followed. Anitha poured everyone a glass, and for Thatha, she made his usual *kashayam*. A concoction of hot milk, turmeric and ginger for times when he fell sick. They all settled in Samyuktha's balcony, the balcony she had hoped to do a very different set of things in.

Samyuktha realized it was of no use. She messaged Abhimanyu and said, Big fat drunk family reunion in the balcony tonight. Today, we cannot meet. Romba (very) sorry.

Abhimanyu was just getting ready and wearing his favourite T-shirt when Samyuktha's message beeped. His heart sank.

Stoically, he replied, That sounds lovely, of course! Have fun with your family. He could faintly hear some whoops from below, Ayaan's being the loudest. The room felt even more silent and empty now.

Samyuktha, Ajay, Anitha and Thatha sat on the balcony, reminiscing about the past. Ajay looked around the balcony, trying to recollect the last time he had been there.

'I can still picture little Samyu cycling around on that small orange tricycle. I also remember that giant brown teddy bear sitting in the centre,' he sighed, patting Samyuktha on her head as he felt a wave of nostalgia rush through.

Over the years, the balcony had become a mirror for Samyuktha's inner self. Anitha could trace different phases of her life spent there. She chimed in, 'Remember that time when the balcony used to look like a small LEGO store? You spent a mini fortune buying her all kinds of LEGO packs and jigsaw puzzles.' She could picture a four-year-old Samyuktha huddled over a dinosaur jigsaw puzzle, with a frow on her face, trying to figure out how to fit the pieces.

Ajay laughed heartily as Anitha perked up, 'I think that's the phase when Ajay spent most of his time with Samyuktha. He fully endorsed her "intellectually stimulating" passion, before her world exploded with a profusion of dolls and sparkles.' Samyuktha flushed, remembering the time she was obsessed with princesses.

'Aiyyo, the scariest was the rockstar phase pa,' Thatha jumped in, tearing up as the laughter, alcohol and nostalgia started hitting from all sides. 'Anitha was able to save money on clothes. All Samyuktha needed back then was black tops and blue jeans.'

Samyuktha laughed along as she remembered the times when a rather concerned Anitha would sit with her and gently ask her for the names of the bands playing on her speakers to strike up some conversation, but in vain. The rebellious streak had hit hard and that was the time Samyuktha had picked up the guitar.

As the wine flowed freely, the conversations became more uninhibited.

Then Thatha recalled tales of Samyuktha running away from dogs in her underpants for the whole road to see. The way Thatha described it, it didn't sound offensive at all. Samyuktha couldn't stop herself from laughing. Her family members were good storytellers, there was no doubt about that.

As Samyuktha listened and looked from one person to the next, she had a very different sense of contentment. *This is my tribe*, she thought. Her mind flitted to everyone in the apartment complex and settled back on this bunch. She then thought of Abhimanyu and all of their conversations. *I am lucky to have these people in my life.*

It was nearly midnight by the time they all went to sleep.

That night, she noted, had a different touch to it. It seemed to mark the beginning of the process of her morphing from a kid to someone who can connect with her family. That night, she was able to see their vulnerable side. She felt more comfortable talking to them. They opened up to her, more than they ever had before. *Is this the 'good' that the virus is doing?* she thought. *Opening up more?* Her gaze shifted to the the road where Abhimanyu usually stood wearing his Ray-Ban. Maybe it is, maybe it isn't. She didn't want to overthink this one.

∞

'So, anything suspicious?' Abhijeet asked the soldier on duty.

'No, Sir,' Dhruv happily reported. *Why did he look upset?* he wondered.

∞

Abhimanyu was particularly looking forward to meeting Samyuktha that night. Watching the glow of lamps across the city and the buzz of families chatting excitedly was making him miss his parents and the feeling of being at home. He called Shalini didi, but she didn't answer.

The jawans had lit up the officers' mess and the ground outside with diyas. There were sparklers, fireworks and music playing as some of the jawans were breaking a leg. Missing home was a constant theme for this band of boys and they spared no effort in bonding with each other at every opportunity. Sukhi, Anish and Ayaan were sitting on the steps with beers in their hand, egging on the dancers.

Ayaan erupted in a loud hoot as he saw Abhimanyu walk in. 'Look, who's here!' he yelled as he dragged Anish and Sukhi into the fray. 'Chalo, now we have no excuse to sit this one out.' They all broke into a jig. Sukhi tossed a beer over to Abhimanyu.

Life was good. For the next hour, all of them let their hair down and danced like no one was watching.

After the crowd thinned down, Ayaan and Abhimanyu sat around and chatted for a bit. Once Ayaan, too, left, Abhimanyu stared at the glow of the city for a while, and then picked up his phone and called his sister again. *Why is she not answering?*

After eight to nine rings, she finally did.

'What are you both upto, Didi? Everything okay?' he asked. He sensed that everything seemed eerily quiet in her background. She was silent for a few seconds.

He could hear a faint sniffle before she started speaking. '*Kuchh nahi* (nothing), Abhi. How are you? Celebrating the mini Diwali?' she asked, trying to be cheerful. But Abhimanyu instantly knew something was up.

'Didi,' he said, his entire protective brother instincts on full alert. 'Tell me. Now,' his voice was firm. Shalini couldn't help but respond to the combination of authority and affection.

She broke down as she told him everything amidst uncontrollable sobs.

⁘

The next morning, Anitha's hospital was in chaos. Most families had gone all out for the candlelight vigil. The smoke from the Diwali sparklers, and consumption of oily food and sweets, was causing discomfort to many with episodes of dry cough, aggravated asthma attacks and other symptoms.

Under normal circumstances, one would have dismissed these as nothing, but with the panic circulating all around, nearly everyone seemed to think they suddenly had coronavirus.

Anitha was more than a little hungover that morning and had a splitting headache. Three bottles of water, a starchy upma breakfast and cups, no, two mugs of chhaas later, she was just starting to feel better. *I really should act my age*, she thought as she nursed her headache. She checked her phone during the break. There was a message from Suhasini.

Anitha, I have had a cough and fever since the morning. I'm pretty sure it's just a routine thing, but I am isolating myself entirely from Sandhya. Is there any chance I can get tested just to make sure? Didn't know who else to ask, hope you don't mind.

Anitha was alert. She quickly called her and asked about her symptoms. They were worrisome. 'Yes Suhasini, please isolate yourself. I've just reached the hospital, will check the status on testing kits and keep you posted.'

She quickly made some calls. Yes, testing kits were available. She called back Suhasini. 'Please come to the hospital as soon as you can.'

She thought of all the activity that would ensue on the WhatsApp groups. Then she did something that she usually would not do. But the minute she did so, she felt better.

⚬⚬⚬

For Abhimanyu, the day had been crazy since morning. There were supplies to be organized, supplies to be collected. They had to maintain a list of every house where even one family member was down with a symptom. *Thank God for army discipline*, Abhimanyu thought. His commander had set a system in place, which had to be adhered to like clockwork.

Around noon, Abhimanyu finally got five minutes of free time. He checked his battered Nokia.

You don't look sleepy at all, the message read. Abhimanyu smiled and sat down, throwing his legs up on the desk as he replied.

It's been crazy since morning. There's so much work to do. But it's a good feeling to be able to help, he replied.

I'm sure. Here at the apartment, there's complete pandemonium. Sandhya has pregnancy complications, Thatha is coughing, Amma is going mad managing the home and work, in-between the 100 baths she takes in a day, Samyuktha texted.

You may want to help her, no? Abhimanyu said, trying to sound like her.

Oye, wannabe-Tam, Samyuktha typed. He laughed reading her response. He had to hear her voice. His mind was spinning after his call with Shalini didi last night. He decide to call her.

'…and that's how it all came to an end. It was so different but lovely,' Samyuktha finished giving the details of the night spent with her family.

Abhimanyu enjoyed hearing her talk on call as he sat outside at his desk during his morning break. He had slept well that night. After four nights of lack of sleep, he had finally been able to sleep like a baby.

He, in turn, told her about how he had made merry with the other soldiers. She could hear the excitement in his voice. *Men need their boys' night-out*, her twenty-year-old brain figured out, rather early in life. Abhimanyu then briefly mentioned about the conversation with his sister. But instead of his usual chirpiness everytime he would talk about her, she sensed a hint of wistfulness. She made a mental note to bring it up in their next balcony meeting.

'Did you miss hanging out with me last night?' Samyuktha asked a little hesitantly.

'Yes,' Abhimanyu said at once. 'But I'm also glad you had a lovely night. So, it's all good,' he added in the same breath, although the last bit wasn't entirely true. He paused and wondered whether he should tell her…

'I just don't know why people get married sometimes. The concept of marriage was created by a patriarchal society, and just doesn't work for educated and independent women,' he said as he sat staring at Jitesh's warli art in his office.

Samyuktha paused as she thought about what he had said. The mention of educated and independent women made her think of Amma. *How do they make it work?* She wondered about her parents. She saw flashes of dinner table arguments, Appa cooking a meal during emergency delivery days, Amma putting a sticky note on the fridge to update the bank passbook when Appa was away for a month on travel. As the images flashed by, she particularly noticed Amma's firm expression and Appa's calm retreat—the tango of two very headstrong personalities.

Seeing her parents' relationship in a new light, she resumed, 'I agree, but why is the onus on the woman when it comes to fixing any issues in a marriage? I am no fan of marriage myself, but when I see my parents, I realize that both of them really wanted to make it work. Amma is rather over-educated and over-independent already,' she rolled her eyes, 'and she sets clear boundaries. Appa respects her for it, and over the years, they've built a relationship that works for them.' Samyuktha paused as he looked at her again, quizzically. She added hesitantly, 'Abhi, I don't know enough about Shalini didi's situation, but I hope she has tried to set clear boundaries.'

Abhimanyu paused momentarily and said, 'Of course she has…' his voice wavered, 'I mean, I am sure she has.' His brow furrowed as he tried to remember if and what Shalini didi had done to set clear boundaries.

Samyuktha stayed silent and let Abhimanyu process it for a few moments. Her mother had always told her to clarify things not once but twice when needed. 'You need to be heard louder than the generations of voices speaking inside your head,' and she wasn't wrong.

Abhimanyu wondered, 'If even I can't remember, is it possible that Shalini didi assumed she was clear when she actually wasn't?'

As if on cue, Samyuktha stated, 'Such a thing does not happen by itself.' Her voice was clear and firm.

Abhimanyu looked at her and the furrows on his brow relaxed a bit as he decided to understand his sister's stance on his next call with her. As he looked at Samyuktha, marveling at her calm yet confident stance, his eyes roved to the picture wall behind her. 'I've always wondered if Michelle set those boundaries or if Barack never needed her to,' he sighed as if he was talking about his childhood friends. 'That portrait and the couple in it are hashtag goals,' he said, using the millennial phrase with panache. 'It is one of the first things I noticed when I gazed into your balcony,' Abhimanyu continued. It was a black-and-white portrait of Barack Obama leaning and looking admiringly at Michelle as she stared confidently at the viewer, her arm supporting her husband.

'Even the most gentlemanly gentlemen and the most ladylike ladies need to be made aware of boundaries,' Samyuktha said. 'Of course, if they've never come close to crossing it in the first place, they probably haven't explored the relationship fully yet, right?' she offered in addition, winking at Abhimanyu as he glanced at her, smiling.

Abhimanyu replied without hesitation, 'Absolutely.'

꒰꒱

Samyuktha was leisurely finishing up her call when she heard a loud knock on the door. She saw Appa's face and immediately sensed something was wrong.

'What happened?' she asked.

'Thatha's cough has worsened and he also has a mild fever. He's self-quarantined himself,' he said flatly.

Samyuktha's heart went cold.

'Appa, is it...I mean...' words failed her, and she just looked at her father.

'I think he's taking a precaution, Samyuktha. I don't think there's anything to worry about.' He himself didn't sound convinced.

Samyuktha felt her throat go dry. She had been coughing this morning too.

'What is this balcony activity that Abhijeet has been talking about?' Ajay asked, coming straight to the point.

Her heart went cold. 'What balcony activity?' she asked quietly.

'Abhijeet asked the guards last night to watch our balcony. He said something has been going on for the last two weeks. Is this something I need to know about or is it just his nonsensical imagination?' he was looking at her with his usual expressionless face.

'You know Abhijeet uncle, Appa. He is always overreacting to the core. This is all stupidity,' Samyuktha managed to blurt it out, observing his reaction closely.

'Yes. I know. I trust you, Samyuktha,' he replied as simply as he had asked.

Samyuktha's composed face crumpled as her father walked out of the room.

Ajay went back to his study. He pulled out some information he had received that morning and started pacing. He tried to piece together the sequence of events. The order did not seem to align with his hypothesis, but then again there were always exceptions. He wondered if the guard outside his house had been careful enough, as he alone could be a threat to so many people.

He wrote to his colleague asking for all the possible

information that could be gathered legally, as he didn't want to raise an alarm without any reason.

What about flight itineraries? Can we confirm the details of the incoming flight from the States? he typed. There was silence for a while, and he waited patiently as he tried to go over it once more in his mind. His colleague was taking longer than usual. *That's unusual.*

When the reply finally popped up on his screen, it almost made him jump.

Are you sure? That seems unlikely. Request to reconfirm, he wrote back.

Absolutely positive, came the reply.

Then how come the police never visited to enforce the quarantine? What do the police reports say? he typed back, frowning.

Sir, there are no police reports on record. This one person seems to have been given an exception for some reason, his teammate replied.

Ajay stared at the screen. He looked back at the Google search report and scanned it thoroughly. His eyes stopped on one, *how can I get tested for Covid in secret?* Slowly, it all started making sense.

✷

Suhasini had never experienced a feeling like this before. Her mouth was dry, she had a runny nose, a splitting headache. And that cough, dry and rasping. She checked the symptoms for the hundredth time. *No wonder Anitha asked me to come to the hospital immediately.*

Honestly, she was terrified of going all alone. She was also worried that if she was not infected already, then she would be at the hospital. Not to mention, she was stressed over the idea of leaving behind her nine months pregnant daughter alone at home.

Sandhya called out to her, 'Amma, *polaya innum* (Mother, haven't you gone yet)?'

Suhasini was quiet.

'Amma, I'm scared,' Sandhya burst out in tears. 'What if you do have it? Does it mean I will too? Who gave it to you, Amma? Is it Anitha aunty? It's all because of me, illa. She came home that day to see me. What if she gave it to me?'

All Suhasini wanted to do was comfort Sandhya, hug her and tell her it was going to be okay. She was suddenly overpowered by a level of resilience that even she didn't know she possessed.

'Kanna, don't worry,' she said. 'I'm going right away. Stay safe. Call me or Samyuktha if you need anything. And don't make up silly nonsense in your head, okay?'

'Okay, Amma,' Suhasini's voice helped Sandhya calm down, and she called Samyuktha, asking her to keep an eye on Sandhya. Samyuktha was more than happy to.

Suhasini wore her mask and gloves, walked straight out of the home, straight to her Maruti Swift car, and drove slowly to the hospital, doing all of this with a burning fever. Abhimanyu had already been intimated at the gate. As she drove out, he gave her a half-smile, half-worried look and watched as she slowly drove to the hospital.

⸱◌◠◌⸱

Anitha sat down at the table, looking concerned. 'I don't understand Ajay. First Suhasini, now Appa. I've met both of them in close quarters recently...'

'Amma, will they both be alright?'

'Yes kanna, I'm sure they will. We can't say for sure till we get the test results, of course. We've all been extra careful. I've made sure Thatha doesn't go out for anything and everyone who comes in has had a full scrubbing ritual. No one else comes into the house.'

A feeling of panic started to set in as the room around Samyuktha started spinning. *No one else has come in…*that was not true.

Samyuktha excused herself and walked back to her room. She couldn't get the one image out of her mind—her grandfather on a ventilator. *And all because of me.* It was only yesterday when someone had messaged on the college WhatsApp group that asymptomatic carriers were the cause of majority of infections.

She closed her eyes and thought once again. Was she responsible in any way? Images of her hugging her mother the previous day, kissing her face, giving her a hi-five and dropping a piece of brinjal that she hated back into Amma's plate, all started flashing in front of her eyes. And then the carousel in her mind stopped on the handshake—she shook hands with him in the hallway a few days ago. Not to mention, his visits to her balcony and that one time he sneezed!

It's quite likely, Samyuktha, her inner voice kept telling her. *He delivered supplies to fifty houses that day. He interacts with everyone on the street each day, especially during their morning training when he is with a hundred other soldiers, who each have to deliver to fifty houses and interact with at least two hundred people.*

Samyuktha was feeling terrible. First, Thatha in isolation, now Suhasini aunty off to the hospital for a test. What was happening here? On top of all that, Appa's question regarding the balcony fiasco kept haunting her.

She called Abhimanyu again. He cut the call. *Of course. He was on duty.* She debated whether she should call Sharanya. She decided against it. Somehow, she didn't feel it would help.

Samyuktha was feeling lost, helpless and scared at the same

time. The world as she knew it was changing. She called Thatha.

'Yes, kanna?' came a weak voice from the other end.

'Thatha, *eppidi irrukke* (Grandfather, how are you feeling)?'

'I'm okay, kannama. But why are you sounding so scared?' Thatha said, after a fit of coughing.

Samyuktha's head was whirling. The full impact of what she had done came hurtling back to her. She had let in a soldier, who was a superspreader, into her balcony. She had met him not once, but twice! Putting her entire family that she loved so much at complete and utter risk. And now it had happened. Her Thatha was sick and his symptoms were exactly the ones she had read about. And ironically, those were on the website that Abhimanyu trusted the most—WHO. She wanted to cry, but couldn't. The guilt burnt all the tears away and what she was left with was an empty feeling.

'Thatha, everyone is sick. Suhasini aunty has gone to the hospital and you, too, are sick. She's asked me to take care of Sandhya,' Samyuktha managed to get the words out.

'You should, Samyuktha. These are trying times. And people who make it good during such times are the ones with fine character, like yours,' Thatha said, slowly but surely.

Samyuktha bottomed out when Thatha said the words 'fine character'. *If only he knew what I had done. It's the very opposite of fine character.* She had placed her own happiness, her own selfish needs above everyone else. Somehow, she managed to hang up the phone and sat on the balcony floor, crumpled, staring bleakly at nothing.

Finally, she picked herself up. She grabbed the Dettol spray and started working on dousing her entire balcony with it. She continued spraying everything she saw, including her Bose speaker, without a care whether she was rendering any gadget useless. Had anyone seen her for those ten minutes, they might have taken her to be a possessed person. She ended up emptying the one-litre bottle of Dettol spray. She tossed it aside, took the Scotch-Brite wipe and cleaned everything with a ferocity that would have put her mother to shame. She then tossed that aside too.

She finally sat down on the floor. The stench arising from the disinfectant, somehow, gave her a bit of comfort. She kept sitting for half an hour.

Looking out of the balcony, she saw Abhimanyu. He smiled at her, but that smile disappeared in a moment when he noticed her disheveled look. He immediately called her.

She told him about her grandfather and Suhasini aunty. Abhimanyu knew about the latter, but was shocked to hear about her Thatha. He tried his best to console her. He had no idea that Samyuktha was considering him to be a possible carrier.

'Let's talk in person tonight, Samyuktha, I'm sure it's not going to be serious. You guys have been so careful.'

'Abhimanyu, are you sure you've been careful enough?' she stammered.

That's when it dawned on him.

'What are you saying, Samyuktha? Of course, I have. It's the first thing we are reminded of every morning. I'm always maintaining a safe distance from everyone, using masks and gloves where needed, and scrubbing regularly. The night I left from your balcony, I was careful not to touch anything.' Abhimanyu found his voice getting louder as he said this.

Silence.

'You can't possibly…look you're just upset right now. I can't believe you're accusing me of…' Abhimanyu said in utter disbelief.

'Abhimanyu, I don't think we should meet anymore.' Samyuktha was in tears. She quickly hung up and switched off her phone.

The Pursuit of Happyness

Samyuktha was up by the time Ajay came to the kitchen in the morning.

'It's only 6.30 a.m., kanna, why are you up?' he asked. Bloodshot eyes, she looked like she hadn't slept all night.

'No Appa, just stayed up late to wrap up some assignments. Their deadlines are nearing, illaya?' She vaguely looked at some pots and pans around her. 'And I thought I'd help make breakfast for everyone.'

'Thanks, kanna,' Ajay, too, looked around vaguely and left.

Shoot, Samyuktha thought. *Now I actually have to make breakfast.*

Samyuktha had spent all night googling how to figure out if she was a coronavirus carrier. She kept playing the past few weeks in her mind, trying to recall every human interaction she had had. Her thoughts kept coming back to her rendezvous with Abhimanyu and the proximity she had shared with him. She wondered whether she had adequately cleaned the surfaces he had touched. The hugs and kisses exchanged with Thatha and Amma worried her. She wanted to stop thinking of the scary possibilities but just couldn't.

As all these thoughts were playing in her brain, she heard a loud series of uncontrollable coughs from the next room. Her heart went cold. She ran to Thatha's room and knocked. 'Thatha, all okay a?' she said, with her face close to the door.

There was no reply. She knocked, more fearfully and louder this time.

'All okay, kannama,' a feeble voice said from the inside. 'Dontuu worry.'

Samyuktha now worried even more. Along with guilt, helplessness took over. She was just twenty after all. She felt frustrated as a result of her guilt about being a probable carrier and was also upset about her mother not being home at a time like this. *Even after her own father is sick, she's still going to the hospital! How irresponsible of her!* She picked up the phone and fell back on her age-old habit of sending her Amma a volley of blame messages.

```
Where are you?
Thatha not well.
How can you be at work at a time like this?
You always do this.
```

As she typed, she tried to fight back anger, blame, worry and guilt, all at once. The situation was hitting her in waves, in a way that her young mind just couldn't comprehend.

Samyuktha could've sworn she had taken every possible precaution, and trusted Abhimanyu to do the same. Could one chance instance of harmless fun turn her entire world upside down in an instant? The wonderful balcony conversation with her parents and Thatha suddenly seemed to be like one of those predictable happy scenes in a movie exactly before the protagonist's parents are killed. Her throat kept drying up at the thought of it, as she tried to shut out the increasingly negative thoughts in her mind. She felt a massive weight on her chest, remembering how they would make fun of Anitha's sanitization routine. *Who's laughing now?* A voice in her head asked caustically.

In his room, Thatha was lying on his bed, feeling weak, tired and feverish. His head was spinning and he was having difficulty in breathing. Hands trembling, he picked up the phone. He was

never one for self-pity, but he knew when situations were dire.
I should get tested, Thatha messaged Anitha.

Anitha checked her phone after coming from the delivery room. She read Samyuktha's messages first and sighed. She had been subject to such messages before. Samyuktha would suddenly start ranting and send barrages of messages, and then not reply at all when Anitha would message or call back. It had almost become a pattern.

She then checked her Appa's message. As the words imprinted on her brain, her heart sank. Somehow, all this while, she had gone by Appa's conviction—that the firecrackers had worsened his asthma. She actually partly believed that. But this message...

Had she been careful enough? Had she been lax about the precautions that she was expected to take as a medical professional? Had she been careless? Anitha played back everything she had done, again and again and again. Maybe Indrani was right. Had she done the right thing by going to Suhas's house? Had Suhas caught it from her? Or had she caught it from Suhas and passed it on to Appa? Her mind started whirling. Had Ajay been right, after all? And all this with a teenager in the house, the one she loved beyond anyone else. Anitha felt the exhaustion, emotion and guilt hit her in one giant wave. She had to sit down.

She felt her world crumbling around her. For her, everything was held together by her Appa. With him being sick since the last few days, she had already started feeling lost. And now with the threat of Covid and ventilators looming in front of her, it just became so...real. *What if something is wrong with him?*

Anitha forced the thought out of her mind and brought back herself to the present.

Coming right away pa, she typed back.

〜∞〜

Abhimanyu shut his eyes. Every time he did so, Samyuktha's accusing eyes staring at him from the balcony pierced him. And all he could hear was her accusing voice over the phone, implying that he was the one who had infected her family.

He opened his eyes again. It was 5.17 a.m. The fist rays of the sun were beginning to hit the apartment. As soon as they hit his eyes, he shut them again. It was the first time he had not wanted to wake up for his morning workout. He looked at his phone. There was no message. He had some WhatsApp messages from friends and some new notifications on Tinder. Not that he cared for any of those. He pressed on the lock button and put his phone away, before curling up on his side.

He closed his eyes and tried to think clearly. He had been nothing short of obsessively careful from day one. And he could surely say the same for his jawans. They had rigorous checks and protocol enforced everyday. He recollected the time when Dhruv had even sprayed disinfectant on a pillow when they had set up their post. It smelled so awful that they burnt it in the bonfire later. *Did I manage to slip up somewhere? Are my boys at risk too?*

As for his encounters with Samyuktha during the grocery store meeting and then the jogs, they had both been wearing masks. He remembered hers was a lavender polka dotted mask that had stood out like a fashion statement in front of his army-provided N95 variety. Abhimanyu racked his brain hard to figure out whether he had taken off his mask, if at all. It was definitely after she had turned around the corner and left. All good there. As for the balcony meetings, he had sat several feet away and used plenty of hand sanitizer. They had definitely not touched each other or sneezed or coughed in close proximity. He opened his eyes and stared at the paisley print that dotted the blanket he was sleeping on. The room was silent except for the gentle hum of the AC, which he found weirdly comforting.

He wondered if he had any symptoms. *I've not coughed or had any trouble breathing. My workout routines have been spot on despite this horrible heat. Could I still be infected?* He rolled over trying to shut out the wave of doubt and negativity that was taking over.

Something buzzed somewhere. He flailed around trying to find his phone amidst the mess of sheets. It was his sister. Talked to the lawyer today. He'll come back with the agreement. Thanks, kiddo.

Abhimanyu shut his eyes in relief. Finally, she was taking the much-needed step. He wished more than ever that he could be with her during this time, and suddenly Ayaan's voice flashed in his head. '*Hamari Didi na, fighter hai* (Our sister is a fighter)...' He knew that once Shalini didi had taken a decision, she would plunge ahead, despite moments of self doubt washing over her every once in a while. And his mind immediately connected back to the person who had helped him and her see it.

Didi, that's awesome. You're so courageous! Way to go, he replied. He wished to take a screenshot and send it to Samyuktha. As he thought of her, his stomach dove again.

Ayaan had texted him. Workout?

Abhimanyu replied, Not today, bro. Sick.

What's the latest from Ms Nose?

Abhimanyu wasn't in the mood for jibes from the boys, especially of this variety. He dragged himself out of bed like a zombie and hit the shower. As he waited for the water to turn hot, he mindlessly kicked the blue bucket below the faucet and it went rolling and clanking to the far corner. Once the water was warm enough, he stepped under it. As the spray hit him, he felt a sense of emptiness. He just wanted to let go of all the thoughts in his head and hit the 'skip day' button.

He again started replaying the events of the past few days.

This is now the second time, he thought as he remembered how she had simply shut him out the previous time over the issue regarding Ahalya. He decided he was not going to go begging to her again. *She didn't exactly do me a favour by letting me into her balcony,* he decided. He had equally risked his health, reputation and career for it, hoping the connection they were building would get stronger if he made the effort. Yet, if it was so easy for her to disconnect instantly…maybe it was not meant to be. *No point belabouring it,* he tried telling himself.

The day went by in a blur. Everything seemed normal. His checkpost, his cabin looked the same. He assiduously avoided looking at a certain balcony that morning. He spent most of the day in his office, sitting on one of the mattresses and looking into the distance. He had trained his unit well. The testimony of a good leader and trainer is when his team does not need him for day-to-day operations. So, it gave Abhimanyu a lot of time to stare bleakly into nothingness.

Abhimanyu missed lunch with the boys, and instead went back to his quarters and buried his head in his pillow. He checked his phone. There was no sign of any message from Samyuktha. *God I hate this torture!* He winced and turned his head the other side.

Abhimanyu was used to speaking his mind. He never shied away from confrontation and instead welcomed it with open arms. Hence, it was the ultimate punishment for him to not be able to express his thoughts. *I'm fine with apologizing or giving her the benefit of doubt if there is a valid concern somewhere in here, but I don't understand her not wanting to even hear my point of view.* He looked away in agony, as if an imaginary Samyuktha was sitting right in front of him. *Even prisoners of war are given a chance to explain before being sent to an isolation chamber. What kind of a person torments someone silently like this?*

As he turned back around and stared at the ceiling, his instinct took over. *I need to solve this, not continue moping. I don't regret anything I did. Not only was I super careful, I overdid the precautions. There is no way it could have been me. How do I convince Samyuktha?* He needed something to validate that it wasn't him. Abhimanyu thought hard for a moment and something struck him. As he lifted his head from the pillow, he took a decision. He went straight to his commander.

'I need the morning off, Sir,' he said, looking him straight in the eye.

Major Verma was surprised. Of all the soldiers, Abhimanyu had never taken a day off during the entire time he had known him. Covered for other people? Yes. Taken off for himself? Never.

'Everything okay, Abhi?' he asked in his booming voice.

'Feeling a bit uneasy, Sir,' Abhimanyu said as he looked away momentarily.

He looked at the boy. His eyes were a little bloodshot. He looked tired and a little…defeated.

Was it a matter of the heart? Major Verma had a strong intuition about these things. *Anyway, the boy never asks for time off. Good kid.*

'Alright. Take care,' he said, looking at him intently, before checking off the daily list on his jot pad.

Abhimanyu gave him a quick salute and left.

༺✲༻

Everyone in Ashok Apartments had sensed something was wrong. There was Suhasini, who was sick. And now Anitha's familiar silver Honda City was back home at eleven in the morning.

Amidst prying balcony glares, Anitha made her way upstairs in a jiffy. Today, her sanitization routine took longer than ever in her head and she did it more meticulously than ever. She walked slowly to her Appa's room, armed with a mask and a full hospital gown.

Thatha was feeling weak and feverish at a different level altogether. Throughout his seventy-four years, he had never experienced symptoms like these. He lay down, breathing heavily. *What a burden I am*, he thought in his feverishness. *That poor girl, Samyu, just came back home and now I might infect her. Anitha has gone through so much* thollai *(pain) because of me... I seem to be the virus here...*

Anitha softly stepped in, fully masked and gloved. She felt tears sting her eyelids. *How frail and delicate he looks,* she thought. *I am the cause of it all,* she thought bitterly. *I am responsible for what happened to Suhasini too. Who will look after poor Sandhya. God, I pray that nothing happens to that kid and her kid as well.* As the guilt brimmed over, she felt tears streaming down her mask.

Thatha sensed this. He looked at her, eyes half open. A bit of his old spirit sparked up. 'Stop crying,' he managed to utter sternly. '*Kuzhandhai-a nee* (Are you a child)?'

Anitha gave a laugh amidst her tears.

౦◦

Apollo Hospital, the sign read loud and clear. As Abhimanyu arrived at the entrance, he was intercepted.

'*Covid aa no Covid aa* (Is it Covid or is it not Covid)???' A moustached security guard yelled at him as if he was an outcast.

'Covid testing,' Abhimanyu said in a resigned tone.

'Go...go...go...go.' The security guard pointed at the back entrance.

As Abhimanyu made his way to the filthy back entrance, he felt a sense of foreboding. As he went in, he saw a giant A-5 paper reading 'Covid Test' pasted on what looked like a dilapidated entrance to a cafeteria from the Neanderthal ages. He went in gingerly.

Once you return from here, please do your job well, Abhimanyu told himself, *and make sure as few people as possible have to come here for getting tested. That's the best thing you can do for this country.*

As he entered, there was a woman standing there, wearing gloves and a mask. She signalled him to wear the gloves and mask placed in the plastic tray. As he put those on and went in, he saw a series of people waiting in a queue, one behind the other.

Abhimanyu walked around like a zombie, shocked at how calm everything appeared outside and how fragile everything seemed inside.

No social distancing norms were being followed. They may as well have been standing in line to cast their vote in an election. Some people were even shoving each other. He stood at the far corner of the room, staying well away from anyone and allowing everyone to enter the queue ahead of him.

At that moment, Abhimanyu saw the true reality of the pandemic. The chaos. The helplessness. The overworked doctors. And what kind of self-discipline was anyone practising? None of the precautions they were trained to adhere to in the army for the safety of the civilians were being followed here by the latter. He looked around. He saw a nurse and signalled to her.

As she walked up to Abhimanyu, he flashed his army badge and said, 'Covid rapid testing, please.'

She saw his badge and ID, and allowed him to skip the queue. *Thank god for some perks,* he thought.

As he went into the testing centre, he was made to sit next to two people, but far enough. One had come from Thailand and the other's roommate had just tested positive.

And then Samyuktha's mother walked in.

As he saw her, Abhimanyu's heart did a double take. And who was that frail gentleman behind her? Must be Samyuktha's Thatha. She had spoken of him so many times that he felt like he knew him.

Anitha quickly scanned the room for an empty space. There was none. Abhimanyu sprang into action. He meticulously took out sanitized wipes and cleaned the seat he had been sitting on. He then offered the space to Thatha, who slowly sat down.

Anitha expressed her gratitude with a flash of smile, 'Thank you.'

Abhimanyu's stomach churned. *Even from behind her mask, he could tell—that smile,* he thought, *that's where she gets it from.*

As Anitha looked at him gratefully, there was a flash of recognition in her eyes. *Where had she seen him before?* Anitha racked her brain.

Abhimanyu quickly picked up. 'Ma'am, I believe I man the street where your apartment is located. Lieutenant Abhimanyu Singh. Pleasure to meet you.'

'How nice, Abhimanyu,' Anitha replied. 'Thank you for looking out for us.'

Why is he here? she thought. But she was too polite to ask. Had she been Indrani, that would have been the first thing she would have wanted to know.

'Ditto, Ma'am,' Abhimanyu said. 'Being a doctor in these times comes with its share of praise and blame.'

Anitha smiled at his incisive comment. *If only he knew how true it was,* she thought. Little did she know that he actually knew.

Thatha tried to say something, but a series of coughs interrupted him. Anitha patted his back with her gloved hand.

Abhimanyu's eyes softened. *I can imagine how stressed Samyuktha must be,* he thought. He started hurting again thinking of her.

'So Abhimanyu, it must be hard work, manning the post out there?' Anitha asked.

'Ma'am, it is and it isn't. It's good to know that we're waging a war against a virus, but if I had to be honest, the discipline that civilians have leaves much to be desired,' Abhimanyu replied.

Anitha smiled. *Tell me about it.*

Just then, Abhimanyu was called in. He saw Thatha, frail and fragile. 'Ma'am, please go ahead of me,' he said. Anitha smiled in gratitude and took Thatha inside. Thatha did a frail namaskaram with his hands and went inside hobbling.

Abhimanyu's eyes were moist. He said a silent prayer.

∽

It was Abhimanyu's turn. The doctor inside was making all kinds of jokes to lighten the mood. She opened the kit and took out two large swabs. She stuck the first in, as far as it could go, into the mouth. Abhimanyu almost choked. She then took the second and stuck it into his nose, again as far as it would go.

Quickly, she took the two swabs, sealed them in an envelope and gestured that the test was done.

'You will get email,' she said.

He returned post lunch and took up his station. He was still numb from seeing the scenes at the hospital. *This is not a peacetime posting. This is war,* he concluded. He took on his duty with renewed vigour, and for a while completely forgot about the balcony, Samyuktha and everything else. When he finally noticed her sitting in that blue loveseat, his throat went dry. He consciously decided not to look at her. Part of him didn't want to be tempted, part of him was afraid he might break down.

As he returned home after his shift, he called his sister. He felt guilty. He hadn't called her at all since the message. *How selfish I am*, he thought. *All I do is think about my own problems when everyone else has much bigger fish to fry.*

He called. After a few rings, a voice answered. 'Hello. Hi, Abhi,' she said.

'How are you, Didi?' Abhimanyu asked as he paced around the street. 'Sorry I couldn't call you earlier. Tell me everything.'

There was silence on the other end for a while. 'I can't believe I'm doing this, Abhimanyu.' Her voice was close to breaking.

Abhimanyu fell silent. 'I know,' he finally said. 'It must be hard.' *Understand and empathize. Ask questions.* Samyuktha's words came back to him. 'What's so difficult, Didi? Is it leaving him, or is it that you have to fend for yourself?'

'None of that. It's the feeling that I failed.' With that, she broke down.

It slowly dawned on Abhimanyu. Of course, his sister was scared of the ramifications: living alone and the stigma associated with divorce. But all of that paled in comparison to the feeling that she had failed at giving it her 100 per cent. And whatever she did, whatever he did, she might never be able to let go of that feeling.

'I get it, but Didi think about it. What else could you have done? Do you honestly think that things could have been any different?' Abhimanyu asked.

'I don't know,' she said, between sobs. 'I'm not perfect, right? There's some things I could have done differently. That's what keeps coming back. I have so much self-doubt.' The voice was muffled, and Abhimanyu could picture his sister sitting on the bed, with her head immersed in a pillow.

Drat this damn lockdown, Abhimanyu cursed. He would have been there in Delhi, in her home, packing her bags for her and getting her out of there faster than she could say Jack Robinson. But he could do none of that.

'Didi, I know,' he said, 'but here's something to think about. I know you deserve better in life. Ayaan knows it. Do you remember how Mummy Papa were with each other? Papa just worshipped Mummy, remember? He just knew what she needed without her even saying a word. Don't you think, Didi, that you deserve someone like that? You do, for sure.'

Shalini didi was silent. He knew she was listening. He went on.

'Didi, I don't know whether you will or won't find something like that. But I do know that if you stay in this marriage, it will start eroding every little piece of assurance, self-respect and self-worth that you have. And I can't see that happening to you and neither should you.'

⁂

Suhasini woke up with a start the next day. Instantly, she started coughing uncontrollably. Her body was burning and she could barely breathe. She said a silent prayer. *Why me? Why now? Isn't it enough that I have to do all this alone?* Her eyes welled up thinking about Sandhya and her unborn baby in the next room. What would she do and where would she even go at this time?

The test results had not come back yet. But Suhasini knew it in her bones. The persistent dry cough, the high temperature, the difficulty in breathing. It was nothing like she had ever felt before.

'Amma?' Sandhya called out, her voice scared.

Suhasini burst into tears, but pulled herself together. Wheezing, she tried to muster up her energy and replied, 'Sandhya, I'm so sorry kanna. The symptoms are getting worse. We should not be in the same house right now. Can you call Anitha and ask her if they can admit you early?'

Sandhya's voice sounded heavy and broken now. She was

crying. 'Amma, I can't leave you like this. I'm sure we will figure something out. I'm calling Anitha aunty.'

She dialled her number. There was no answer. She called the next best person she knew—Samyuktha.

Samyuktha shook herself out of the Abhimanyu fantasy as her phone rang. *Sandhya akka*. She immediately picked up.

'Akka, are you okay?' she asked, half fearing what she might hear next.

'Samyuktha, Amma is sick, wheezing and coughing. I'm terrified.' Sandhya was sobbing.

Samyuktha's mind started whirling. She just didn't know how to process this anymore. Here was Thatha, gone with Amma to get tested. Suhasini aunty was sick. Sandhya, the one she looked up to, was asking for her help now. And to top it all, she herself may have been the cause of all of it.

She said what her mother usually would on being faced with something like this, 'Please don't cry, Sandhya akka. I understand. I'll call you right back. Okay? We'll figure this out.'

She hung up, buried her head in her hands, and started crying uncontrollably. *Let me get it all out,* she thought, *before I talk to her again.*

Her phone rang once again. It was Abhimanyu. She looked down and saw him signalling to pick up.

'Why are you crying?' he asked her in a curt tone.

'Sandhya akka's worried she'll catch the disease. Amma's not here. And I don't know what to do or tell her,' Samyuktha replied flatly.

'Get her out of the house. Get her admitted to a hospital. Ask your father to drive her there. Separate them as soon as you can,' Abhimanyu replied in a cold yet assertive tone.

'*I* should do all of this?' Samyuktha asked in disbelief as she stopped sobbing.

'Of course,' Abhimanyu replied. After a pause, he added, 'I know you can.'

Samyuktha started getting her spirit back. 'Thanks, Abhi...'

He had already hung up.

Samyuktha watched from the balcony as Abhimanyu gave out orders to his jawans. *Why was he absent in the morning?* she wondered. *And it was thoughtful of him to call her when he saw her crying with no resentment and no malice.* Samyuktha felt guilty when she thought of what she had done. *But what else could I have done? He might have been the superspreader. How can I even take a chance?*

She forced herself out of her own self-wallowing misery and focussed on the problem at hand. Abhimanyu was right. As usual, he removed all the fluff and told her the only logical thing to do. She got up off the loveseat and went inside. Abhimanyu saw this from the corner of his eyes. *Good*, he thought. *I knew she would.* He felt good that he had been able to help her, amidst all his heartache.

'Appa.'

Her dad looked up, surprised to see Samyuktha looking pale yet resolute.

'What happened, kanna?' he asked as he tried to read her expression.

Samyuktha explained the situation to him, clearly and calmly. As she spoke, talking about Sandhya, her options, peppering the argument with fact and what she consequently thought needed to be done, Samyuktha felt a sense of relief.

And Ajay felt pride welling up inside him. *My daughter...* he thought. Such presence of mind at twenty. He quickly saw the logic behind Sandhya being admitted as soon as possible to St. Isabel's Hospital. They rummaged through Anitha's cupboard and found the hospital gowns she always kept as spare.

Samyuktha knew Amma's sanitization routine by heart now. The father–daughter duo went through the steps laboriously and then sprinted up the stairs to Suhasini's house. As they crossed the second floor, they came across Abhijeet uncle, smoking blissfully (or was it stressfully?) in the landing.

He saw both of them and stopped them short.

'What are both of you doing?' he asked in a demanding tone.

Ajay cursed silently. *Of all the people.*

'Sandhya's not keeping well, Abhijeet. We are taking her to the hospital as a precaution. There's no time to explain. I'll talk to you later.' Ajay looked him straight in the eye as he spoke.

Samyuktha had never seen her father run before, but she could have sworn that she saw him scurry off. She meekly scurried off behind him.

⋘⋙

'Papa asked him, beta. He said he didn't see anyone at all,' Indrani was trying to reason with her daughter.

Ahalya was going mad. Her infatuation for Abhimanyu had multiplied her hatred for Samyuktha many times over. 'That's impossible, Mumma! I know her. She must have found another way. I can guarantee you that a soldier visits her at night. If not by the balcony, then maybe straight up the stairs!' Ahalya had no idea that her absolute fantastical imagination was true, albeit with zero proof.

'Ahalya,' Indrani chided her. 'Beta…' she had a weird sense of deja vu as she tried to reason with her daughter and saw her own face momentarily in Ahalya's. *The apple doesn't fall far from the tree.*

Ahalya took no notice and relentlessly ploughed on. '…her parents are so engrossed in their own lives, I'm sure they don't even notice, or maybe they do notice but don't care. Maybe he actually lives in her room!'

'Ahalya!' Her mother's voice was stern now. 'Stop it now, *paglamo koro na* (don't be crazy).'

Despite her frustration, Ahalya stopped herself at her mother's stern tone. She had crossed a line. She went into her room and out on to her balcony. There he was, standing as if all was normal.

Why wouldn't he respond to me, what does Samyuktha have that I don't?

He looked up at her momentarily, his face expressionless. His gaze calmed Ahalya down, and she raised a hand to wave to him. Just as momentarily, Abhimanyu looked away, ignoring her. A sense of emptiness filled Ahalya. She kicked the poor flower pot next to her leg.

Just as she went outside, Abhijeet strode inside. 'That Kumar family is crazy,' he said. 'I'm calling MLA sir.'

You've Got Mail

The WhatsApp group of the apartment was set ablaze.

Dear Residents,

The Safety and Security Committee has consistently sent out guidelines to keep everyone safe during the pandemic. Despite reminders, violations have been observed and reported. We would like to bring to your attention one such critical violation that occurred on the afternoon of 16 April.

A resident sneaked into C-31 when it is clearly a violation to be entering any other apartment. This may have gone undetected if a well-wisher had not observed the attendant in full sight. While he pleaded with the violator to go back, no attention was given to his pleas. Left with no option, the said well-wisher had to complain to the society.

We are sharing this incident to drive awareness among the residents. Please adhere to the lockdown requirements and guidelines shared by the municipal corporation, so as to avoid inconvenience to yourself and others. Our only objective is to ensure everyone's safety. Let's work together and

defeat this pandemic, so that we can all
go back to our normal lives soon.

Regards,
Mr Abhijeet,
C-25, Ashok Apartment

—

This irresponsible action by one resident has now
endangered the health and safety of the entire
community.

While the security committee has confirmed this
serious violation, there is no clarity on the
actions being taken to safeguard the interests of
the community.

As a resident, I now look forward to a detailed
report on the incident from the president/secretary,
along with action taken to protect the safety of
the residents.

Ganesh,
B-45

—

I, too, agree. Had all the necessary precautions
been taken, there wouldn't have been such an
increase in cases.

After all, we had voluntarily published our
names (three family members) with the MC and
followed a strict self quarantine protocol in the
larger interest of the community.

Pradeep,
A-22

—

This is simply outrageous.

The concerned resident needs to be exposed, and compulsorily needs to undergo isolation or quarantine.

The entire complex cannot be put at risk because of one irresponsible resident.

As a resident, it's my right to know, failing which I would not mind taking the next logical step.

Regards,

Easwaran,

B-22

⊲∞⊳

Abhijeet went into the balcony and called MLA Balasamy. He closed his eyes, listening to the calming sound of the phone ringing, enjoying the rare moment of something predictable amidst the uncertainty around.

'Abhijeet, how are you pa?' came the booming voice in the predictable Tamil accent.

'*Romba nalla irruken, Sir* (I'm very well, Sir). All thanks to you!' Abhijeet slyly reciprocated in Tamil. 'Hope you're taking good care, Sir,' he said.

'It's all a *tapasya,* Abhijeet, these people are my God and this city is my temple. How can anything happen to a true bhakt in his temple?' he said, with sounds of incessant chewing of paan in between. This was exactly the kind of talk that would have made Samyuktha and Abhimanyu laugh and cringe at the same time. But Abhijeet nodded wisely.

'Absolutely, Sir. A true bhakt can never be touched, correct? On that note, the last time we spoke, you told me to let you know about anything suspicious, right?' Abhijeet came to the point, after all the sycophantism. *Matters like this must be addressed,* he felt.

'Of course. Tell me?' MLA Balasamy cocked up his ears at the thought of something juicy that he could sink his teeth into. Lockdown had proved to be boring for him till now.

'Er….just…er…so in our building, there is this lady doctor who spends all day at the hospital, Sir,' he said, looking at Indrani next to him and smiling indulgently. 'My wife is suspicious that she may be infecting other residents in the building, Sir. And Sir, you know how much I trust her,' he said as he gave her hand a squeeze.

'Abhijeet, let's be sensible, pa. Doctors are required. Now we cannot blame her for going to the hospital at such times, no?' the MLA grandly conceded, as if it were perfectly alright to blame them at other times.

'We are also fully supportive of her.' Abhijeet straightened his back to show his support. 'In fact, we help them in any way we can….*dharam to karma hai, na* (work is worship, after all)?' Abhijeet felt pleased with himself. 'But I feel,' he said as if making a grand concession, 'she should at least get tested, Sir.'

'She should definitely get tested,' the MLA agreed, adjusting the rudraksh on his neck correctly. 'What house number did you say, pa?'

Abhijeet hadn't, till now. He faithfully said, 'C-11, Sir.' He paused, before saying, 'Er…Sir, I hope you will not tell anyone that I gave you this information.' He looked at his wife, who faithfully nodded. In such matters, they were the epitome of partnership and solidarity.

'Of course. You relax,' the MLA laughed. He was pleased. Now here was something to do. There might be some gold at the end of this tunnel.

Abhijeet lit up another cigarette and heaved a sigh of relief as he looked out at the tree-lined colony around.

꩜

Samyuktha woke up with a start. She saw she had slept with an open book on her face. Quantum Mechanics. She groaned. She was lagging behind in every subject.

What a day yesterday had been. She had gone with Appa and a sobbing Sandhya to the hospital, and managed to admit her safely. Luckily for Sandhya, her company had pre-booked the room and had had everything ready. She had admitted her, spent some time chatting with her and tried to keep up her spirits. She herself had hit rock bottom after her situation involving Abhimanyu and her Thatha's condition. Now she had to ensure she helped make Sandhya feel better.

Carry your own sunshine everywhere, Turtle, Abhimanyu's voice kept echoing in her head. And that's what she did. She had started talking to Sandhya about nostalgia, how jealous she had felt when Sandhya had walked out looking like a flower outside while she had been busy mugging for her boards...*Abhimanyu would have been proud of me,* she thought wistfully.

She came home late in the evening, scrubbed and sanitized, and almost immediately fell asleep. She checked her messages. There was nothing from him. Her heart sank. She had earlier texted a `Thank you for all the help`.

She opened her email and scanned the tonnes of emails, Google sheets, docs and slides she hadn't looked at in the last two days. She was almost ready to shut her machine, when on an impulse, she clicked on the 'Promotions' tab. Amidst all the emails from Facebook, Instagram, Hinge, Tinder and Bumble, her eyes settled on one.

Environmental Defense Fund!

Her heart did a double take. Trembling, she clicked on it.

Dear Ms Kumar,

I am delighted to inform you that the Committee of Admissions has admitted you to the Class of 2020 under the Young Environmentalist Programme. Congratulations on your outstanding achievement.

This year, nearly ten thousand students applied for the fifty spots on this programme. We looked not only at extraordinary talent, extracurricular and personal strengths but also a passion for the Earth. We find that you 'tipped us over' on the passion quotient, as we love to describe it. With a majority voting to offer you admission, the Committee puts a lot of responsibility on the contributions you can make during your college years and beyond.

By early July, you will receive an invitation to visit the Environmental Defense Fund from Monday, 31 August, to Wednesday, 2 September. We'd love to have you over, but completely understand if you cannot given the current challenging circumstances. If such is the case, we would be happy to have you visit us at some other time if you are unable to join us in August.

You have until 15 June to respond to our offer. A complete admission kit will be sent in early September.

We look forward to having you join us in December.

Gerald Dickens,

Dean of Admissions

'We do not inherit the Earth from our ancestors, we borrow it from our children.' Ralph Waldo Emerson

Her head was whirling. The biggest dream of her twenty-year-old life was in front of her on her laptop screen. She smiled and as she did, tears started falling down her cheeks and she started sobbing, half with joy, half with fatigue. She covered her face, sobbing and smiling at the same time, in alternating circles.

Finally she looked up and read it again…*'you tipped us over in the passion quotient…'* and her mind travelled to that one person who had brimmed her passion quotient over for the last two weeks, not just for the environment, but for everything…

Simple. And true. As she dried her eyes and looked at her tired, yet happy and hopeful face in the mirror, Samyuktha smiled and gave herself a pat on the back. She knew whatever she did in life ahead, she would be proud of herself in ten years' time looking back at herself. She went outside to tell her Amma.

As she walked into the kitchen, her Amma was busy doing the dishes.

'Samyuktha kanna, I'll need your help today. Things are not looking good for Suhasini aunty…and Thatha is just the same. I'll need your help….' she said looking at everything around her. She was hassled and tired, and looked more worried that Samyuktha had ever seen.

'Amma, see the email, I…' Samyuktha started excitedly, when Ajay strode into the room, furious and seething.

'Did you see the WhatsApp messages?' he thundered, still in his *veshti* and *banyan*.

'What emails?' Anitha asked, tired and puzzled.

He brandished his phone.

'This is from your sister. She's attached her PAN Card like you asked her to,' Anitha told Ajay.

'Oh,' Ajay quickly checked the right message and brandished it back.

With every message Anitha read, she grew redder and redder. 'Those jobless, up-to-no-good human beings,' she spluttered in anger. 'I'm going up there immediately…'

As she said that, the bell rang. They all looked at each other. Samyuktha opened the door. Three plainclothesmen were waiting outside, wearing masks and gloves.

'Mrs Anitha Kumar? Is that your mother?' one of them asked patronizingly.

'Yes. Why are you here?' Samyuktha asked suspiciously.

'Just ask her to come to the door, ma?' he said.

'Amma,' Samyuktha called out, 'someone is here at the door.' Anitha came out.

'Madam, we are from the Chennai Corporation. We heard you are violating norms. Is it true that you went to meet residents of C-31 two days ago?' one of them asked.

Anitha's eyes grew wide.

'Yes, but that's because she had pains and she is pregnant. I'm a gynaecologist, a doctor who delivers babies,' she clarified as one of them interrupted her.

'Okay, Ma'am. But is it true that your husband and daughter also went to that house yesterday?' the second gentleman asked.

'Yes, but it was to admit her to the hospital! She's in danger because her mother is sick!' Anitha's voice started getting high pitched.

'And is it true that your esteemed father was also taken for a coronavirus test, ma?' By now Ajay had joined her.

'Yes, it's true,' Ajay said quietly. He knew there was no point in beating around the bush with these people.

'Madam, your entire family is quarantined for the next twenty one days.'

'What?' Anitha's voice had reached a high pitched squeak now. 'I am a medical professional. I am authorized to...'

'Madam, please mind the tone. We are letting you off with a quarantine only because you are a doctor. Otherwise, it is a fine of 250,000 rupees.' The man sanitized his hands and took out the stamp. He looked ready to mark that stamp on anyone who would go near him.

By now, Anitha had tears in her eyes. Samyuktha couldn't believe her ears. Ajay put his hand on Anitha's shoulder. 'Okay,' he said, holding out his hand. The man stamped it on Ajay, then Samyuktha and then Anitha. Then one of them went in to stamp it on Thatha. 25 May, it read. They had to be quarantined for the next 21 days till 25 May.

'Please keep your WhatsApp locations on. We will check it at eight in morning and eight in evening,' the man said in a more mellow tone.

'Yes, Sir,' Ajay said.

The three men looked at them. 'Such irresponsible miscreants,' one of them muttered as they shook their heads and went down.

⌖

Sandhya's phone rang. It was her husband, Suresh.

'How are you, kanna?' he asked as Sandhya started sobbing on hearing his voice. 'I know. I know,' Suresh said in his calm reassuring voice. 'I know it's hard, baby.'

'Hard? I can't even tell you. Amma is sick and I don't know whether she has coronavirus. Neither of our results have come in yet. No one is here. No one else is allowed to visit. I'm all alone, and...' Sandhya's voice broke... 'I didn't ever imagine it would be like this...' she just stopped there, unable to go on.

Suresh mentally cursed the helplessness he faced. 'Don't worry. I got my travel permit today. I will be there as soon as I can, driving as fast as possible. And you already know that I drive like a maniac.' Sandhya smiled between her tears as she heard this. 'It'll take me two days to drive from Mumbai to there. But I'll be there as soon as possible. Okay?'

'But Suresh...' Sandhya paused.

'Hmm...?' he encouraged her to speak.

'What if I also have it?' Sandhya burst into tears again, 'Our baby…Suresh what if—'

'You'll be fine, Sandhya, please don't worry and strain yourself,' Suresh interrupted her emphatically. He went on to remind her of all the measures Suhasini had taken since she had begun suspecting, and patiently responded to more anxiety-driven fears and paranoia that Sandhya fired at him. Sandhya eventually calmed down and asked him to drive safely, and then hung up.

The doctor on duty came to check on Sandhya and saw her sobbing.

'Mustn't cry, ma,' she said, clicking her tongue. 'You smile, okay? This hospital is known for happy ammas and healthy babies. Don't you worry!' She gave her a smile.

Sandhya couldn't help but smile. 'Where's Anitha aunty, doctor?' she asked.

'She's taken the day off, ma. Didn't say why.'

Sandhya's head went into a whirl again. She had never known Anitha aunty to take a single day off since Sandhya was a girl. *Did it mean…? How was Thatha? How was Amma?* Quickly, she called her Amma's number after the doctor checked her blood pressure.

'*Eppidi irrukke, kanna* (How are you, darling)?' a rasping voice answered.

'Amma, what's wrong with you?' she asked.

'Nothing, ma. Just some fever and breathlessness. I'll be okay. You tell me.' Suhasini felt much worse, but played it down.

'Anitha aunty didn't come to the hospital today, Amma,' Sandhya told her with hesitation.

'Oho. Must be some emergency, ma.' Suhasini didn't say a word about Indrani's conversation with her.

'Amma, do you think she's positive? Is that why she has not come?'

Suhasini, too, started fearing. This could definitely be possible. Anitha had come, not once, but twice to their house. She wearily checked her phone. The WhatsApp groups confirmed her worst fears.

—Anitha and family have been self-quarantined for 21 days. Apparently something about Covid symptoms. Don't know the whole story.

—Ramanathan uncle went for a test for sure. I saw them leave in Anitha's car yesterday.

—Aiyyo, the entire apartment is in danger of infection. I think we should all move to a hotel.

—How irresponsible! They seemed to be educated people.

Suhasini saw all the messages and said as clearly as she possibly could, 'I think you're mad, Sandhya. There's absolutely no way. You just relax, okay, ma?'

She went up to the kitchen, barely able to walk. The wheezing had become even worse. Her usual strong, melodious voice had become a croaking version of itself.

She boiled water on the stove. *Let me drink some warm water with lemon and honey*, she thought. As the water was coming to a boil, she felt her head spinning out of control. She clutched the kitchen slab just in time, avoiding from spilling over the boiling pan of water.

Chocolates. She remembered what Rajagopal always told her. Eat some chocolate for instant energy. They then started keeping a few Dairy Milks in the fridge. She tottered over to the fridge and took a Dairy Milk out. Leaning against the fridge, she slowly unwrapped and ate it. She felt better, probably just mentally.

She mustered up the strength to look at her phone. As if on cue, an email from the Covid testing centre flashed on the screen.

Rajagopal, Suhasini. Covid positive.

⟨∞⟩

Anitha and Ajay were sitting in the living room balcony. He had never seen her look the way she did in that moment. He knew that the events of the day had exhausted her both physically and emotionally.

'Anitha, what are you thinking?' He reached out and put his hand on hers, wishing he could blurt out everything about his project to her. A slew of Covid tests had popped up on his team's radar, including one by a soldier posted outside Ashok Apartments. *Were they just precautions, or was there more to this? Why did the soldier suddenly decide to get tested?* He would've loved to discuss this with Anitha, but couldn't for confidential reasons.

'I'm furious,' Anitha said without any trace of anger. 'How could they?'

'Anitha, they're not wrong, you know. They have a right to be paranoid. We actually violated all precautions we possibly could. Now I'm not saying that you didn't have valid reasons, but they aren't wrong given where they are coming from.' Ajay tried to reason with her, desperately hoping she would get the hint that things were actually rather serious with a superspreader lurking right around them somewhere.

Anitha looked at Ajay. She hoped he wasn't so logical each time. Everything he said was true. *But there is always a time and a place to say anything, isn't there? Not when I am down and out. He is making me feel small about myself when I am already low, that whatever I do, I don't quite get it right. Does he mean to? Or has it just become his second nature? Here I am, doing everything right by my family, my profession, my craft. And yet I feel like someone who is just about that small in front of his eyes.*

She went in to check on her Appa. He was battling it like a true champion. He had holed himself up in his room since the first day of his cough, refusing to come out. He insisted on meals being sent through the door. After having food, he would wash his utensils in the bathroom and then keep them outside whenever it would be time for the next meal. Rest of the times, he would keep the door fast shut.

'Yes, ma?' he asked on hearing somene knock on the door.

'Appa, it's me. How are you?' Anitha made no effort to hide the fact that she was crying.

'I'm better, ma,' came the voice from behind the door. 'How come you are at home?'

Anitha told him, between sobs. Her resolve to be stoic under the present situation seemed to fall apart. She leaned against the door and told him everything.

Thatha felt angry and guilty at the same time. He believed she had been forced to undergo the self-quarantine partly because of him. *That Ganguly! He has no sense whatsoever. Pandering to his spoiled wife and daughter.* He pitied his daughter, who did so much and deserved so much more, and was instead being subjected to this.

'This too shall pass,' he said in his frail voice. '*Nee dhairyam a iru* (Be brave).'

Anitha smiled and it took all her resolve not to go in and hug him. Just then, an email notification popped up in her phone.

Kumar, Anitha. Covid Negative, it read.

౸

Back in his room, Thatha woke up with a fit of coughing. 'Parvati,' he groaned referring to his late wife. She had been dead for almost fifteen years now, but he would still take her name every once a while.

He looked at her photograph, hung at the vantage point of his bed. He smiled looking at her.

'*Enna ma, paakare* (What are you looking at)?' he asked her fondly. 'At any given chance, you want me to come to you, illaya?'

With her beautiful saree, combed back hair, large pottu, she glanced back with her delightful smile. Her smile was no different than that of Anitha and Samyuktha.

'I am really sick, kannama,' he told her. 'What do I do? *Inga burden a irrukken naan* (I'm a burden here). Should I just come to you?'

He paused and started again.

'Anitha is so wonderful ma, you should see her now. She's so accomplished. She's one of the best doctors in Madras now, one of the best gynaecologists in the country.'

'*Samyuktha kutti a paakanom nee* (You should see Samyuktha). She was two when you went away. She's all of twenty now, a beautiful girl who knows what she wants. And she is so smart and intelligent. Aana, she still can't identify Thodi ragam.'

He lay back, exhausted. But he did not call out for anyone. With a shaking hand, he felt his head. It seemed to be hot. He took a Dolo 360 and some water along with it. Some of that water trickled down his chin. And so did a tear, on to his pillow.

꼬◎꼬

It was 6.30 p.m. The doorbell rang. It was the sound Samyuktha had been waiting for all week.

Her father opened the door. There he was.

Abhimanyu gave a quick salute to Ajay. His face was expressionless. Was she imagining it or did his eyes look tired? He consciously averted his eyes from Samyuktha and focussed on the job at hand as if his life depended on it. Diligently, he listed out the usual to-do's and updates, with a calm voice. *He is so good at this,* she thought, feeling a surge of pride and admiration.

Ajay took the groceries into the kitchen. As he did, he asked

Samyuktha to shut the door. Samyuktha was trembling and her heart was beating at triple the speed. Could Abhimanyu see how nervous and flushed she was?

She stood at the door in silence. With glove-clad hands, he gave her a pad with the receipt to sign. She signed it and handed it back, and looked at him briefly, not believing their eyes would meet. He briefly glanced at her.

'How are you?' he asked her. He looked at her and gave her a hint of a smile. All of what he felt for her peeped out for a brief second.

Samyuktha felt she might burst into tears any moment. As she opened her mouth to reply, Kamala aunty from C-12 opened the door to ask Abhimanyu whether there were any extra packets of thayir that someone didn't want. *Of course.* For the likes of Kamala aunty, thayir was the sustenance and source of all things good. BUT NOW? Samyuktha quickly averted her face and not trusting herself, quickly shut the door and looked through the peephole. The last thing she wanted was Kamala aunty to catch her crying. It would just become more fodder for gossip.

Abhimanyu noticed it: the struggle in her eyes, the anger and the dilemma. His own anger had simmered down when he had seen her Thatha at the hospital. It was one thing to prescribe and tout the mantra of being brave and resilient but totally another when you helplessly watch your loved ones become afflicted by a rogue virus, or in case of his own sister, a rogue. Abhimanyu was reminded of his own anger and helplessness when Shalini didi had first told him about her decision.

Over the years, with the sudden loss of his parents and the slow and painful unraveling of his sister's marriage, Abhimanyu had adopted a 'no regrets' perspective to ensure he lived life king size. He didn't want to be hurt anymore, so he eliminated all possible causes—attachments and expectations.

Samyuktha had infused a breath of fresh air that had blown away this façade to reveal the vulnerable child within him that was longing for attachment. He began to understand Samyuktha's point of view of wanting to 'protect everything that's dear to me'. And she helped him kick-start it with Shalini didi. Knowing that his sister could be free from her shackles and live a full life gave him boundless joy and a newfound hope.

He was grateful to Samyuktha. Even in his anger and hurt, Abhimanyu wanted to look out for her. She had valued and considered his perspective, and imbibed it in her life. It was a new journey for her, and he had egged her on to embark upon it. How could he let go at the first sign of a storm? Abhimanyu realized that his feelings for her were too strong to be shaken by a fleeting moment of doubt. This was the time for him to be the bigger person, and if a time comes for her to do the same, he believed that she, too, would do the same.

As Kamala aunty stood there, waiting, with her hands on her hips, Abhimanyu forced himself back to the 'critical' issue at hand and explained to her that there were no other extras available. Kamala aunty hemmed and hawed, requesting Abhimanyu to *try* if he could. Abhimanyu nodded that he would. He put the jot pad back and headed down the stairs.

As Samyuktha gazed from the peephole, she saw Abhimanyu signal something with his hands. Or did she imagine it? As soon as he left, she opened the door, just when Kamala aunty closed the door after giving her a 'dirty' look accusing them of being an 'infected family'. Samyuktha found a crumpled piece of paper lying in a corner in front of her house. She quickly picked it up and went back in, her heart pounding.

She slowly made her way to her room. Hands quivering, she opened the paper. It was a coronavirus test report.

Singh, Abhimanyu. Negative.

Fight Club

The phone rang. It was Suhasini. Anitha picked it up in an instant.

'Anitha, I tested positive, ma,' she said with a croak.

Anitha's heart sank. She knew it was coming. She somehow gathered her composure and said, 'Suhasini, I'm calling an ambulance immediately. They will come in, take you and leave. Don't worry. You are healthy. Covid cannot get to you.'

'But Sandhya…?' Suhasini's hoarse voice interrupted Anitha.

'Sandhya's test just came in, and I was about to call you myself. She has tested negative, Suhas. Sandhya and her baby are absolutely fine, and you will be too,' she finished as Suhasini burst into tears of relief. 'We will take great care of her and her baby, Suhas, I'll keep you updated…'

Suhasini knew that she had to get it off her chest. 'Anitha, were you the one who gave it to me?' she asked directly.

Anitha replied in a second, 'I didn't, Suhas. My test came out negative today. It must have been someone else.' She understood Suhasini's concern. It wasn't doubt or anger. She just needed to know.

Suhasini smiled amidst her fever. 'Thanks ma, I always knew…I just wanted to…' she croaked…collapsing back into the bed in relief.

Anitha cut her short. 'Of course, I know, Suhas,' she said. 'You don't need to explain anything. Now you just wait till the ambulance comes and rest, seriya? Don't strain yourself.'

Suhasini smiled thinking of the rock-solid friendship and understanding they had nurtured over the years. Anitha made her next call to Sandhya.

'Sandhya. I have bad news, kanna. Amma has tested positive.' Simple. Plain. No point beating around the bush.

There was silence on the other end as Sandhya processed this news. 'That's…that's not good,' she faltered. 'What are… wh—what are we going to do, Aunty?'

'Kanna, you don't worry about a thing. Suhasini called me as soon as she knew. I've already called for an ambulance. She immediately needs to be shifted. She'll pull through beautifully. She's strong and her immunity is good.' Anitha was back to business, with her calm and crisp demeanour, and her bedside manners intact, even through a phone call.

Something about Anitha's calm voice immediately soothed Sandhya. 'I trust you, Aunty. Is there any way I can help?'

'Yes,' Anitha said caustically, 'Come over this instance and drive the ambulance.'

Sandhya laughed amidst her tears. 'I love you, Anitha aunty.'

'Love you too, kanna. Take care of yourself.' Anitha hung up, feeling a little guilty. She wasn't so sure about Suhasini. That rasping voice definitely didn't sound good by any means. *Ashwatthama the elephant,* she reminded herself of the battle of Kurukshetra. This, too, would be a lie for everyone's good.

After making all calls, she sat back, sighing with relief looking at her test results. An enormous load of guilt had been lifted off her. *Bless the sanitation routine,* she thought. *Even if it saves one life, it's worth it.* She called the hospital president. He picked up in one ring. He was waiting for her call. Back at the hospital, everyone missed Anitha—her cheerfulness, her competence.

'Anitha, tell me. How are you keeping?' he asked in his deep voice.

'I'm keeping well, Doctor Ram. I've tested negative. Can I resume work tomorrow?' Anitha asked the question, even though she already knew the answer.

'Anitha, I'll check, but the orders have come from an MLA. So I really can't predict the next course of action that we can take. How's Appa doing?" he asked. Anitha knew this would be his next question.

'He's the same, Doctor. His results should have come in yesterday. They haven't yet. They should come in anytime now,' she told him everything she could.

'We'll wait for that, Anitha, before we can make a case to the Board on your rejoining. In the meantime, take care. All your patients are doing just fine. Take care of your plants for a change.' So saying, Doctor Ram laughed and hung up the phone. She sat in silence, looking at the empty space in front of her. Ajay quietly came and sat next to her.

She looked at him. There was so much she wanted to say, but it was a lot to process and she didn't quite know how to get it out. She took a deep breath and held his hand, looking at him.

'I'm so used to tackling every situation, for every pregnant mother, for every problem that Samyuktha has thrown at me. Ajay, my life seems to be crumbling down since the last two days. If I try to go solve one thing, somethings else falls apart the very moment. And now Appa too...' she choked up and continued after a pause, '...and on top of that, those accusations. These people have known us for YEARS, Ajay, decades. Our children have grown up together, and they never hesitated to call in the middle of the night for any and every problem. All it took was a virus to break that trust? I mean, they accused me of being a superspreader?' She felt hurt. Leaning her head on Ajay's shoulders, she continued, 'What and who is one to trust anymore?'

Silence. Ajay, after all, wasn't much of a talker.

'Appa is my rock, you know. Sorry, no offence meant to you, but he is.' Ajay had known since a long time that he was not capable of providing the emotional cushion that Anitha needed. 'If something happens to him, I don't know what I'll do. But…I think he's doing okay because he has not been showing any worse symptoms. And moreover, he has not come in contact with anyone for a while now.'

Ajay tactfully didn't mention any rumoured stories about the balcony, or that of his team's latest update about the soldier who got tested.

Sir, his phone is left at the barracks all day, but one night it seemed to be at Ashok Apartments. Maybe he was out for night patrol, but something seems off, the message read. *Could it be…?*

'Somehow…' Anitha hesitated.

'Hmm?'

'If Appa's test is also positive then I'll blame myself for putting him in danger.' A gush of emotion welled up in Anitha's throat.

'How is Appa doing?' Ajay asked. 'He seems to be very adamant about staying in isolation and not evening opening the door.'

'Well', Anitha said with a small, tense laugh, 'He refuses to tell me anything. I've been asking him every two to three hours, and all he says is that he is fine. I hear him cough all the time. He says he is taking a Crocin to control the fever. Last night that shifted to Dolo.'

They both sat in silence for a minute.

'Anitha, I think you've been immensely strong through all this, as always. You're always such a pillar of strength for everyone, me included. I'm so proud of you, and I know you will figure out a way to help Sandhya and Suhasini as well. You probably don't need it, but you know I always have your back.' It had taken different kind of strength for Ajay to say so. This was honestly the most he had spoken in years.

Anitha squeezed his hand tighter as she closed her eyes and wondered. Ajay and she didn't share a deep understanding with one another. She had put that part of herself, which needed love and patience, somewhere far away and never ventured near it because it was too painful. She could never watch romcoms, as she would later feel overhwlemed with a sense of wistfulness. She'd always tear up reading a romantic book because she felt that they were just...lucky to experience it. She shut her eyes, mind, soul, to all of that because it was just...easier that way.

But she also knew that he always had her back. He'd be there for her when the chips were down. He always took care of their needs and provided for their bread, no, rather the sourdough. She laughed thinking of it. Was that enough? Anitha threw that eternal question into the universe. There was no right answer, she believed.

Back from a distance, Samyuktha saw the two of them. And instinctively and naturally thought of the one who she shared some understanding with. As she looked at her mother, she realized that she and her were similar, and both were in want of a deep connection. *Amma doesn't need someone who will have her back. She has her own and everyone else's back. What she needs is someone who will encourage her, push her, nurture her desire to keep growing and becoming a better version of herself. Amma needs a champion and so do I,* she continued thinking as memories of her conversations with Abhimanyu flashed in her mind.

The Samyuktha who had returned from IIT around two weeks ago always thought in black and white. She remembered how she had judged Abhimanyu for winking at her, or for his lack of response to Ahalya, or for climbing into her balcony.

But Abhimanyu had not given up on her. He had questioned, debated, asserted and coaxed her into making room for a different possibility, a different perspective. Abhimanyu's insistence on talking things out had made her appreciative of the fact that a bold and adventurous soldier could also have a socially awkward side to his personality. Such had been his impact that she now found herself advocating for the relationship her parents had built with each other and was trying to gauge their vulnerabilities. There was once a time when she had dismissed the entire institution of marriage based on theirs.

As the world around her had entered a lockdown, Samyuktha had set her mind free, and Abhimanyu was her champion. She had learned to loosen up a little. She had learned to speak about her passion for animals from a place of love and joy that was deeper and more genuine than the place of morality that she was operating from. Expressing this in its most raw and vulnerable form had fetched her the prestigious EDF internship. That's the level that Abhimanyu operated at, and relentlessly had pushed her till she got there.

She had taken leaps of faith with him. Did he get hurt as she clung on to him for her dear life? Yes. But she was learning how to not hurt him anymore. What a shame it would be to give up now, when the worst was over. She looked back fondly at the vision of Abhimanyu winking at her. She cheered on that older Samyuktha who had given him a chance, the Samyuktha who had decided to hear him out when he had climbed into her balcony, and the Samyuktha who had taken his advice and poured her heart out into the internship application.

As she looked back at her parents, she now had a newfound fondness for them. Though her own circumstances were different from those of her Appa and Amma, she knew they would always have her back.

Staring at the silhouette of her parents amidst the sunrays around dusk, Samyuktha did what she knew was the right thing to do. `I got into EDF. I wanted you to be one of the first to know,` she messaged Abhimanyu.

⋙∘∘∘

Just as he was putting finishing touches on the Aarogya Setu 2.0 report and was about to log off, a new message popped up. *Subject: Mission Aranya-Expedite.* Curiously, Ajay opened it. A Tibetan leader recently alleged that China was keen on capturing more than just Tibet, it wanted all of Nepal and Bhutan. Other parts of three Indian states were also on their radar. Ajay frowned as he remembered the death of some Indian soldiers in Ladakh the past week as Chinese and Indian forces had clashed briefly at Galwan.

`Request to dispatch asset within 30 days,` the message said.

This ruling party is really serious about investing in security, he thought as he racked his brain trying to think of anyone who could pick up Ladakhi dialects as well as Mandarin easily.

`Noted. Do you have a list of potential candidates from the new recruits?` he replied. Within minutes, a list of three candidates came up, ranked by suitability. Ajay clicked on the first name and stared at the profile and picture that popped up.

⋙∘∘∘

As the ambulance with its loud siren came to a halt in front of Ashok Apartments, all the residents came out on to their balconies to watch. They all knew. Anitha had already asked the hospital to make the best of arrangements, and so they had.

Nurses in pale blue contamination suits got out of the ambulance and made their way to Suhasini's house. They did not allow anyone anywhere near the house citing protocol. They escorted Suhasini to the ambulance. After shifting her to the ambulance, they disinfected the house, especially her room, as best as possible. They also had to test Sandhya for Covid; all the nurses and attendants who had come in contact with her were to self-isolate for forty-eight hours.

As the shocked residents saw Suhasini going out on a stretcher, Ganesh, Ranjini's husband, created another WhatsApp group called 'Ashok Apts minus Kumars'—an extremely creative group name, of course.

Ramesh: I've known Anitha for fifteen years, but what she's done is so irresponsible. I cannot believe that she endangered us like this.

Indrani: I can't believe that the corporation officials had to come here to quarantine them. Don't they have any sense of self-responsibility?

Ganesh: Poor Ajay. I guess he doesn't have a say in any of this.

Indrani: They infected Suhasini, of all people. Poor innocent lady.

Kamala: This is extremely unfortunate. I feel very sorry for Suhasini. But Suresh, how are you so sure it was Anitha? Let's please not jump to conclusions.

Sunil: Guys, do you have any proof that it was her? Are we really saying all this with ZERO evidence?

Krishnan: Who else could it be? Suhasini and Sandhya have not stepped out anywhere, and Anitha is the only one they came in contact with. She actually visited their house and personally checked on Sandhya. Anitha's father is showing symptoms

too. I think their entire family should do the
world a favour and self-quarantine.

Ramesh: I agree with Suresh. All evidence points
to Anitha. While I appreciate the service she is
doing as a doctor, I think it is irresponsible
to infect building residents just because of her
carelessness. She should know better about the
dangers of being an asymptomatic carrier even if
she doesn't have the symptoms.

It went on and on and on. Locked up and nearly with nothing
concrete to do, they stayed busy on their phones.

Samyuktha, Anitha and Ajay watched the ambulance leave.
She knew Suhasini would be well taken care of. Dr Ram had
said he would see to that. Also, both mother and daughter were
in the same hospital. Somehow, it felt right.

As they all came inside their house, Anitha saw Thatha sitting
in the living room and reading *The Hindu*.

'Appa, what are you doing?' she asked, with fear in her eyes.

'I'm done ma kanna, done with the whole thing. Whatever
will happen, will happen,' he said in a defeated, resigned voice.

Anitha and Ajay looked at each other, and then at him
in despair. Samyuktha looked at him curiously. And then she
shrieked in happiness.

'Thathaaaaa! You tested negative, illaya?'

Suddenly, Thatha's expression broke into his toothless smile.
That's all Samyuktha needed to see.

Where there's life, there's joy and there's hope. And that's
what happened to the Kumar family in that instant.

Samyuktha descended on top of him and gave him a bone
crushing hug. Anitha suddenly went mad with joy, with tears
streaming down her eyes. Of course, she knocked down the
corner lamp in the process. One could never believe that she

deftly performed caesareans for a living. And Ajay—he just kept clapping his hands in glee.

At that moment, suddenly, the stress just…dissolved.

It felt like the movies. What was missing was a song playing in the background. But given the elation that the Kumar family felt at that moment, they swore they could hear it.

Ajay switched on the news for the 8.00 p.m. address by the PM. It had been eight weeks since the lockdown. The virus curve was still on the rise, but the government recognized that lockdown couldn't be imposed forever. So, they announced a marginal lift of the lockdown. People were allowed to go outdoors, but only in a group of three or less; wearing masks and carrying santizers were still mandatory. No restaurants and bars were to reopen yet.

As everyone watched and listened intently, they realized that the lockdown was largely about self-discipline, self regulation and self-care more than anything else.

⌒∞⌒

It was time. Samyuktha showed them the email that she'd been waiting for. Thatha, of course, was elated, and her Appa beamed with pride.

As soon as her Amma read the email, tears rolled down her cheeks. She looked at her tenderly and held her close. *This girl will go places I've never been*, she thought. *If there's anything I can do, I will help her clear her path and mind, so that she can march ahead boldly. She's more than capable of taking care of the rest. She'll scale greater heights, and fall deeper than I ever have. After all, both are two sides of the same coin.* When Amma and her eyes met, Samyutha needed to tell her nothing. Everything had already been told.

Anitha then proceeded to finally make the call she had been wanting to for quiet some time. 'Doctor Ram, I'll see you at work tomorrow.' Samyuktha squealed and hugged her Amma.

In the meantime, the WhatsApp messages on Ashok Apartments minus Kumars continued.

∽∾

As the mother and daughter went to Abhijeet's room, they saw him sitting on the edge of the bed, his head hung down, coughing.

'Finally woke up? Those Kumars are infecting the entire building and instead of helping me fight them, all you want to do is sleep without a care?' Indrani asked, annoyed at her husband's lethargy.

'Stay back, Indrani,' his voice sounded rasped. They froze. Looking up at them, he said, 'I have a bad fever and a mild cough.'

The Gangulys looked at each other, fear filling their eyes.

'Mumma, I think we should get Papa tested.'

'*Ekebare na* (Absolutely not)! He is absolutely fine. He is coughing because of his smoking habits and also because there has been a change in weather recently. He has taken a Dolo for his fever, he will be alright by evening. Just don't enter his room, that's all, to be safe, but nothing has happened to him. Where will he get coronavirus from, tell me?'

'Mumma…he returned from the US a few days ago!' she blurted out. 'It could be…'

Ahalya was terrified. Her mother's extreme anxiety had taken over all logic. She wondered if she should let anyone else know. As she stared at the armymen below, she wondered if she should let Abhimanyu know. She dismissed the thought, but it lingered in her subconsciousness.

Abhijeet mustered whatever strength he could and called Indrani. The strain on his lungs brought on a bout of whooping cough. Uncontrollable and progressively increasing, it left him breathless. He pulled himself up to sit straight on his bed, struggling to breathe, wheezing, just as she appeared at the door. He looked at her with tired, guilty eyes.

'Indrani. It's now or never.'

His raspy voice interspersed with uncontrollable cough and the feeling of heat in the room quite likely exuding from his high fever, finally did the trick. Indrani's eyes filled with tears as she looked at him. She nodded in agreement.

✧

Suhasini was staring at the ceiling. The nurse was saying something incoherent in the background, but all she could hear was silence amidst a weird feeling of emptiness. *How had it come to this?*

'...if the symptoms worsen...short on ventilators...fever should reduce...stay calm...' she could intermittently make out what the nurse was saying from behind her masks, head gear and gloves, looking at her with dead and hopeless eyes. *She is probably saying this for the hundredth time today,* Suhasini thought.

She looked sideways at the nurse and nodded gently. Nobody seemed to be telling her what she really wanted to know. What could she do to get better? She tried asking the doctor but they just brushed it off saying she should just relax and rest.

If only they knew that relaxing and resting had never been part of Suhasini's DNA. Since decades, she had been getting up early before dawn for her morning practice before the household woke up. Cooking three meals a day along with giving music lessons to eager young minds struggling to find the right note or the right beat was not an easy task. Her husband used to be the one taking care of all money matters, but after his death, Suhasini had had to take command. It was hard, but not worse than this feeling of helplessness. All she could do now was lie down and wait to get okay soon. There was, after all, Sandhya, who she had to look out for. Her first grandchild was going to be born. Suhasini had been waiting so eagerly to help Sandhya through a time that was both difficult and delightful, just like her own mother had helped her. *Will I even make it?* she wondered as she lay staring at the ceiling.

Suhasini's phone rang. It was Suresh.

'Amma, I'm right here. Arrived an hour ago. You brave girls don't have to worry anymore.'

Suhasini felt a wave of relief amidst her condition. She mustered up all her strength and said, '*Appada* (Oh my goodness),' before falling into deep sleep.

As Anitha drove to the hospital, she gazed out of the car (she had stopped using a driver as a precautionary measure), the streets were calm. The trees seemed greener. The birds were chirpier. Or was it just her imagination? Was it the immense relief of finding out that her family had taken every precaution it could and had tested negative? Was it because her father was now going to be okay soon? Or was it because her daughter had achieved her dream? Anitha laughed and turned up the music as Ziv Zaifman's innocent voice filled the car with the strains of 'A Million Dreams' as she slowly turned towards St. Isabel's Hospital.

In stark contrast to the streets she was looking at till now, St. Isabel's Hospital seemed to be in utter chaos. Panic-stricken patients, visitors, staff and nurses were everywhere; they were clad in masks and gloves, yelling out instructions. What had transpired in the last three days? Amidst all the gratitude, Anitha had a very keen awareness of her mortality at that very moment. She said a silent prayer for everyone, the humans, the living beings and the world at large.

⌒∽⌒

'Shut up,' Samyuktha said into the phone. Abhimanyu had finally called her back, after seventeen missed calls from her.

'What?' Abhimanyu said blankly. 'I haven't said anything.'

'That's your problem. You don't say anything.' Samyuktha cut him off. She was so relieved that she was resorting to snapping at him. *Why not?*

He continued, 'And congratulations again, Turtle... So happy for you. You must be so proud—'

'Why didn't you call me and blast me about how immaturely I have been behaving?' she cut him off unceremoniously. 'Instead, you just stopped speaking with me. How...why did you do that?'

'Because...' Abhimanyu said softly, 'maybe you needed time. And honestly, I don't blame you. After seeing your Thatha at the hospital...'

Samyuktha cut him off again, 'Thanks, *Professor*,' she said scathingly. Now that everyone in her family was doing okay, she could feel her old self returning back. She even felt a little brazen.

'Yes, so the "messers...become the messies"? Is that right?' he asked, quoting her favourite F.R.I.E.N.D.S. reference, rather sheepishly. His cold temper had caused her pain and he was feeling bad about it. He wanted to make up for it in his own way.

'That's completely wrong usage. So like I said, just stop talking,' Samyuktha said. But the edge had been taken off by now.

'Okay. By the way, it's kind of windy out here,' he said wickedly.

'Where?' Samyuktha asked, her heart leaping.

'Outside in your balcony, Turtle,' he said, in a whisper.

She heard a soft knock and opened the balcony door. And there he was.

The next thing they both knew, they were crushed in each other's arms, inextricably.

A few minutes or hours later, none could tell, both Samyuktha and Abhimanyu gazed at the stars at the dead of the night. It was perfect—just the two of them and a soft, humid breeze rustling the trees in the dead of the Mylapore night. As Abhimanyu held her close, he couldn't imagine a time when he didn't know her. And it had been just ten days since they had met.

As for Samyuktha, she was in a state of bliss. All the stress, the worry, the guilt was replaced with a deep sense of contentment. She knew they shared an electric chemistry—one that comes with not just attraction but also a sense of oneness.

'How's everything at home?' Abhimanyu asked her as he kissed her for the hundredth time. He tucked her hair back.

'Finally, manageable. Amma is back at work. Appa has started standing up for Amma, which is awesome. And Thatha is getting better. I went to his room last evening after four days. So weird no? And he had kept it spic and span. Thatha is so awesome.'

Abhimanyu was used to hearing the last sentence as a blanket conclusion to most things. He smiled and looked at her. He just couldn't get enough of her.

'I sometimes wish I had such a lovely family,' he said a little wistfully. 'In my family, Didi is probably the only one like that.'

'What about your aunt in Canada?' Samyuktha asked. Abhimanyu smiled because she remembered.

'Yes, she's awesome. But she's so far away,' he replied, gazing into the distance.

'Distance makes the heart grow fonder,' Samyuktha teased.

'Is that so?' he asked, pulling her closer.

She went on, 'And listen, your friends are your family. Look at them. They'll die for you. Family comes in all shapes and forms, you know.'

'I know,' he said, looking at her. 'Okay. Let's make this night count.' He had the same up-to-no-good look on his face that he had had when he first had entered her balcony.

'What do you mean?' Samyuktha asked, puzzled, but snuggling up closer.

'I'm Covid negative and so are you. And the PM just announced the lockdown relaxation as of...' he checked his watch, '...midnight. Let's hit the city, I say. And paint it red!' Abhimanyu's eyes gleamed.

'How? When? What?' Samyuktha asked. Her mind was in a whirl.

'Meaning...' Abhimanyu gave her a wicked look. 'Today is the practical exam. Theory is done. You told me all your precious Madras. Today, you SHOW it to me. Okay?' he said as he stroked her elbow.

'And what do I get in return?' Samyuktha shot back. 'I'm a selfish, cunning girl, you know.'

Abhimanyu smiled at how untrue that was. 'Of course. The same rule applies to me too. Whatever I've wanted to do with you in theory, I will apply it in practice.' He gave her his crinkly smile. Samyuktha blushed, turning a shade of beetroot.

'Okay, now to be systematic,' he said solemnly. He went in and opened her laptop. 'Unlock this for me.'

'What are you doing?' Samyuktha asked, surprised while she typed her password.

Abhimanyu didn't answer. He connected her laptop and his phone through a video call. He plugged her laptop on charge and removed the 'Sleep after ten minutes'. And just to be safe, he placed her teddy bear on the track pad.

'Now we're set, kanna,' he said, mimicking her expression of endearment, while she was busy comprehending his actions. He kissed her and said, 'Your room...' he shook his hand with a flourish, 'and me are now on a video call. We'll keep checking every once in a while as we paint the town deep crimson.' Samyuktha laughed at his audacity. And suddenly, she was game.

All at once, she could see the next hurdle ahead. 'But...I don't know how to climb down an entire floor,' she said, genuinely terrified. 'I've only scaled walls before,' she said, thinking of the low walls back in her campus.

'I'll teach you,' Abhimanyu said confidently. He sprang down on the pipe and gave her his hand. She looked at it with some hesitation and then at his reassuring eyes. On impulse, she took his hand and climbed down. Thank God, she was wearing her joggers and ASICS.

Masked and carrying a sanitizer, they crept down the apartment. As they got into his jeep and reached the check post, Dhruv was standing guard. He looked at them, and comprehension slowly dawned in his eyes. He checked his watch and said, 'Sir, lockdown lifted, Sir!' He stood up straight, and unflinchingly gave a full army salute to his boss, despite the latter not being in his uniform. Abhimanyu gave a hint of a smile and saluted back. Samyuktha glanced in part wonder and part admiration at this quiet exchange, where very little was said, but all was understood.

As they raced down the street towards his jeep, Samyuktha gave a peal of laughter. All of it felt surreal to her. They were finally, after weeks of intense restriction, doing what she had been imagining, for real.

They sat in the jeep and looked at each other foolishly, panting. Abhimanyu said, 'Let me kick-start the practical exam.' He then pulled her close to him and kissed her, first gently all over her face, and then, more intensely. Samyuktha closed her eyes and succumbed in kind, gently, then eagerly. They looked back softly at each other.

'Hmm…' Abhimanyu said, after he caught his breath. 'Four out of five, I think,' he tried to say it in jest, but his voice broke at the five. Samyuktha smiled and leaned on his shoulder.

'Now, my turn, right?' she asked. 'You know where I want to go first.'

Abhimanyu didn't reply and Samyuktha didn't need him to. He started the ignition and made his way to Marina Beach. As he parked the car near the Kannagi statue, they both looked in silence at the beautiful beach, waves lapping in the distance.

'Race you,' Abhimanyu suddenly said. Samyuktha smiled and started running effortlessly. Abhimanyu smiled, waited and watched her slim elegant figure race ahead, admiring her silhouette against the moon. He now had to race to catch up with her.

As Samyuktha's feet hit the wet sand, she threw her arms wide open, taking in the newfound freedom and liberation after weeks of staying cooped up at home. Abhimanyu caught up, and they both ran alongside till they collapsed panting and lay there looking up at the stars.

'You know,' Samyuktha began, still breathing heavily. 'If I'm feeling so free, without my own species around glaring at me, I can imagine how the penguins and peacocks must be feeling right now. So, a yay for them,' she yelled out the last bit.

'I agree, especially since they can run so much faster than a turtle.' He noticed Samyuktha glaring at him, but continued anyway as he stared into the sky, 'Do you think turtles also swim that slow, or is it just the waddlin—Ouch!' he was interrupted by a sharp jab to his ribs.

He laughed as he dodged a second jab from Samyuktha and got up to leap aside. She, too, laughed and then decided to start walking along the water. Abhimanyu joined her and they held hands as the conversation drifted to EDF.

'Will you actually get to work with animals or will you be a desk jockey running numbers and presentations?' Abhimanyu asked as he stopped to trace an 'A' in the sand.

'Please. I wouldn't have applied if all I would be doing is sit at a desk,' she stepped over and put an S before the A and then an M after it as Abhimanyu glared at her. 'Question is, do

I get a choice on which animals? I'd love to work with pandas. They're so clingy and cute!'

They started walking again. 'What's your scene? Are you ever a *turtle* about anything or always annoyingly hyper-organized?' Samyuktha jumped on to an incoming wavelet before it receded.

'Being hyper-organized and disciplined is not a choice for me. I'm in the army, remember?' Abhimanyu stepped closer to the water as more ripples came in. 'But I'm definitely exploring whether I want to be in infantry or communications or intel, etc. We'll see.' He drew her closer, wanting to change the subject. Samyuktha had no idea what any of those things meant and wanted to ask, but changed her mind as she leaned against him, feeling his rock-hard army-trained body.

They lazily walked some more, silently taking in the gentle sea breeze.

'Didi finally moved out today,' Abhimanyu told her. 'Ayaan got one of our regiment officers to go to their place. She's out of there and in my Maasi's house as of now.' His voice had a sense of relief.

Samyuktha held his hand tighter, waiting for him to say more.

'She deserves better, you know,' he said, looking at the waves lapping against the beach. 'She's so much more. She needs someone who wakes up every morning and says...'

'I'm...with *Rachel*!' Samyuktha completed the thought for him.

Abhimanyu smiled. 'Yes!' he said, getting the *F.R.I.E.N.D.S.* reference instantly. 'She needs someone who sees her for everything she is, not a dwindled down, sad version of herself.' His voice cracked with emotions.

'I know,' Samyuktha said quietly. 'She's better off being alone, than becoming a lesser version of herself, don't you think?' She looked up at him.

'Yes, and thank you for teaching me that,' he said smiling back. Samyuktha brushed the hair from her face and looked into the distance. *It is so true,* she thought. *Never let anyone make you think less of yourself.*

Soon they reached their favourite place—each for very different reasons—The War Memorial. They sat down at the entrance of the Memorial, cross-legged, and looked at the marble epitaphs in quiet solemnity. Abhimanyu put his arm around her and she leaned in naturally as if she'd been doing it for years.

They sat in quietude, not having to say anything, but fully understanding each other at that moment. It was one of those rare moments when one is completely happy. They needed nothing else but each others' company in that moment. They occasionally looked at each other, exchanged a kiss and lapsed back into their quiet reverie.

'Where next?' Abhimanyu asked her gently, an hour later.

Samyuktha roused herself. 'Besant Nagar,' she said with a smile. 'And this time, I want a glass of wine in my hand,' she said with a flash of mischief in her eyes.

Abhimanyu drove to Besant Nagar and parked near the edge of where Adyar and Besant Nagar met. They poured wine and Glen in their paper cups, sitting along the massive, tree-lined avenue. As the heady mix of alcohol and unfettered romance hit their young minds, they burst into laughter at the silliest of things.

'Say *vazha pazham kizha vizhindhudhi* (the banana fell on the floor),' Samyuktha challenged him.

'Please. I already know it,' Abhimanyu replied as he tried to utter the words in his Delhi accent. Samyuktha clutched her stomach howling in laughter as he tried to wrap his drunk and slurring tongue around the alien syllable.

'Okay, your turn,' Abhimanyu was not to be outdone. 'Do this,' he said as he started air DJing with one hand and bouncing an imaginary ball with the other. Samyuktha's eyes widened as she tried to process. She balanced her glass on a red post box sitting quietly on the side of the road, and tried to imitate him. It was Abhimanyu's turn to laugh now as he doubled up at her hilarious attempts at ambidexterity. It didn't take long for her to give up and burst into laughter again.

'That's really difficult, how did you do it so easily?' she exclaimed amidst peals of laughter. 'You are one geek, I tell you.'

They picked up their glasses and started walking again. Abhimanyu felt Samyuktha's hand first on his arm, then shoulder as he quietly smiled. At one point he spoke up, a bit shyly. 'It's the daily workout regimen. I'm glad you love it.'

Samyuktha blushed a deep red. 'I'm so sorry, didn't mean to be weird.'

Abhimanyu laughed and drew her close, 'It's totally cool, I love it. Just wanted to say you don't have to be so shy about it.'

Samyuktha looked at him dreamily and gave him a long passionate kiss. 'That body's so hot,' she started off hesitantly, the alcohol spurring her on. 'I've fantasized about armymen. But talk about reality being way sexier!' she said with a sparkle as she drank from her glass, the other hand still around his neck.

Abhimanyu just laughed, with a hint of a blush, enjoying the moment. 'I know what we should do when I visit you in the balcony next,' he said in a half-whisper as she playfully pushed him away. They continued half-teetering towards nowhere.

As they approached the beach, Samyuktha squealed and pointed to the distance. 'Broken Bridge!' she cried out.

Abhimanyu looked at where she was pointing. There was a lone solitary bridge, which just…stopped in the middle of the ocean. With water lapping all around, it was a serene structure, seeming to lead one to all kinds of possibilities. Abhimanyu drank in the sight hungrily. Somehow, that was like a balm to his soul, which deep down still ached with all the tragedies of his childhood.

Samyuktha saw that look from the corner of her eye. She

moved her face towards him, looking in his eyes, and gave him a giant, bear hug, like she never wanted to let him go.

As Abhimanyu held her close and tight, he felt a comfort like he had never felt before. He didn't want to let go. They both stood there as one, for a while.

'Let's stand at the very edge,' Abhimanyu said, finally releasing her and looking gently at her.

Samyuktha nodded and they both made their way to the bridge. As they went to the very edge, they looked around. All they could see was miles and miles of sky up above and miles of sea below.

Samyuktha took in a deep breath and said, 'I want to stand as close to the edge as I can without going over. Out there on the edge, you see all kinds of things you otherwise cannot see from the centre,' she paused and then added, '...and that's one of my favourite quotes.'

Abhimanyu looked at her with unbridled admiration. Here was this twenty-year-old who was sweet, beautiful, sorted, intelligent, ambitious and so much fun. She was everything rolled into one. And she...wanted to be with *him*. Abhimanyu Singh. He looked at her in quiet admiration as Samyuktha looked into the distance with dreams and hopes in her eyes.

Finally, the first rays of pink started appearing against the sky. They both knew that it was time to go back. They made their way quietly to the jeep and back home. As they reached Ashok Apartments, they were forced out of their reverie.

An ambulance came to a screeching halt outside Ashok Apartments. The siren continued wailing. The nurses and attendants rushed in. *Which house is it?* Samyuktha wondered, as she crept into her house. *And what has happened?*

To their horror, they saw Indrani come out with Abhijeet on a stretcher.

The Greatest Showman

Abhijeet lay, out of breath, too weak to get up, coughing repeatedly. He was unsure if he would make it out of this alive. As he lay there helplessly, he regretted the string of decisions that had led to this moment. He somewhat knew that Ajay and Anitha were extremely selfless and decent people, sometimes he wished they had raised Ahalya and Arun like Ajay and Anitha had raised Samyuktha. *All that shines is not gold*, he remembered his father telling him. And yet he went for the gloss. And then he got that high-flying job of an international sales representative for a large company and all that came with it, whether he liked it or not. His mind wandered back to the time he had landed in Chennai.

As the impact of the landing had woken him up, he had reached out instinctively for his phone. It was 1.00 a.m. 'Hello, Abhijeet?' He could sense from Indrani's voice that she had not slept at all. She had clearly been waiting for his call.

'Just landed, shona. Duty done. Can you please go to sleep now? It'll take me a couple hours to get done with immigration, pick up the baggage and get home,' Abhijeet had said as he yawned and got up to stretch.

'Abhijeet, it's different now. There's apparently a fourteen-day mandatory institutional quarantine one is supposed to undergo after they land from abroad. I'm worried. Can you please call someone who can help you avoid all this?' Indrani had been awake and alert as she rattled out the research she had done all day on this new rule.

'It's just routine checking Indu, nothing serious. They don't have the facilities to quarantine me. It'll mostly be a mandatory quarantine at home for two weeks, what's the harm?' Abhijeet had sounded nonchalant as always, ignoring Indrani's worries and oversimplifying the situation.

'What's the harm? Abhijeet! *Tumi ki bolcho shona* (What are you saying, darling)? You will be in some medical facility full of infected people. Any healthy person can catch Covid in such a place! I can't let that happen to you or us, shona! Think of Ahalya and Arun! Just come home, and we will anyway quarantine ourselves for fourteen days. I promise. No one will even step out. Okay?' Indrani had been alarmed.

Abhijeet had been quite sleepy and this wasn't the conversation he had wanted to be having. He had known Indrani wouldn't budge. Also, he had not been particularly enamoured of going to an institutional quarantine in God-knows-where. 'Okay, I'll talk to him. You're getting unnecessarily paranoid. But promise that we will follow the quarantine strictly, okay?'

And then...Indrani had given that parcel to Suhasini. The parcel, that had possibly led to Suhasini getting infected, as he now realized. He cursed himself. He was probably responsible for that. That lovely lady, with a pregnant daughter at home. Was Sandhya infected, too? He couldn't bear it anymore. He shut his eyes and prayed for forgiveness.

Indrani hung up as she stood outside the Covid ward at St. Isabel's Hospital, tears streaming down her face as she frantically paced around, anxious and nervous. Despite her pleas and crying, they wouldn't let her in. Her mind wandered to Anitha, and a surge of irrational anger bubbled up. Without thinking, Indrani called for an emergency meeting of all residents.

⁂

Abhimanyu woke up promptly at 5.30 a.m. after exactly an hour of sleep. As he switched off the alarm, he lay in bed processing the first moments of consciousness. He could hear sparrows chirping, pigeons cooing and a solitary koel singing in the distance. *Has this been happening everyday and I never noticed, or has the animal kingdom finally found its freedom as the humans stay locked in?* He felt a sense of calm and joy as he looked around his brightly lit room with the sunlight streaming in.

He closed his eyes for a moment and thought about the previous night and morning with Samyuktha. He remembered how he had held her face in his hands and kissed her passionately. Then he opened his eyes, sensing his imagination getting wilder, and got up to stretch and get ready for his morning workout.

Abhimanyu was feeling extra energetic this morning, even with less sleep than usual. He did thirty more push-ups and two more sets of plank jacks, going overboard with his usual routine. Ayaan gave him a goofy smile.

'Look who's back!' he said, as he looked at his friend, who looked sleep deprived but happy. '*Kya hua, bhai* (What is the matter, brother)? You seem over the moon today!'

Abhimanyu told him about last night, tactfully leaving out the intimate details. Ayaan listened in amazement. It was so unlike Abhimanyu to speak this way. He had known this guy forever and yet had never heard him speak of anyone with such...was it passion, reverence or just fun?

'Holy moly, Abhi,' he said, 'You're in love! Not movie love, but the real deal.' He picked up a weight with one hand and punched him with the other.

Abhimanyu looked at him in surprise. *Is that true?* Ayaan had never said these words to him, ever before. Even during those times when Abhimanyu thought he was in love, Ayaan had seen through it immediately.

'I'm serious,' he said. 'This is special. Keep this safe, okay?'
Ayaan looked at him long and hard before resuming his push-ups.

Dhruv came running up to him, panting. 'Sir, Major Verma
has asked you to come to Ashok Apartments as soon as possible.'

'My shift starts in thirty minutes. *Kya hua* (What happened)?'
Abhimanyu didn't wait for the answer. An order from Major
Verma was like gospel truth. *Ours is not to question why, ours
is but to do and die.* The lines from 'The Charge of the Light
Brigade' flashed in Abhimanyu's mind.

He raced to Warren Road to find that Ashok Apartments
had an unusual visitor. MLA Balasamy had come to know about
the lady who had tested positive, courtesy Indrani. Abhimanyu
watched in intrigue as a white government car with a rose flag
hoisted on the bonnet rolled to a stop outside the building.
Two *veshti*-clad men in pure white clothes, with moustaches
and *veeboodhi* (sacred ash) on their foreheads and masks on
their mouths stepped out.

*Sarkar meets Grey's Anatomy. If not for the pure white
attire, they could pass off as goons in any Indian movie,* thought
Abhimanyu as one of them beckoned him, 'That virus case, this
building no? One lady, correct?'

৵৹

Thatha woke up feeling better after a long time. He looked at
the clock. It was 7.30 a.m. He had slept for ten hours straight.
He stretched and realized that this was the first time in the last
four days that he hadn't woken up with a fever. He looked at
Parvati's picture and winked.

'Not coming to you today, ma. Have to go out and see
your family.'

He went out, feeling sprightly. He saw his family sitting
there looking sombre. '*Enna aachu* (What happened)?' he asked,

stretching. 'Why do you all look like dead ducks?'

'Appa, you look so much better. How are you feeling?' Anitha sounded tired yet relieved.

'Back to normal, ma. Just a matter of a few days.' His eyes now twinkled as before. 'But why are all of you looking so grim?'

'Abhijeet Ganguly fainted and had to be taken to the hospital late at night, Appa...' Anitha said. 'We all got to know in the night.' *That last part isn't entirely true,* Samyuktha guiltily thought. She said nothing.

'I wonder what is wrong? The man seemed fine just two days ago,' Anitha said. This time, Ajay didn't say anything.

'Thatha, come and have breakfast.'

Samyuktha was the happiest to see Thatha hale and hearty once again. Seeing him weak and tired had completely messed with Samyuktha's mind, the depth of which she only realized when she saw him healthy again.

'Samyuktha made breakfast?' Appa asked with a smile.

Samyuktha had taken Abhimanyu's advice seriously and made a resolution to help more around the house. After her night out, she went home deliriously happy and sanitized every inch of herself and then took a quick shower.

Soon, it was dawn. She then headed straight for the kitchen. She looked up the upma recipe, painstakingly ferreted out the ingredients and prepared it all from scratch. She was proud of it, until she looked at the kitchen.

It was a disaster—pots strewn around, rava on the floor, vegetable peel everywhere. *How did it get on top of the cabinet there*? Samyuktha wondered. She was blessed with her mother's klutziness. She looked around and sighed, and then started cleaning. *Even the gods can't unscramble eggs,* she thought. *The mess I make, I need to clean.* Strangely comforted by her literal and figurative statement, she started scrubbing.

As she sat down for breakfast, she saw Amma's and Thatha's smile and watched Appa relish the food. All her tiredness vanished.

'*Pramadhama irukku* (It tastes brilliant),' Thatha said, enjoying the breakfast, with his old appetite returning.

After breakfast, Samyuktha sat next to Thatha and watched the news like old times. Covid-related deaths had surpassed 200,000 in the United States. People in Maharashtra were gathering in crowds to protest lack of essential supplies promised to them. Starvation deaths were rising in North India as the virus had left daily wage labourers jobless. Though she was drained, she couldn't stop smiling. Anitha noticed her looking happier than even before. *It must be EDF,* she thought, incorrectly for a change.

Sitting in a corner, Anitha was busy writing up some discharge papers when she asked Samyuktha, 'Did you get to speak to Sandhya today?'

'She's better Amma. Her mind is, at least, off Suhasini aunty, now. I bored her with inane details of quantum physics and other nonsense,' Samyuktha said, smiling. She was thinking of Abhimanyu and what he would have done in a situation like that.

Anitha smiled for a brief second and then said solemly, 'If it doesn't get better, soon she may be put on a ventilator, Samyuktha. I think she'll pull through. But it doesn't look good, to be honest. But,' looking at Samyuktha's face fall, she steered the course of the conversation, 'there have been way more cases than the media has reported of people recovering despite being put on a ventilator.'

Samyuktha frowned. None of what Anitha said was very reassuring. She yawned. 'I am so tired, Amma. Didn't slee—' she stopped mid-sentence.

Anitha looked at her daughter and paused. It was as if

Samyuktha knew something already. 'Why didn't you sleep?' she asked.

Samyuktha felt her hands go clammy under her mother's suspicious gaze. *Nothing escapes her, damn.* 'No, Amma, just. The ambulance noise. The late nights studying…'

'It's time for Indrani's emergency meeting, Anitha,' Thatha said, prodding her to get up. They all trooped into the balcony with their devices and saw that everyone else had also done the same.

'Nosey parkers everyone,' Anitha said in frustration. 'No work, only all this drama.' Thatha agreed, but he secretly loved the drama.

⤜∞⤛

Suhasini woke up in a cold sweat. The soft humming of the patient monitor with its intermittent beeps was the only sound in the cold, white-walled room with a solitary window on her left. The IV tube ended in a small contraption that was taped to her wrinkly hands with the veins popping out. She had always hated being in environments like this. *I should've continued the yoga routine the past two weeks,* she thought, wondering if her immunity had been affected. She had briefly forgotten about herself as she had been busy pampering Sandhya with four meals a day. *Where did all the time go?*

Three masked doctors had put her on a potent blend of medication, hoping to control the symptoms. Though there had been some relief initially, she could feel the raspy breathing and cough coming back, and her body was heating up again.

As she lay on the bed, Suhasini tried hard to imagine something pleasant to keep her spirits high. She would not let this virus defeat her, not now when her daughter needed her the most.

She did what she loved to do best. Alapana in Kalyani, Sandhya's request.

It turned out to be a bad idea. After a few cracked opening notes, she suffered another uncontrollable bout of coughing.

Just then, a nurse came in to check on her and left after checking her vitals. Within a few minutes, another battery of masked doctors came in as Suhasini's cough refused to abate and her fever kept rising. She realized she wasn't being able to breathe as she tried to respond to the doctor's questions. She wasn't sure if it was even her own voice. The dry grated rasp that emanated was both painful and alien to her.

Minutes later, Suhasini was put on a ventilator. A feeling of panic gripped Suhasini as she felt lonely and helpless amidst a set of masked humans, unable to breathe or speak. She wanted to see a familiar face or hold Sandhya's hand. It was disconcerting to be lying down with one hand debilitated by the IV, a plastic contraption covering half your face, with no loved one nearby. Tears started rolling down her face as disturbing visuals started popping up in her mind. Slowly, she started wondering if she would ever see Sandhya again.

৵৹

As Abhimanyu reached the scene, all residents were on their balconies, each of them with their phones, waiting in anticipation for their own Netflix original to start.

The State versus The Kumars.

Samyuktha pinged him. *Major showdown on Zoom and on balcony, she said. Don't know why.* Major Verma, his commanding officer, who was in charge of all of Chennai, was there.

As if on cue, a white Accent drew up and two moustached men in masks got out. One of them was MLA Balasamy.

Indrani logged in from St. Isabel's Hospital, looking distraught and red-eyed, amidst the hustle and bustle of nurses and patients milling around behind her.

Abhimanyu peered at the screen. *Ah there she was.* Samyuktha was the prettiest on that screen. Abhimanyu bit back a lovestruck smile.

Indrani greeted the MLA in tears. 'I've been telling everyone in this building for days now but no one has bothered to listen. My husband has tested Covid positive. And so has poor Suhasini.'

Ganesh chipped in to show his support. 'Because of Anitha's carelessness, why should Abhijeet have to be in this situation? They're infecting everyone.'

Abhimanyu's colleagues beckoned to him and he took his position in the army cordon surrounding the drama at the centre.

Easwaran, the treasurer, helpfully chipped in, 'I demand immediate action, Sir. That family needs to be isolated or sent to live elsewhere. Who will it be next? I, for one, am not waiting to find out,' he said with an air of finality.

MLA Balasamy nodded. His job was to 'dispense justice'. He looked around to see who he could pile on to. He turned to the Major.

'Is this how you guard the community, Major Verma? Is this your duty to the country? How are you allowing this family to happily infect everyone in the building? What is the protocol?' he spit out the last few words, wetting his mask.

'Sir, we are doing our duty as stipulated. We got a notification from the Medical Board to allow Dr Anitha Kumar to resume services. As far as I have been briefed,' Major Verma tried to spit the words out, but his dignified demeanour didn't allow it, 'that is the protocol.'

Major Verma spoke addressing everyone on the Zoom call. Even if he hadn't, everyone would have heard him. He had commanded many battalions with that voice.

Ganesh was in full form now. 'She must have manipulated it,' he said. 'Did you ask her to get tested? That family is a bunch of liars. Do you even know what Ajay does in his secret office room that no one is allowed to enter? No one does. One big secret operation is running in there.'

'I have seen that secret room when I have visited the house,' Mr Parameswaran from B-26 said feebly.

'Sir, honestly that is not the army's business,' Major Verma said. *And it shouldn't be yours,* he thought, but was too much of a gentleman to say.

Indrani was having a full-fledged anxiety attack by now.

'And did you know that one of your soldiers climbs into her balcony at night. *Pata bhi hai aapko* (Do you even know about it)?'

Abhimanyu, expressionless, looked at the floor. Samyuktha went pale but was smart enough not to react. Ahalya smiled.

And then someone said on the Zoom call.

'Enough!'

⁖

Sandhya was squirming in pain. Suresh had gone down for lunch. She pressed the bell. Promptly, the nurse came in.

'What's the matter, ma?'

'Shooting pain… contractions…' was all Sandhya was able to manage.

The nurse took one look at her and called the duty doctor.

Soon, a platoon came in. Anitha had trained her battalion well. BP. Check. Fetal heartbeat. Check. A slew of machines were connected to her.

As the doctor on duty checked her, she said, 'She's six centimetres, nurse. Start an epidural drip and call the father. And, please call Dr Anitha immediately.'

Meanwhile, Suhasini woke up with a start. She knew

something was happening. *Something was up.*

She immediately pressed the buzzer next to her. The nurse, fully clad in protective clothes, came in immediately. 'What's happening? How is Sandhya? My daughter. She's in Room 3048,' she croaked.

The nurse checked Suhasini's vitals. For the first time in six days, she didn't have a fever. However, she was tired and groggy. 'I'll check on your daughter, Ma'am,' she said.

After what seemed like an eternity, the nurse came back. 'Ma'am, your daughter just went into labour. They are wheeling her into the OT.' The nurse kept checking Suhasini's IV, assiduously averting her eyes from the emotion welling up in her eyes. The nurse was keen enough to know that she didn't want it to be noticed.

Suhasini tried to sit up straight. *That moment is finally here*, she thought, overjoyed. She looked at the nurse. 'Has Anitha been told?' she asked in a croak.

The nurse smiled as if she were pre-empting the question. 'Yes, Ma'am, and she's coming in shortly,' Suhasini fell back, relieved. That's all she needed to hear.

⁘

Everyone was curious to know who was it who had said 'enough'. And then it was obvious to all. There was Ajay Kumar in the list of participants, unmuted.

'Anitha has tested negative. And so has my father-in-law. There is absolutely no infection in this house, lady,' referring to Indrani for effect and respect. 'Please explain on what basis you are accusing us.'

'I don't believe you,' Indrani screamed.

Anitha had had enough. She beckoned to Samyuktha. 'How do I...?'

Samyuktha didn't need to hear anymore. She shared her mother's Zoom screen with everyone, showing the two emails that she got stating that both her and her father were negative.

'Then if the Kumars are all safe, then who has spread this?' the logical Mr Sreenivasan from A-12 asked.

Silence.

'Abhijeet Ganguly,' a voice said.

Everyone furiously checked their screens to see who was speaking. It was Ajay. Again. The silent man had suddenly become the centre of attention now.

'He was the first one to get infected, and hid it from the building. He's the one responsible for Suhasini's infection.'

Everyone fell silent and looked at Indrani in disbelief. At that moment, Anitha's phone rang. She listened. And quickly wore her protective gear.

'It's Sandhya,' she told Samyuktha. 'She's in labour. You fill me in on this saga later on. We have a baby coming soon.' Saying so, she hugged Samyuktha and ran out of the door, knocking a stream of books and that poor lamp in the process, again.

Anitha, showing her medical pass and getting out of the gate, caused the next stir. Dhruv smartly saluted her and helped her make her way out. As she left, everyone shifted back their attention to what was going on. It was like an opera, and everyone had balcony seats.

MLA Balasamy looked at Indrani and then looked up at Ajay. The former had fear on their faces for the first time.

'It is true,' Ajay said calmly. 'And it is this MLA who helped him hide his infection when he returned from abroad.'

'What do you mean I was involved, man? Don't drag me into all this. I barely know their family, and strictly follow the government's instructions,' MLA Balasamy was shouting as he looked at Major Verma, Ajay and the army personnel around.

'Tell me,' Ajay continued, 'Did anyone know that Abhijeet Ganguly returned from abroad a few days ago? Everyone who returned were mandatorily quarantined with a stamp. Why did Abhijeet not get the stamp?'

Indrani froze with fear at this point. *How did this man know all this?*

MLA Balasamy looked at Ajay and spoke. 'Sir, this is quite a serious allegation. I hope you understand the consequences of such a statement. Do you have any proof for what you are saying? I can have you thrown in jail—'

Major Verma interrupted him, 'Sir, I don't mean to be rude, But I can guarantee you that he has proof of everything he is saying. I definitely would not challenge him of all people.' Seeing his expressionless cold gaze, the MLA piped down.

Indrani continued on.

'So...well what if he returned...many others did too...doesn't mean he had anything. What proof do you have? Anitha is the one who is exposed to hundreds of patients every day. And that soldier who climbs into your balcony, the one who probably meets hundred other people on the streets each day...'

She was interrupted again by Ajay's voice.

'Careful, Indrani, you are crossing a very dangerous line here. Do you have any proof for any of your accusations? Show me proof and I will take the blame.'

Indrani paused to think and looked at Ahalya. 'Beta, tell them.'

Ahalya knew when she was cornered. She blurted out incoherently, 'Yes unc—uncle...I know a soldier climbs into her balcony sometimes at night. I've seen them smile at each other during the day when Samyuktha is in the balc—'

'Do you have proof? Are there photos or videos of this said soldier climbing up?' Ajay demanded. '...before you malign my daughter's character.'

Ahalya froze. She had never seen Ajay uncle speak like this.

❧

Anitha wore her scrubs, sanitized herself and rushed straight into the operating theatre. Her efficient team was already there. She checked the vitals and the stats. Everything was normal.

Good girl, she thought. *And her girl too,* she smiled. Anitha had known it was going to be a girl all along.

'I need to make a call,' she said. She dialled a number and was quickly put through. 'Suhasini,' she said clearly, 'your girl is about to become a mother.' She heard sobbing at the other end.

'Please take care of her.'

'You know I will,' Anitha said and hung up.

She came into the OT and saw Sandhya smiling weakly at her. Suresh, too, was there, wearing scrubs.

'Everything is fine, kanna,' she said patting her head.

'Does Amma know?' she asked.

Anitha uncharacteristically had tears in her eyes.

'Yes. And you know what? Her temperature was reported to be normal for the first time in four days. Your little unborn baby has already brought so much luck.'

❧

Ajay repeated his question. 'Ahalya. Do you have proof? Are there photos or videos of soldiers climbing up into the balcony that is right below your house?'

Ahalya slowly spoke.

'N—no...I don't but I'm sur—'

'Has this entire family lost their mind? You think with the army standing guard outside, one of the soldiers can possibly climb up into a balcony without being noticed?'

'Indrani,' he calmly looked at her. 'Shouldn't you know better than to believe made-up theories from a teenager who in all likelihood was bored? And then you bring it up with absolutely no proof or verification?'

None dared to respond. Finally, Mr Sanjay spoke up.

'Mr Kumar,' he said, 'I think all the residents of Ashok Apartments owe you an apology, and an unconditional one at that. We're sorry for even remotely doubting your or your wife's intentions and actions. Believing a lot of lies and fabrications reflects poorly on us.'

He paused. He was impeccable with his words.

'I'd request if you can put this behind you… and…'

'Sandhya had a baby girl!' Samyuktha squealed into the Zoom call. 'Amma just messaged!'

Suddenly, the gloom, the doubt, the anger, all of that dissolved. All the residents slowly broke into smiles and then laughs, one by one.

That newborn at St. Isabel's Hospital managed to bring everyone at Ashok Apartments together again.

A Whole New World

'Thatha, just move back a little,' Samyuktha said as she adjusted Amma's iPhone to capture a portrait photograph of him. Thatha stepped back and gave his smile, posing amidst the glorious fare that he had cooked.

'This is a perfect thumbnail for "Tiffin with Thatha"!' Samyuktha said as she clicked the picture. Anitha looked at her Appa with a smile. Who knew that a seventy-four-year-old could start his own YouTube channel?

After watching Thatha everyday during the lockdown, Samyuktha felt that MasterChef was an understatement for his talent. So she had pushed him to start a cooking channel. Thatha had poo-poohed the idea initially, until Samyuktha had filmed him in secrecy one day, edited it and showed him the final video on a YouTube link. Thatha had seen it, and smiled and laughed with a childlike glee.

After that, he had been the most enthusiastic of the lot! They had four episodes out already, six waiting to be edited and had plans for two more before Samyuktha returned to her campus in two weeks' time.

Samyuktha came up with the name 'Tiffin with Thatha'. In every video, Thatha would make some improvization or the other to his dishes, whether it was a dash of salsa with appalam, or a hint of jaggery to sambar, or even crushed chia seeds in the beans poriyal!

As Samyuktha looked at the beautiful photograph with

Thatha smiling amidst *urulai roast, vengayavetha kuzhambu* and *mango pachidi,* she reflected on the last month.

Little Sandhya was about to turn a month old. Shruti Suresh, as she had been named, was coming home, discharged the same day as her grandmother.

Anitha ensured that Suhasini's home had been scrubbed by professional cleaners. Thatha had made extra food for everyone. Samyuktha had been tasked with welcoming them and dropping off the food at their house.

After the apartment showdown, Abhijeet Ganguly's condition had worsened very quickly. He had been put on a ventilator immediately but passed away within six days. While his entire family had also been Covid positive, it turned out that they had been asymptomatic carriers.

Abhijeet uncle's death had shaken Samyuktha and the entire apartment complex. She had grown up with Ahalya and Arun, and had many fond memories of Abhijeet uncle. Indrani was devastated, but had handled the shock as bravely as she could. Her brother had flown in from Delhi and taken the three of them back with him. He was a lovely person, who cared for his little sister beyond anyone else.

Before she left for the airport, Indrani had called Anitha. 'I'm sorry, Anitha. People like you should be celebrated, and what I did was...just the opposite,' she had said, sobbing.

Everyone in the complex had then been tested. Luckily, the infection hadn't spread any further. Ashok Apartments had heaved a collective sigh of relief. One death. One hospitalization. Three asymptomatic carriers. They had had their fair share. The building had been sealed for fourteen days right after Abhijeet had gotten hospitalized and nobody had been allowed to enter or exit.

Samyuktha and Abhimanyu, who could hardly stay apart, hadn't been able to meet each other for those fourteen days.

Be it the hastily exchanged messages, poking fun at each other, sharing the most inane of things during their work or study hours, the chai break phone conversations, the nightly Zoom calls, they were inseparable in mind and spirit. They were both deliriously happy.

Once the fourteen-day seal was lifted, Abhimanyu and Samyuktha were able to go out on proper dates. She would head out under some pretext—to meet friends or to clear her mind. They would spend hours together. She showed Abhimanyu her favourite spots in Chennai, her school, her college, her favourite chaat place, her favourite cafe, her favourite pub... Abhimanyu drank it all in, loving how close she was to him and how he got the chance to see her world from her eyes.

One afternoon as they were lazily strolling through the lanes around Chamiers Cafe after a sumptuous meal, Abhimanyu commented, 'Chennai feels like a city that is trying hard to keep the balance between the old and new.'

Samyuktha thought for a moment and asked, 'Tell me more. What makes you say that?' They passed by yet another temple. *I haven't taken him to a temple yet,* she thought to herself.

'Well,' Abhimanyu paused to think. 'Chennai has been a metropolis for almost as long as Delhi and Mumbai have been.'

She smiled and continued, 'Yes, so your point is that it doesn't look as metropolitan as those other cities?'

'Yeah, but not in a bad way. It almost feels like Mumbai doesn't really have much history left except for the architecture in South Bombay or a few ancient campuses, like IIT Bombay,' he added tongue-in-cheek as Samyuktha gave him a jab in the ribs. 'Remember learning about the ancient university of Takshashila?' he chuckled. 'But seriously, it's dotted with malls and skyscrapers and all things new and modern. Delhi possibly has a lot more in terms of monuments, but there's a clear line between the modern and the old in both cities. Meanwhile, Chennai seems to have the best of both worlds. We just ate at this Italian cafe and stepped out to walk amidst residences that haven't been converted yet into some luxurious open-layout villa while a cow passes us by,' he watched the bovine citizen with amusement.

'Yes and I love that about this city,' Samyuktha added as she looked more keenly at the markers of legacy all around. 'There are certain things that make Chennai as we know it, or Madras rather, and it wouldn't feel like home if they suddenly morphed into something I would see in Singapore.'

'There's a quote,' Abhimanyu began remembering, 'about the feeling of coming home. When nothing changes, and everything looks, feels and smells the same, you realize what's changed is you.' He paused as they both thought about it. 'It's nice to have a place that reminds you of your past self sometimes, just so you realize how much you've changed. I returned to Ambala last year to visit my childhood home and refresh my memories, but the challenge with army quarters is that it goes through many families, and now nothing from my childhood remains there,' he said wistfully. But he instantly smiled again and said, 'I hope Mylapore and Ashok Apartments retain their identity long enough for you to write a book about them that resonates with those who live here then.'

Samyuktha felt a newfound appreciation for all the things she could still recognize in her city and how she could relate moments from her childhood with each of those things. She remembered how her eyes would open wide at the mere mention of ice cream at Freez Zone when she was all but a seven-year-old, how she loved having chaat at the stalls on Marina Beach as a thirteen-year-old and how she loved exploring the city with her friends.

'Do you miss not having a childhood home to go back to?' she asked Abhimanyu. He looked at her fondly for a moment before replying, 'I do. But maybe next time I'll just visit Chennai to feel like a child again,' he winked before adding, 'I'll land up at C-11 and demand to be fed idlis on the balcony.' Samyuktha laughed. He then added after a pause, 'I have Shalini didi, and as long as she is happy, I will remain fond of my childhood memories.'

'How is she doing?' Samyuktha asked softly.

Abhimanyu updated her on his sister's new life. Shalini Didi had moved in with her childhood friend and they were both living as young, carefree ladies. It was definitely difficult for her, but with each passing day, Abhimanyu could sense her old sunny and cheerful self returning back.

'Look at her,' he showed Samyuktha an Instagram story. Shalini didi, wearing a charcoal pack on her face, could be seen laughing till she cried, with her friend Dhanya by her side. Samyuktha looked at it and smiled. Shalini didi did look happy and carefree. She had the same eyes as Abhimanyu, and gorgeous curly hair along with a lovely dimple. Samyuktha looked at Abhimanyu looking at the picture and her eyes softened seeing his love for his sister. Instinctively, she gave his shoulder a squeeze.

'What are you staring at?' he said, keeping the phone away and looking at her.

'The photograph,' Samyuktha said untruthfully. Abhimanyu laughed. They were staring at the moon, sitting on the patio of Sera. This was the first time they had stepped out for a drink, and Samyuktha was amazed at the precautions that were being taken. She had already sanitized her hands. The waiters were all gloved. There was a gap of two empty tables after every table. The glasses, the bowls, everything they needed for their meal, was sanitized in front of their eyes. On the one hand, she was impressed, but on the other, she cringed at the amount of waste that was being generated with all the cleaning.

'I know you're worried about the environment with all this

plastic and waste, Turtle,' Abhimanyu said as he read into the small frown forming between her forehead. 'You're forgetting that you probably wondered the same about the lockdown a few months ago. Hasn't that ended? You worry too much for no reason.' Abhimanyu looked at her with a smile. He then leaned forward and slipped his hand in hers. 'This too will, if fine people like you work to make a difference.'

They paused as the masked, glove-clad server brought their drinks and food. A Long Island Iced Tea for Samyuktha and a Black Label on the rocks for Abhimanyu.

She looked at him wistfully. 'Just like our time together.' His smile weakened as he grasped her hand tighter. 'I know we've been avoiding the topic. But it hurts to think that I don't know where you will be posted next. As if the thought of you leaving wasn't bad enough already...' she looked away as her eyes moistened.

'You know, I've never hated that part of army life in all these years...' She looked back at him. '...until now,' he added softly as he lowered his eyes and then looked up again. 'I never imagined doing anything else for a career.'

'Maybe become a spy?' Samyuktha mustered a smile, wanting to cheer things up a bit.

Abhimanyu looked at her, amused, 'Why do you say that?'

'It just struck me the other day,' Samyuktha said lazily without thinking, tracing frost patterns on the glass. 'You climbing into the balcony while your own colleagues and my cyber security expert father never noticed, your burner phone being untraceable, you leaving me that crumpled test result on the landing.' Samyuktha had looked up at the sky again. 'I just felt you could be a good spy if you wanted to.' She didn't notice Abhimanyu stiffening up the slightest bit.

❧

Ajay eyed Samyuktha in a new light as she walked into the kitchen. Minutes later, Anitha came out, dragging her feet and yawning. Samyuktha, Ajay and Thatha were amused.

Samyuktha had finally convinced Anitha to take a break from work after a rigorous month. While the number of coronavirus cases continued, hospitals were now inundated with patients for regular concerns, such as blood pressure, fertility issues, diabetes. There was no respite. Dr Ram had insisted, fortunately, that his staff take a break when they can, else Anitha would've never been the one to ask for leave. Samyuktha said a silent thank you in her mind to Dr Ram as she watched her mother teeter into the kitchen and plonk herself at the dining table like a hungover teenager.

Without a word, Samyuktha picked up Anitha's plate and loaded it with generous portions of idlis, vadas, sambar and chutney, and placed it in front of her mother. Anitha's eyes grew wide, 'Thanks, kanna,' she looked fondly at her daughter. 'But I'm also not Jambavati, illaya?' she said as she put back a few idlis before starting to eat in good earnest.

Thatha and Samyuktha exchanged glances and smiled like kids as they watched Anitha eat.

'What date is it?' Ajay perked up suddenly as he looked around at the others. 'Is it the twenty-fifth already?' he put his spoon down.

'That's tomorrow.' Thatha squinted at the Kalanjali calendar hanging on the wall before looking back at his son-in-law. Samyuktha looked at him curiously, 'Why Appa?'

'We need to book your flights back to Mumbai. Airlines will be starting bookings again soon,' he said as he went back to his half-eaten idli.

Samyuktha felt a tinge of pain at the thought. *Back already?* She looked at her father, eating away. She then glanced at her

Amma, who was looking at her keenly.

'How about that Velveteen afternoon sometime, kanna?' she asked her with a wicked smile.

'I say, no time like the present!' she whispered back. A small smile began to form on Anitha's lips and the mother–daughter duo smiled wickedly at each other. Anitha winked. If there was one thing the virus had taught her, it was to not miss out on the small joys.

⌒⌒

Abhimanyu and the gang were walking around the narrow lanes of Burma Bazaar. In two weeks, he was meant to leave. He wanted to spend some time with his buddies, exploring the city the way they wanted to. He loved the hustle and bustle of grey markets in the narrow lanes as much as the monuments and museums, or probably more. He observed the locals in this crowded part of Chennai's George Town and how they seemed different than the rest of the city. The spirits brighter, the buzz chirpier. As he stopped to have Irani chai at a hole-in-the-wall thela, he saw a group of four lungi-clad youth chattering away while sipping their coffee.

Abhimanyu, with his jawans, went to the same thela and had coffee together, discussing the events of the last month. They all had a great time as always, but were unusually quiet. They knew their time together was coming to an end, and each of them was trying to process it in their own way.

Sukhi was planning to visit his village near Lucknow. '*Eat maa ke haath ka khaana,* (eat home-cooked food) sleep and drink. That's the only plan for two weeks, bhai,' he said merrily.

Ayaan was planning a vacation with his parents and sister 'somewhere not this hot'. Anish was due for a promotion, so his commander had already sent him orders to report in three days to Meerut Cantonment.

'*Aur Abhi, tu* (And Abhi, you)? What's the plan?' Ayaan asked him. Abhimanyu shook himself out of his trance as he thought of life beyond Chennai and Samyuktha. He knew he wanted to go to see Didi, for sure. He was sure of that. And then…after that… He tried to shake away the wistfulness as it struck him that there was no guarantee their next posting would be together. His mind went back to his last conversation with Major Verma the day before.

'Quite some drama that afternoon, eh?' Major Verma had said, referring to the day of the showdown.

'Yes Sir, I remember.' Abhimanyu had replied in his usual brief and to-the-point tone.

'As Abhijeet Ganguly passed away, Mr Ajay Kumar did not want to file the report.' Major Verma had explained, detailing how the MLA had also gone to great lengths to cover up his wrongdoing. Abhimanyu marvelled at how easy it was for someone in a position of power to change a narrative, and even lives in the process. Someday he knew, he, too, would have to deal with such characters.

Major Verma seemed to have read his mind. He continued, '*Achha*, so with the lockdown being lifted, we are all going to be heading back soon. I see you have put in a request for something rather challenging for your next assignment, Abhi?'

Abhimanyu perked up. 'Yes, Sir. I have, Sir,' he smiled.

'Very well then. All the best Abhimanyu. Hope you get what you are aiming for. I'll make sure to put in a good word,' Major Verma smiled back. Abhimanyu felt a surge of delight. First Samyuktha, then Shalini didi's liberation and now this. *Good things come in threes,* he thought as he marched out. *Not bad, Chennai!*

Samyuktha's college WhatsApp group was abuzz with messages. Even though dates had been announced for the new semester, it had come with the caveat that it depended on how the situation would turn out to be eventually.

—Denmark has reopened schools.

—Ya dude, US is also not extending its lockdown any further.

—Big surprise. NOT. Their leader is nuts.

Wow such mature debates. Samyuktha's eyes glazed over the flood of messages with no interest.

Sharanya's text came in, 'Samyu! Let's start planning that karaoke party, girl!'

'Sharan, the last time you got this excited about it, a virus took over the world, remember?' Samyuktha replied along with a facepalm GIF.

Sharanya replied with that of a stern-looking lady glaring back at her disapprovingly. 'Shut up. Don't be a bore. Let's get that list of songs sorted soon, anything to start feeling like it'll all be normal again. What do you say?' Samyuktha didn't know what to say, but Sharanya could hear her even in silence. 'Oh God. Please don't tell me this is about having to leave that soldier. What are you, Preity Zinta in *Veer Zaara*?' Sharanya sat down to calm herself and her tone, tugging at her hair.

Samyuktha took a deep breath. 'I know. Remember when I told you I've only known him for two months?' her voice trailed off as tears rolled down her face. She just needed to blurt it out, and that's what she did over a good part of the hour with her best friend.

∽∾

As Abhimanyu climbed over the railing and landed on the balcony floor, silent as a cat, he found Samyuktha staring out into the distance. He stood there for a few moments in silence, taking in that picture of her in the moonlight. She was dressed in a simple white sleeveless kurta, paired with jeans. She wore a bindi, as she would only on rare occasions, and a thin bracelet of gold. She had done up her kajal on both upper and lower eyelids, which made her eyes look even more striking than usual.

'It's unfair that you're so beautiful,' he said quietly as they both gazed out of the balcony.

Samyuktha blushed and looked at him. He was wearing a white linen shirt over navy blue khaki pants, his shirt glowing in the moonlight.

'The world isn't very fair, I guess.' She smiled with a look of wistfulness in her eyes as she walked into his open arms. He kissed her and she gave in to his crushing embrace as her tears fell on to his white shirt. He looked at her, long and hard, and brushed away the tears from her eyes. They hugged again, without saying anything. As the wave of emotions passed, Abhimanyu led her to the loveseat, where they snuggled, staring at the full moon in silence.

'What are you thinking?' Abhimanyu asked her, mindlessly tousling her hair after a few moments of silence.

Samyuktha paused for a moment. 'Well. It started with how things would never be the same again for Ahalya and Arun, but then I went on to how things won't ever be the same in the world either, or for me, for that matter,' she said in a tone devoid of any emotion.

'How come?' Abhimanyu asked as he made a mental calculation. He was leaving for Delhi in two days and she, for Mumbai. They had forty-four hours together.

'I have learned not to take anything for granted. The freedom I have, the parents I have, the opportunities…I have learned that life is a series of moments that need to be experienced without regrets…' Samyuktha glanced up at Abhimanyu slyly. A small smile formed on his face as he looked into the distance. '…that every kind of situation is an opportunity to grow. It's just about finding out how.' Samyuktha looked into the distance along with him, as he tightened his arms around her.

'…that it's important to set boundaries, however close you are. That true love isn't about possession, it's about helping someone be and grow into who they are meant to be, and being their champion…' Abhimanyu completed her thought, holding her tightly.

They gazed at the distance for a while. Finally, Abhimanyu smiled his goofy smile again.

'But there are so many good things, illaya?' he said as Samyuktha's face broke into a smile. He continued, 'The Ganga is pure again, all the animals had a blast…'

'…Thatha has his own YouTube channel…' Samyuktha added.

'And I met you.' Abhimanyu cupped her face with one hand before giving her a long kiss.

As he leaned back, their eyes met again. Then without a word, Samyuktha stood up, and taking Abhimanyu's hand, led him into her room.

⌒⌒

The Kumar household was abuzz the next morning. Samyuktha's flight was in less than two days, which meant it was Ajay Kumar's time to shine—organizing, packing and helping Samyuktha get back to her campus life. With overgenerous helpings of upma and tomato chutney, he outlined his plan.

Samyuktha was still basking in the glow of the previous night and her mind kept wandering back to every detail of it, only to be interrupted by Appa's gruff 'seriya' every few minutes. She would nod her head and get lost in her thoughts again.

Anitha interrupted occasionally to ask if she could still pack a lifetime supply of Dettol in the bags and if the airlines would allow it. Thatha wanted to make room for chutneys and podis, so Samyuktha could avoid eating in the mess for as long as possible.

Samyuktha looked around at her family and had this sudden urge to announce that Abhimanyu had been in her room last night. She wondered what would happen if she did that. She let go of the idea, quite sure that Appa would most likely just ask why he didn't stick around to help pack.

She cleared her throat and sat up in her chair and kept looking at her father till he paused and asked, '*Enna aachu* (What happened)? Why are you staring at me like your flight just got delayed?'

'Appa, I know packing bags perfectly gives you great joy. It will happen, this evening we will finish it in two hours, I promise. But I don't want to spend my last day here talking about packing and baggage fees and dabbas, Appa. Let's talk about something else please,' she said with an air of finality that reminded Ajay of his mother. He looked at her bewildered and then broke into a smile. Thatha laughed as Anitha came around and gave Samyuktha a kiss on her head

'Okay. Fine. Whatever you want, kanna,' he said.

'What's on your mind, Samyu?' Anitha asked, giving her a quizzical look as she sat down next to her.

Samyuktha paused to collect her thoughts as she looked around at the three people she loved the most in her life. Well...

'Nothing, Amma. And that's precisely what I mean. This lockdown has made me realize the value of the things we mostly take for granted. That stupid bag will get packed, Appa, and I can buy Dettol from my hostel store if needed,' she said, looking around at them. They were all keenly listening. She went on, this time more calmly, 'I wish we didn't need the PM's Janata

Curfew to finally sit down and talk about my childhood, like we did that night, and all of yours. That is what I want my time with you all to be about. And I get it that till last year, I needed help with all of this and still do, and I love you all for it, but…' She paused, thinking.

'But you also want to be treated like an adult,' Anitha said, reading her mind.

'It gets hard to keep up with how fast you kids grow up. Someday you'll know. But also don't let this pandemic make you cynical or feel hopeless,' Anitha said and then held Samyuktha's hand. 'I know how it must have felt with Thatha getting tested.'

Samyuktha's eyes welled up as she looked at Thatha, his sparkling round eyes looking at her, smiling. She took a deep breath and looked back at her mother. 'Yes Amma, it was terrifying. But I was also amazed by how he pulled through, how strong you were during that whole phase. And…' she looked at her Appa, 'I love how you stood up for Amma at that showdown, Appa. So many character-defining moments for me.' Samyuktha tried to blink her tears away and smiled.

'Your Paati would be proud to see you today, Samyuktha,' Thatha piped up. 'This virus and all comes and goes. I have seen so many epidemics, cyclones, earthquakes in my life, ma. Each time we used to think that life and the world as we know it would come to an end. But life goes on, kanna.' As he said it, Samyuktha got a glimpse into his years of wisdom and she slowly realized what strength of mind meant.

'It's so hard to see things from the larger perspective at times, especially when we see it everyday on our Instagram and WhatsApp screens,' Amma said. 'We all think it's doomsday, and this social media makes it seem like the end has arrived,' she pondered thoughtfully.

'For someone who's at an age where everything seems like I've seen it before, I have never, ever seen myself in a YouTube video before!' Thatha said with a flourish. Everyone laughed. 'Thank you for that, Samyu,' Thatha said. 'If not for you kids, there was no way I would've added this to my already impressive resume.'

'What are you thinking, Appa?' she asked, wondering if he was upset that she interrupted his excitement around packing her bags.

'Hmm?' He looked up and then after a moment added, 'Nothing kanna, just listening to you all. And wondering why we didn't spend more time chatting like that night. I'd have so loved to, but one doesn't realize how fast time flies I guess.' He smiled a bit wistfully. Samyuktha was about to say something but he continued, 'But I am also super relieved, ma. Now that the bag will pack itself, I can take a nice nap and chat with you all evening. Don't have to worry about that anymore, what say Anitha?'

Samyuktha looked at him and blinked, digesting what he had just said, and then her eyes widened as she blurted, 'Wait.. wha...? No! That's not what I meant. Of course, I need your help with that.'

Ajay burst out laughing as he saw her panic-stricken face and Anitha joined him as she pulled Samyuktha's cheek. Samyuktha realized her father was joking and broke into a smile as she heaved a sigh of relief. It felt good to be both an adult and a kid while she still could.

The rest of the day was spent in a flurry of folding clothes, being fed and fawned over, and packing her guitar and the thousand-piece jigsaw puzzle, again. Her father remained as obsessive as ever about the packing, but occasionally reminded himself to throw in some conversation and a joke or two. The former was good, the latter made Samyuktha wonder why she roused the devil. In response to 'Wait, Appa,' he had said, '72 kilograms' with a triumphant smile. *Facepalm.*

Her phone, meanwhile, seemed to have a life of its own. It kept buzzing all day. There were lots of texts from Abhimanyu, messages on the college WhatsApp group, email notifications from college, airline updates and then there was Sharanya being Sharanya. She talked to Abhimanyu, with the instant sinking feeling that tomorrow would be the last day she would see him.

Finally, the two big suitcases were packed and ready. Anitha brought out some wine and they all sat in her balcony again to chat for some time. They talked about her upcoming semester and what inter-hostel events she was going to join, when Anitha would head back to work, what the post-Covid routine would look like and how Thatha planned to build his new Spotify playlist. Ajay asked her about her EDF internship and what she would be doing there. Samyuktha slowly dazed off, gazing at the fading stars on her balcony ceiling.

⌘

'She looks just like you, Sandhya akka!' exclaimed Samyuktha as little Shruti wrapped her tiny fingers around Samyuktha's little finger and held on.

It was 10.00 a.m. and Suhasini's house had the aroma of sambrani and Johnson's baby powder all over. She had been singing a beautiful ragam that they could hear from outside, and Samyuktha felt bad disturbing her. The joy on Suhasini's face was palpable. She loved singing to her granddaughter, and hearing her make baby noises in response. As she saw her Amma play with the baby and share Suhasini aunty's joy, she remembered how Suhasini aunty's trust hadn't faded in her mother even for a brief moment through the lowest of times.

Anitha and Samyuktha quickly went around to visit and bid farewell to a few other neighbours before returning for lunch.

Late afternoon, she told her Amma she wanted to take a quick walk around the neighborhood. As she turned around the corner, Abhimanyu was waiting for her as decided. They took a walk around the same place they first met. There wasn't much to say, except avoid moments of gloom and despair by holding hands and smiling as they looked at each other.

They walked back in silence towards Ashok Apartments. Abhimanyu felt a wave of nostalgia as he looked at the place where their check post had once been. And finally, they were at the gate. They looked at each other for a few moments. Samyuktha had tears in her eyes as Abhimanyu gave her a hug. 'Don't cry, Turtle. We'll talk soon, and often. Until...' Abhimanyu stopped short.

Samyuktha didn't register the last word. She came home and went straight to her room and into her balcony. Abhimanyu passed by, waving to her till he was out of sight. Samyuktha stood there for as long as she could, craning her neck to catch a final glimpse. Then she stood staring at the under-construction building, where his office had been for the last two months.

From the little window in his study, Ajay saw Abhimanyu pass by. He kept looking out of his window for a few moments, deep in thought. He had a large brown envelope in his hand. With a deep sigh, he walked back to his table and set the envelope down. In it were pictures of Abhimanyu and Samyuktha on her balcony.

Ajay sat down at his desk and continued to read an email that had just come in. And sighed.

'...to hereby assign Lieutenant Abhimanyu Singh to Mission Aranya with immediate effect. Asset to not have any contact with the outside world for three years...'

Acknowledgements

We would like to thank Dr Shanti who inspired us for Dr Anitha's character.

Thanks to GSN Aditya and Sush for giving us copious feedbacks on every draft; the army official who gave us details on how the army and R&AW are set up; Malini aunty who connected us with publishers; Apparao Emani for ensuring everything in the book made sense; Janaki for giving us incisive comments on the book and pointing out the minutest of errors.

We would also like to thank Linishya Vaz, Radhika Tadinada and Maalika Tadinada for giving us a great insight into one's life growing up in an army family; Sravanthi Emani for her childlike excitement to read each chapter as it got done!

We are also grateful to Rudra from Rupa Publications—he replied to our cold LinkedIn message, read our manuscript, and here we are!